ALSO BY TALIA

UNTOUCHABLE

Ravenswood Book 2

TALIA HIBBERT

Nixon House

For everyone who's ever been left.

ACKNOWLEDGEMENTS

All the thanks on Planet Earth to Aysha and Divya, ninja editors extraordinaire. Thank you to my patrons Ellen Baier and Adina Taylor for all the support; you are the sweetest and I do not deserve. Thank you to everyone who asked me about Hannah, or begged for updates on her story, or squealed about her general amazing-ness. She's not exactly a typical romance heroine, but she's valid and you remind me of that. I appreciate you.

PROLOGUE

MOST PEOPLE DIDN'T LIKE WALKING in the rain.

Especially not this kind of rain, the sort of icy spray that barely seemed to fall, yet soaked everything in its path within seconds. *Sly rain*, Nate's mum called it. You might look out the window and think, *Oh, that's alright to go out in* —but as soon as you stepped outside, you'd realise it absolutely wasn't.

At least, it wasn't unless you were Nate. Unless you needed something damp and dour to soothe your scorched bones. Only on days like this, when the sly rain fell and the sky was a sad, blue-grey and the earth smelled fresh and clean, did he stop feeling so fucking furious. Only on days like this did his strange, empty rage—the rage he had no reason to feel—go away.

He'd turned fourteen last week, and his mum had bought him a birthday cake. His ever-cheerful little brother had stuck fourteen candles in the round, white sponge. Nate had blown out the candles and tried to seem excited. Later

1

that night, he'd snuck out of the house to watch the stars and wondered why he was such an ungrateful, miserable, angry motherfucker when he had no right to be. They loved him, but all he had room for was rage.

He'd decided it was this fucking town. This tiny, suffocating town and everyone in it. *Ravenswood*. It wasn't his fault; it was Ravenswood's fault. He wouldn't always be like this; he just had to leave. And the minute he'd made that decision, something in his chest had eased. That was all. He just had to leave.

So, Nate was biding his time until adulthood came along, and he could fuck off out of here. He'd run away to somewhere huge and awful like Manchester or London, and… and become an artist. Or a photographer. Something that didn't involve words or reading, since he couldn't even do that right. His jaw still ached from the effort of clenching his teeth in Geography class that morning. That fucker Mr. Meyers had called him stupid again—and since Nate had been too angry to speak, and since he'd promised Ma he wouldn't throw chairs at school anymore, he'd just had to sit there and take it.

Which was why he'd decided to spend his lunch break wandering the school grounds in the rain. It calmed him. He passed by the music block to circle the mammoth obelisk of the science tower, dragging in gulps of cool, wet air. Later, he'd turn up for maths with rain dripping from his nose and the tips of his too-black hair, and some clever twat like Dan Burne would probably call him a *demonic drowned rat* or whatever.

Didn't matter. Nate felt water leak into his battered old school shoes as he stepped purposefully into puddles and relished the shock of cold. He turned his face up as he walked and let the raindrops bathe his wide eyes like someone else's tears. Which is why it took him so bloody long to notice Hannah Kabbah walking in front of him.

But once he saw her, he couldn't focus on anything else. He didn't really want to. He liked watching Hannah—he liked Hannah full stop, not that he'd ever tell her so. If he did, she'd probably just roll her eyes and turn away, which was kind of why he liked her. She was so… *direct*. Forceful, even. Like right now: she walked like she had somewhere to be, somewhere way more important than mere mortals could possibly imagine. She *strutted*, but not like a super-model. More like that one frantic P.E. teacher who always had someone to scold.

They'd been in the same classes all their lives—which had always struck him as odd, because the classes were split by ability, and Hannah Kabbah was a hell of a lot smarter than him. She was smarter than everyone, and a stuck-up sort of know-it-all besides. A textbook teacher's pet, so on the nose it was almost funny. He might even think she was faking it, if it didn't make her so unpopular. And if *he* weren't naturally a textbook teenage outcast.

Sometimes being a cliché came too easily to avoid.

She hurried in front of him on her short little legs and rounded the corner of the science block, disappearing only seconds after he'd noticed her. By the time he turned that same corner, she should've been long gone.

But she wasn't.

Nate pulled up short, raising a very wet hand to swipe the water from his very wet eyes. Unsurprisingly, the whole manoeuvre was largely ineffective. He squinted and wondered if he was hallucinating or something. He'd tried weed three days ago, down at the park with the older girl who lived at the end of his road. Maybe this was some kind of delayed effect. Because surely, *surely,* he wasn't seeing Hannah Kabbah facing off some massive Year Eleven lads.

Only he didn't think weed worked like that, and his head felt just fine. So he supposed he must be seeing exactly what he thought he was.

Just a few paces away, Hannah stood at the centre of a sparse, scattered circle of older kids. She was glaring up at Lee Beech, a boy almost a foot taller than her and a hell of a lot meaner. The people around them seemed tense and quiet, the rain whispering through the air, putting out their illicit cigarettes. Everyone's green blazers were sodden, almost black with wet. Except Hannah's, because she was all wrapped up in a sensible, lavender raincoat that matched the barrettes in her hair.

Honestly, it was like she *wanted* to be bullied.

But she wasn't the only odd figure lurking at the back of the science block, he realised. There was a girl hovering behind her, a really small girl in a teal raincoat that looked like Hannah's. The girl looked like Hannah too, like a little carbon copy, but with thick, turquoise glasses plonked on her snub nose. He wondered if she could even see through the rain-spattered lenses.

Then his wondering was cut short as Lee stepped closer to Hannah, his posture threatening. "You better watch what you say to me, Bugs," he growled.

Bugs as in Bugs Bunny. Because Hannah had these teeth —well, never mind.

Hannah frowned at Lee—she was always frowning—and

Nate wanted to shout at her. Something along the lines of *"Run away, you bloody idiot!"*

Because, if she didn't, Nate would have to step in and rescue her. And he might be big for his age, and pretty used to fighting, but he didn't really fancy his chances against a Year Eleven.

Unfortunately for him, Hannah's fight or flight instinct was shit. Instead of backing away from the scariest kid in school, she set her shoulders and snapped, "You watch what you say to my sister and we won't have a problem."

The girl, who must be her sister, said, "Han." That was it. Just a single syllable, not even a complete word.

But Hannah turned around and answered as if the girl had given a full-blown speech. "Don't start! What did I tell you about *talking*? Huh? Now look! Look what I have to do!"

The sister shrugged, and the action lifted the massive rucksack on her shoulders. Its fabric was darkened by rain, but Nate was pretty sure he could make out some kind of comic book shit on the side. His little brother loved that stuff. Suddenly, he understood exactly why Hannah was being so reckless. He'd put himself in a world of trouble to protect his dorky little sibling, too.

In fact, he was about to put himself in a world of trouble to protect *hers*, never mind his own. With a sigh, Nate shrugged off his rucksack and let it fall to the ground, ready to draw the boys' attention.

Then Lee stepped forward and pushed Hannah, spitting, "Yeah? What you gonna do, Bugs?"

And Hannah stumbled back. No; she *fell*, landing square on her arse with a strangled little sound that made his heart sort of... stutter. Like when a car jolts over a pothole in the road. And suddenly, the anger Nate had managed to soothe with his rainy walk burst back to life, burning brighter than ever.

Who the fuck would push a *girl*? A *little* girl, for that matter? Hannah Kabbah, for all her sharp glares and superior attitude, was basically a tiny ball of fluff. Like a kitten. A newborn kitten that couldn't quite open its eyes yet.

Nate did not like boys who stepped on kittens.

So he marched right up to Lee Beech, who was two years older and a foot wider than him. He met those cruel, smug eyes with his own. And when Lee sneered, "What the fuck do *you* want?" Nate answered by punching the bastard in the face.

For a moment, things moved as if in slow motion. Lee staggered back, clutching his nose, face slack with shock. Nate thought, for a moment, that things might end there. That he'd turn around, grab Hannah and Tinier Hannah, and they'd all leave.

But then a savage sort of roar went up, and Lee's friends charged. They surrounded Nate all at once, like a wall of lanky teenage violence, and he had just enough time to think *Ma's gonna throttle me for this* before the fight began.

Nate went home early that day with two black eyes, a dislocated shoulder, and a week's worth of detentions.

And Hannah Kabbah—unbeknownst to him and much to her own discomfort—went home with a crush.

CHAPTER ONE

Ruth: Evan wants to know if you're coming over for dinner.
Hannah: Aren't *you* supposed to invite me to dinner? Since you're my sister and everything?
Ruth: Do you want his fancy triple-fried chips or not??

As soon as the woman said, "*Excuse* me," Hannah knew there would be trouble.

Maybe it was the way her razor-sharp bullshit-ometer shrieked like a newborn. Maybe it was her years of experience working with kids, AKA masters of pushing their luck and shirking responsibility. Whatever the reason, Hannah's muscles tensed and her smile froze into place before she'd even turned to look at the customer. The customer who, according to her instincts, was about to try some nonsense.

It was the *four-chai-tea-lattes-thanks* blonde from five minutes ago, said chai lattes sitting on the counter in front

7

of her. She pushed her honeyed fringe out of her eyes with a hand that bore a rock the size of Gibraltar. Then she tapped the counter impatiently with one French-manicured claw, just in case the solar flare coming off that ring wasn't enough to alert Hannah to her presence.

"Can I help you?" Hannah asked sweetly, knowing very well that her patience was about to be tested. For the ninth time that day.

God must be punishing me for staring at Emma Dowl's arse in church last week.

"I didn't order these," the woman said. "I wanted plain lattes. Not chai." She spoke with such casual confidence, Hannah almost forgot that she was lying through her expensive teeth. But that blip of confidence passed quickly as Hannah's memory whirred to life.

"No," she said pleasantly. "I gave you exactly what you ordered. You came in…" she glanced up at the clock. "Seven minutes ago. You waited in the queue behind two other people—an older gentleman who ordered a teacake for his wife, and the gentleman in the suit who had a double espresso to go—and when it was your turn you ordered four chai lattes, double shot in two, caramel syrup in the others, one of the double shots 20 degrees cooler. I charged you £14.95, and you paid with a black Santander Select."

The woman stared blankly at Hannah for a moment, like a robot forced to recalibrate. Then her pretty face twisted into an unattractive scowl, and she spat, "I don't appreciate the way you're speaking to me."

Hannah maintained her calm smile and pleasant tone. "I'm sorry you feel that way." She *should* keep her mouth shut and make the damn lattes. Again. But she'd been at work for eight hours, and she'd spent the last three manning the café alone. They were ten minutes from closing. Her shoes pinched and her uniform culottes—yes, *culottes*—dug into her hips awfully, because she'd gained weight again and the damned things didn't come higher than a size 16.

Frankly, Hannah was Not in the Mood.

Apparently, neither was Ms. Latte. She huffed so hard, her fluffy, blonde fringe fluttered. Then she deployed the seven most dangerous words in customer service. "I want to speak to your manager!"

Oops.

Hannah hadn't been a barista for long, but she *had* been waitressing for almost two years before this. And yet, she still hadn't gotten the hang of this whole *be nice to people who don't deserve it* malarkey. She'd never planned on a career that would require her to interact with adults, and certainly not with adults who considered her inherently beneath them. She had *planned* to spend the rest of her life looking after children—preferably babies—because they didn't mind being bossed around or managed, and because they gave credit where credit was due. Give a kid your time, energy and care, and they'd repay you with trust and happiness.

Give an adult the best fucking chai lattes they'd ever tasted, and they'd ask to speak to your manager. Honestly. The ingratitude.

As if summoned by some demonic magic, the man in charge, Anthony-but-call-me-Ant, emerged from his office. He'd spent the last few hours in there doing Super Important Official Things—like playing Candy Crush on his phone—and every time Hannah asked for help, he'd waved her away with a load of supercilious bullshit about how *busy* he was. But the moment he sensed a chance to reprimand her, the tit popped out like a mole from the earth and asked brightly, "Everything okay out here?"

No, Ant, everything is not *okay. It's even less okay now you've shoved your round, shiny, bowling-ball head into things. Why do you exist? Why do you selfishly breathe the precious oxygen that could be better used to sustain a local mischief of rats or perhaps an especially large ferret?*

This was what Hannah thought. Angrily. She could be quite an angry person, at times. Even her depression manifested as anger, which was always fun. But she'd been managing her medication quite wonderfully for the last few months, so she didn't think that was to blame for today's mental fuming. No, this was just her baseline rage talking.

Luckily, Hannah had a lifetime's experience in hiding her baseline rage. Which is how she managed not to fly across the counter and commit a murder when the blonde pouted like a child and said, "No, actually. Everything's not okay. This *person* is being extremely rude to me."

Well. *Extremely* was laying it on a bit thick.

Ant grimaced sympathetically at the customer, then glared at Hannah. "I'm so sorry to hear that. What seems to be the problem?"

"The lady would like to change her order," Hannah said with as much sweetness as she could manage. Which, admittedly, wasn't much.

"You got my order *wrong*," the woman snapped.

I am Hannah fucking Kabbah. I go to the supermarket every week without a shopping list. I once memorised an entire psychology textbook the day before an exam after realising I'd been revising the wrong module for weeks. And guess what? I got an A. I spent the first few years of my professional life keeping multiple toddlers alive. Do you know how hard it is to keep toddlers alive, Ms. Chai Latte? It's really fucking hard. And I was good at it. I do not get things wrong. I do not make mistakes. I do not fuck up FUCKING CHAI LATTES. DO YOU UNDER-STAND ME?

This was what Hannah thought. But what she said was…

Oh. Wait. Shit.

Judging by the looks of utter astonishment on the faces of Ant, the blonde, and the elderly couple sitting over by the window, what she'd *said* was…

Every single word that had just run through her head.

Out loud.

Oh dear.

"*Hannah,*" Ant choked out. He sounded like he was having a heart attack. She didn't blame him. She should be feeling the same way. She should be drowning beneath a tidal wave of shock and panic and embarrassment, frantically grasping for ways to take all of that back and, you know, not lose her job.

But she wasn't. Instead of terrified, Hannah felt peaceful—relieved, actually.

And elated. And free.

Once every few years, Hannah experienced what she privately referred to as a *break*. Whether one chose to interpret that as a pleasant, holiday sort of break, or the more negative *oh-dear-I've-snapped* sort of break was neither here nor there. It didn't matter what she called it or why it occurred, because the outcome was always the same: Hannah's tightly leashed temper broke out, she did something extremely ill-advised, and in the aftermath of her terrible behaviour, she experienced the sort of carefree, unconditional happiness that was usually out of her reach.

Her last break had arguably been the most extreme: she'd smashed a fancy vintage car to pieces with a cricket bat, been arrested, lost her career…. yeah. That one had come at a pretty high price.

But she didn't regret it. Which meant, Hannah realised, that she probably wouldn't regret this, either. And as long as she was riding high on a wave of euphoric adrenaline… might as well enjoy the ride.

Both Ant and the blonde's mouths were hanging open so wide, she could see their fillings. Trying not to smile, Hannah reached beneath her apron and undid the button on her culottes.

Oh, that felt great.

Then she grabbed a little takeaway bag and unscrewed the jar of marshmallows sitting on the counter. They were good fucking marshmallows. She shoved as many into the bag as she could—which turned out to be a decent amount —and popped a few in her mouth, too.

"Hannah?" Ant's smooth, round face was caught comically between astonishment and fury. His pale skin had turned a rather fascinating sort of raspberry colour. "What on *earth* are you doing?"

He sounded like a school teacher preparing to scold a naughty pupil. But Hannah had never been a naughty pupil, and she'd never been scolded at school. Maybe that was why she didn't have the constitution to take it.

"Catch," she said.

"I beg your pardon?!"

She tossed a marshmallow directly into his mouth. Impressive, if she did say so herself.

The blonde gave a little shriek and stepped back, as if she expected a sugary projectile to come her way, too. Smart girl. The elderly couple in the corner, meanwhile, let out an adorable cheer. Hannah loved old people. They were almost as sensible as children, but far more fun. And that was saying something.

"Mumpf aft orffff?!" Ant fumed around the marshmallow wedged in his gob.

"It was a good shot, wasn't it?" Hannah was quite proud. Which made a nice change, actually. She hadn't been proud of herself in a long bloody time.

The feeling grew when she walked around the counter clutching her bag of stolen marshmallows and headed for the door. The old man who'd ordered the teacake winked at her as she passed, and—rather scandalously—she winked back. Good gracious. Perhaps she'd been possessed by a demon with a sense of humour and a spine of hell-forged iron.

"I quit," she called over her shoulder. "You probably gathered that, but men can be rather dense."

"AFFA! TOPF FA—"

"Ant, darling, I can't understand a word you're saying. Don't speak with your mouth full."

The poor man spat out the marshmallow and shouted, "Have you *lost* your *mind*?!"

"Not exactly," she said pleasantly. "It's a free-range sort of arrangement."

∼

"Joshua Davis," Nate said, "you spit that out right now."

Josh did not spit it out.

Probably because his older sister, Beth, was giggling helplessly at the sight of the tulip in his mouth. It was Beth who'd told him to eat the damned thing in the first place, and five-year-old Josh thought his seven-year-old sister was the queen of the world, so of course he'd done it.

Perhaps that was the key. Maybe if Nate appealed to the mastermind rather than the loyal solider…

He turned his best parental glare on his daughter and said, "Bethany. Don't feed your brother random plant life."

Beth stuck out her tongue.

Sigh.

The problem was, Nate decided grimly, that his kids weren't scared of him. Not even a little bit. Probably because he sucked at discipline. Like right now, for example —it was 6:30, so they should be in bed reading. Instead, they scurried off deeper into the meadow with squeaky little laughs and shouts of "Bye bye, Daddy!"

Ah, well. At least they were happy.

They'd been through a lot, recently—finding out Grandma was sick, moving across the country, starting a new school. Nate was so happy to see them laughing again, he didn't even notice the stranger walking through the meadow.

Until Josh, and then Beth, barrelled into the distant little figure like a pair cannonballs. Nate watched for a second, frozen, as they all collapsed into the tall grass.

And then he ran.

He'd been loping after the kids like some cartoon monster before, but now he actually sprinted, carving through the distance between them in seconds. It still didn't feel fast enough. He reminded himself that this was Ravenswood, not London, and the person his kids had just bumped into probably wasn't dangerous…

But that didn't really help. For one thing, no matter who it was, they'd all fallen over. The stranger *and* the kids. What if someone was injured? What if Beth had broken her arm again? Or what if the person they'd bumped into was frail or old or something, and now they'd cracked their head open and were currently bleeding out into the grass, and it was all Nate's fault because he couldn't keep his damn kids under control—

"Daddy!" Josh popped up out of the grass like a teary daisy and launched himself into Nate's arms.

Beth picked herself up with far more dignity—she *was* seven, after all—before scurrying away from the person in the grass with a wary look. The kids had this whole *stranger danger* 'thing down. Nate's wife had always been firm about that.

He sank to his knees and wrapped an arm around Beth, his other arm busy holding Josh. Nate ran his hands over all the important parts—heads, ribs, and so on—while he asked questions. "You hurt yourself?"

"No." That was Beth.

"Yes!" That was Josh, using a tone of voice that actually meant, *No, but I need attention.*

He held Josh closer and kissed his head. "There you go, kiddo. You're okay, right?"

Josh sniffled reluctantly.

"Good. Missing any teeth?" He poked at Beth's cheek.

She swatted his hand and giggled. "No. You're silly."

"You sure? Show me." She grinned wide, and he faked a gasp. "Where's your front tooth?"

"It fell out, Daddy!"

"It fell out? Well, where is it? Let's look!"

Josh chuckled. "The other *day*, Daddy! And we left it for the tooth fairy, remember? Not *now*!"

"Ohhh." Nate slapped a hand over his chest and sighed. "Phew! You had me worried!"

The kids shared a look of exasperation. They so pitied their oafish father. Josh wiggled out of Nate's arms and stood, holding Beth's hand as always—and then, as if by agreement, all three of them looked at the stranger on the ground.

She was looking right back, watching their antics with a slight smile on her face—and what a face. It thrust Nate's mind instantly into photographer mode. He saw her as if through a lens, his focus flitting from the way shadow and light danced over her dark skin, to the smooth sweep of her round cheeks into her broad nose, the curve of pouting lips into pointed chin.

She was wearing fuchsia lipstick and her eyes were dark and hot and startling as a shot of espresso. Everything about her was practically daring him to pull out his phone—God, where the fuck was his camera? — and take a picture. Just one. That wouldn't be *too* weird, right? If he explained that she was walking art and it was his job to capture it?

Actually, that would definitely be weird.

"I'm sorry," she said to the kids. "I didn't see you coming. Would you like some marshmallows, to make you feel better? If you're allowed, I mean."

The kids perked up, all supposed injury to person and

dignity forgotten. "Can we, Daddy?" Beth asked. "Can we can we can we—"

"Yeah, yeah," Nate said absently. But the truth was, he'd barely heard the question. Recognition had just hit him in the chest. He'd seen that face most days since he started pre-school for Christ's sake—only back then it had been softer, smaller, childishly undefined. Even when they'd hit their teens, she'd still looked like a little kid. She didn't look like a kid anymore.

But he knew those sharp eyes. The full lips slightly parted by those too-big front teeth. That steady, strident tone…

And the energy snapping about her like an electrical current, as if all that cool composure held back something more intense than he could imagine.

"Hannah," he said, suddenly certain. "Hannah Kabbah. Right?"

"Hello, Nate," she said calmly, as if they bumped into each other on a regular basis. As if this wasn't their first meeting in—God, almost fifteen years? When had he last seen her? The final day of school, maybe? He had no idea. Long enough that it had taken him minutes to recognise a face he'd once seen every day.

Although, he admitted, she did look different now. The same, but… yeah. Different.

Over the past week or so, he'd gotten used to bumping into people he'd once known. None of them had ever been his friends. Every single one had fallen all over themselves to act as if they were long-lost buddies.

But Hannah… he'd actually *liked* her. She hadn't known it, because he'd never told her—and there'd never been any indication that she liked him, of course. But still. He had the oddest urge to ask her some clichéd, bullshit question like *How've you been?* or *What are you up to these days?* yet she was busy helping his kids pick out the biggest marshmallows, barely sparing him a look.

Which, now he thought about it, was just like her.

If she was still the same Hannah he'd known—or even slightly similar—she wouldn't speak to him until she'd finished what she was doing. So, Nate sat there, and waited, and watched. He studied the way she smiled at the kids, noted the calming effect that her voice seemed to have on them.

She spoke so slowly—not in a boring way, but as if she had control of everything around her. As if the world could very well wait until she finished her sentence. And the kids reacted like they'd just been pumped full of Calpol and put down to bed for the night.

He wished any of the nannies he'd been interviewing recently had been half so effective. Christ, he wished the nannies he'd been interviewing had actually talked to his kids at all, instead of talking *at* them.

But he noticed other things, too. Like the hummingbird flutter of her lashes, and the slight dimple in her chin, and the careful precision with which she held herself. It was a precision that spoke of hesitation, of restraint. It made him wonder.

Once the kids were laden down with marshmallows, she finally looked up. At him. It felt sort of like being electrocuted. He had no idea why. Maybe that was why he blurted out, "We should catch up."

The kids shared a meaningful look at those foreboding

words. Beth mumbled around a mouthful of marshmallows, "Daddy, can we go and play?"

"Sure. Don't go past that tree, okay?" He pointed to a nearby beech, close enough that he'd have them in his line of sight, well-lit by a streetlight.

"Okay!" They ran off together, sticky hands clasped, cheeks stuffed full of marshmallows like hamsters with grain.

Leaving him and Hannah on their knees, Nate suddenly realised, staring at each other like lemmings.

"Catch up?" she repeated faintly, with the sort of tone he might use to say *"Eat mould?"*

"Uh... yeah." He ran a hand through his hair. Christ, he needed a haircut. He stood, and she followed suit, which made him realise how short she still was. Or maybe she just seemed that way because he was tall. Whatever. He should've stayed on his knees. He felt like some kind of ominous, oversized thing, looming over her in the half-light.

She cocked her head slightly as she looked at him, like a bird considering an unsuspecting worm. The shadows shifting over the smooth planes of her face were giving him ideas. He hadn't shot anyone professionally in years, but all of a sudden, he could see a thousand images in his mind's eye. Something about her...

"I don't think we have much to catch up on," she said.

Nate forced himself to focus on the conversation, since he was the one who'd started it. "We don't?"

"No. I know everything there is to know about you."

CHAPTER TWO

"I know everything there is to know about you?" Why in God's name had she said that?

Well, it's true, Hannah's mind offered up. But it seemed to have missed the part where *true* did not mean *appropriate*. Nate was staring at her with an odd expression on his face, as if he wanted to frown and raise his eyebrows at the same time, but was struggling to manage the feat.

She didn't blame him. How the hell had she blurted out something so utterly embarrassing? Oh, but she'd almost forgotten. She was having a break. Tomorrow she'd be all wrapped up in her own self-consciousness again, like an inescapable set of handcuffs, but today she was a wildcard. Typical. According to her sources—her sources being his brother, Zach—Nate Davis had been in town for a week. But of course she'd bump into him now. Of *course*.

"Okay," he said slowly. It wasn't *I'm backing away and calling 999 in my pocket* slow, though. It was more, *I'm a complete badass and nothing can faze me, so I'm happy to calmly question my stalker* slow.

And he *was* a complete badass. He'd been a complete badass when they were kids, and now he was all grown up and absolutely enormous with tattoos peeking out from the sleeves of his shirt. He gave her a lazy grin, one that softened the harsh lines of his face into something achingly handsome and slightly less intimidating. He pushed back his silky black hair with one hand and she realised that he had a tattoo *there* as well—on the back of his hand, like some TV gangster.

Usually, when Hannah saw that sort of thing, she rolled her eyes. But for some reason, the swallow inked into Nate's skin seemed less horrifying/comical/pathetic and more...

Sexy.

Oh dear.

Thank God it was growing too dark for her to see those eyes of his. She remembered them anyway, ice blue with that dark ring around the iris—even though it had been years since he'd left, years since she'd been freed from the daily torture of his casual confidence and tightly leashed, oh-so-enticing anger.

How she'd envied him that anger, soaring wild and unrestrained while hers festered inside.

Now here he was, back like acid reflux, twice as sharp and thrice as unwanted. A thirty-year-old woman should not look at the man who'd once been her teenage crush and feel the horrifying stirrings of that sweaty-palmed, heart-pounding, baffling attraction. She totally did, though.

If God was *still* punishing her for staring at Emma Dowl's arse in church, He was frankly being petty.

"If you know everything about me," Nate said wryly, "we definitely need to catch up."

She blinked, her usually rapid-fire mind suddenly stopped up with concrete. "We... do?"

His smile widened, and a dimple appeared in his right cheek. That dimple had caused enough heart palpitations before he was capable of growing facial hair; now that it peeked out from beneath stubble, Hannah might actually be in danger of feeling... something.

How absolutely heinous.

"Sure, we do," he said. "You—" He broke off, his gaze focusing on something behind her. "Bethany! Stop feeding your brother plants! You're gonna make him sick!" And then he calmly returned to the conversation. "You know everything about me, but I know nothing about you."

Apparently, he wasn't going to pull her up on the supreme creepiness of her earlier statement. Maybe God *was* on her side.

Then Nate said, "So what've you been up to since school?" and she realised that God had nothing to do with this day after all. It was quite clearly the devil's work.

"Um... not much," she lied. "Would you like a marshmallow?"

He blinked. "I don't know. I feel guilty about my kids cleaning you out."

Her bag *did* feel kind of light. Or rather, lighter. Marshmallows were never exactly heavy in the first place. "Don't worry about that," she said politely, while internally she chanted *Please don't eat my marshmallows. I was just being nice. They are the only thing that will help me recover from today's numerous disasters and I do not want to share.*

Maybe he was psychic, because he shook his head and said, "Nah. I could never take a lady's mysterious and questionably packaged sweets."

She blushed. "They're, um… they're totally safe, by the way."

"That's good to hear, since my kids just inhaled twenty of them."

"Right!" Hannah's laugh was a little too loud and brittle, even for her. She was surprised he didn't wince. "Well, I hate to dash…" *I hate to dash?* Now she sounded like somebody's grandma. Not for the first time, Hannah wondered what it was about human contact that turned her into a brisk, clipped, painfully awkward version of herself. She was either utterly embarrassing or unnecessarily harsh, and sometimes she couldn't decide which was worse.

"Alright," Nate said easily. "I'll let you go, then."

She tried not to look *too* grateful. She also tried not to sprint away like Usain Bolt. In fact, she tried so hard things went in the opposite direction. Hannah ended up walking painfully slowly, as if she were some stately matron making her exit.

Which gave him time to call after her, "You know, I didn't think you'd still be here."

Here in Ravenswood. Here in the town they'd grown up in, the town that had stifled them both—him obviously, and her secretly.

Sometimes everything about Hannah felt like a secret.

There was no judgement in his voice, but there didn't need to be. Hannah judged herself all the time. Her mind supplied words he hadn't said: *I thought you were smarter than this. I'd thought you'd follow in my footsteps. I thought you were good enough to escape.*

When she didn't answer, he filled her silence. "I mean... I suppose I just assumed you'd leave."

She looked over her shoulder at him, dredging up her long-suffering, plastic smile. "Like you, you mean?" He frowned, opened his mouth, closed it again, and her smile became harder to hold on to. "We're not the same, Nate. Not even close."

She knew that now. Even if, once upon a time, she'd dreamt otherwise.

"I'm sorry," Ruth said carefully. "I think I misunderstood. It *sounded* like you said you quit your job."

Hannah sighed, propping her elbows on the kitchen table and cupping her face in her hands. "That's not at all what I said, love."

"Oh." Her sister gave a relived little smile. "I must've gotten confused."

"What I *said* is that I went on a foul-mouthed rant, stole a ton of marshmallows—" Hannah nodded at the bag on the table "—and threw one into my boss's mouth. And *then* I quit my job. Or maybe he sacked me. It was hard to understand him, what with the... you know, the marshmallow."

"The marshmallow," Ruth repeated.

"Yes."

"In his mouth."

"That's right."

"The marshmallow you *threw* into his mouth."

"Mmhm."

Ruth stared for a moment, clutching her Spider-Man mug of tea for dear life. Then, abruptly, she shouted, "Evan!"

Like a particularly handsome Labrador, Ruth's enormous boyfriend came happily into the kitchen. The layout of Evan's place still made Hannah feel strange. Since he and Ruth had been next-door neighbours, this flat was a mirror image of the one Hannah had spent so much time in over the years.

The one where Hannah now lived, for very low rent, since Ruth was only using it to store her massive comic book collection.

Evan leaned against the doorframe, gave Ruth a look of sickening adoration, and asked, "Yeah?"

"My sister," Ruth said calmly, "has been possessed."

"See, that's what *I* thought," Hannah said.

"So, you agree. You think you've been possessed."

"It is a possibility," she admitted.

"We should call Mum. She'll know what to do."

"Sweetheart," Evan said gently. "I don't think—"

"Shush. I only called you in case the demon breaks out and tries to murder me."

Evan sighed. "And what, exactly, would I do to defend you from a demon?"

Ruth gave him a withering look. "Punch it in the face or something. Show some initiative, please."

Hannah popped a marshmallow into her mouth to muffle her laughter.

"In all seriousness," Ruth said—which was the only indication that she *hadn't* been utterly serious before— "I am concerned. This is quite unlike you."

"What?" Evan asked. "What's happened?"

"Hannah quit her job. And stole these delicious marshmallows."

Evan's jaw sort of... dropped. In fact, it appeared to be in danger of falling off his face completely, which would be a shame. It was a handsome face—if one liked charming, bearded blondes.

Which, Hannah supposed, most people did.

"Oh," Ruth added, with a sort of horrified glee. "And she threw a marshmallow into her manager's mouth!"

Evan appeared to be choking. Possibly on his own disbelief.

"How many people are you going to tell about this?" Hannah sighed.

Ruth rolled her eyes. "Just Evan. And Laura—"

"Please do not tell our archnemesis that I assaulted my boss with a marshmallow."

"She's not our archnemesis anymore," Ruth said. "I've been texting her. We had coffee. We're friends."

"Ruth. She has hated us both for the past two years."

"It was a misunderstanding." Ruth waved a hand about. She was disturbingly laid-back these days. Hannah suspected that 50% of this new attitude was down to Evan's handsomeness, and the other 50% was down to his obvious devotion.

Now, Hannah was not a jealous person, exactly—but Lord, it would be great if she, too, could find someone to shag the stress out of her. Of course, that would require her to find a human being who didn't irritate her 90% of the time, which had proven difficult thus far. And someone who could actually do half as good a job in bed as she did with her own hand, which had *also* proven difficult.

But she held out hope. Sort of. Sometimes. Maybe.

Nathaniel Davis didn't irritate you. And his hands are much bigger than yours.

Hannah didn't even flinch at that unruly thought. She was used to her mind misbehaving.

Instead she said, "Tell the world if you must, but don't tell mother."

Ruth rolled her eyes. She was an epic eye-roller. "Why? She's not going to spank you."

"Oh, be quiet. She'll worry."

"She absolutely will not. You do all the worrying in the Kabbah family. Mum is physically incapable of worrying."

"I think she worries secretly," Hannah said.

Ruth looked openly skeptical.

"Just don't tell her, okay? I don't want…" she trailed off, far too embarrassed to say the real reason. *I don't want her to be disappointed in me.*

Hannah hated disappointment more than anything on earth. Even the threat of it made acid froth in her stomach. The idea of her mother's soft, dark gaze turning distant, despondent even…

Oh, now she felt nauseous. Maybe a marshmallow would help.

"I don't know what you're so worried about," Ruth said. "It's not like you'll be sent off to the workhouse."

Evan, who had drifted off toward the fridge and was now rifling through it, said, "We don't have workhouses anymore, love. You know that, right?"

"Be quiet, you horrible man."

His head appeared over the top of the fridge, and he winked. Ruth responded with the sort of flushed and bamboozled smile no woman should ever have to see on the face of her stoic little sister. It was damned unnatural. And Hannah was definitely jealous.

Ruth took a sip of tea and tried again. "What I mean is, you don't need the money."

Evan's head reappeared over the door of the fridge. He frowned over at Hannah and asked, "You don't?"

"I do," Hannah said firmly.

"She doesn't," Ruth argued, just as firmly. "She has a trust fund."

Evan gaped. "You do?"

"We *both* have trust funds." Hannah corrected with a glare. "And I don't want to use mine, thank you very much."

"I don't see why not," Ruth said. Sometimes, Hannah didn't understand her sister. Ruth knew very well what their so-called 'trust funds' actually were: hush money. You know, *take this cash and don't tell my wife that you exist* money. *Now you have no reason to bother me with your incriminating presence* money. From their father, of all people. Their shitty fucking father.

Hannah had grown up in the shadow of shame. She hated it, even more than she hated disappointment. Which is why she meant every single word when she said, "I'm not touching that man's filthy fucking money."

Ruth rolled her eyes. "Do be sensible, Hannah. All money is filthy."

"Is this something to do with your dad?" Evan asked.

Hannah shot him a glare.

He slowly disappeared back into the fridge.

"Oh, Hannah," Ruth said, "please don't be difficult. Just… pretend today was a cosmic sign instead of the inevitable result of your goody-two-shoes repression." Ignoring Hannah's gasp of outrage, she went on: "Take this as an opportunity to find a new career. A long-term career that doesn't make you want to commit murder on a daily basis. Maybe we should Google 'jobs that involve bossing people around'."

"Now you're just trying to piss me off."

"I certainly am not. Oh, I know! You should do something creative. It will be good for your general mood, I think. You have an excess of self."

Of course, Ruth would bang on about creativity. She made a living—*more* than a living—through, of all things, her space opera webcomic. Which surprised no-one who actually knew her, but still.

Silence fell quite abruptly, because Ruth had nothing else to say and didn't believe in unnecessary words. Hannah wanted to speak, but she was too busy over-analysing everything her sister had just said, and also the past thirty years of her life. You know, the usual.

It was Evan who eventually restarted the conversation. "Or," he said, "if you *don't* want to choose a new career all at once… you could work for Zach's brother."

Hannah looked up so fast, it was a miracle her head didn't snap off of her neck. "I beg your pardon?"

"You know. Nate." Evan produced a mountain of parsnips from the fridge. "Are you staying for dinner?"

Usually, Hannah would politely decline—she did hate to be a bother—but she'd had a traumatic day and required carbohydrates. "Yes. What was that about Zach's brother?"

She was pleased with how the question came out. Not too sharp, not too desperate, not too astonished at the fact that Evan had casually brought up Nate Davis not two hours after she'd literally bumped into Nate Davis.

Or rather, bumped into his adorable children.

"Zach said they've been interviewing nannies or au pairs or something… what's it called when you live at someone's house and watch their kids and clean their shit?"

"Drudgery," Ruth muttered.

"Marriage," Hannah suggested.

"Hey, now," Evan said with determined cheer. "Marriage isn't all bad!" He gave Hannah a significant look from behind Ruth's back. If she had to guess, she would say that the look meant *Please don't turn your sister off marriage any more than she already is, because I'm really hoping to put a ring on that.*

Hannah cleared her throat. "I mean… um… a live-in nanny. That's what you're talking about. I think."

"Right." Evan gave her a grateful smile. "Well, Shirley's appointments are pretty random…" His cheerful demeanour faded a little when he mentioned Shirley Davis. Her recent cancer diagnosis was the reason Nate had moved back home after all these years. And since the family was small—just Shirley, Zach, and Nate, plus Nate's kids—Hannah didn't doubt that they'd need help.

"Things are kind of complicated," Evan went on, "so they want someone who's accessible all the time. In case of… emergencies. Apparently, the interviews haven't been going well—but you could do it, right? You worked with kids, before. Right?"

Hannah blinked. *Could* she do it? Be some kind of

private nanny, two years after her career in childcare had collapsed as spectacularly as an under-hairsprayed bouffant? Frankly, she had no idea.

But something bright and hopeful and awfully excitable sparked inside her at the thought. Which was sad, and ridiculous, and dangerous, because, "I highly doubt Nate would want me watching his kids."

Evan frowned as he started peeling parsnips. "Why the hell not? You're exactly the sort of person I'd want watching my kids."

Well... that was sweet. So sweet she might do something painfully embarrassing, like thank him. "I can't, Evan. You know I can't. I can't even pass a DBS check."

"Is that necessary," Ruth asked innocently, "if you're working privately?"

"I have no idea," Hannah lied.

"Really? That seems like the kind of thing you'd know."

Hannah sighed. "Fine. No, it isn't technically necessary. But the legal aspect doesn't matter! I just... I don't think Nate would want someone with violent convictions around his children."

"*Violent convictions*," Ruth snorted. "You're so dramatic. It was just a car."

The car of the town's wealthy, handsome, beloved sweetheart. Which Hannah had destroyed in a fit of rage. With a cricket bat. In front of almost a hundred people.

Sometimes she thought she should've destroyed the bastard's kneecaps for what he'd done to her sister. But it was a good thing she hadn't; she was too uptight to survive in prison.

"Whatever," Hannah sighed. "Look, it's a nice idea, but… I just don't know. I don't see it happening, that's all."

"But if it *did*," Evan said, "you would be…?"

She huffed. "I don't know." *Over the fucking moon and highly suspicious of my own good fortune.*

She couldn't say that, because Hannah would rather die than ever be so openly enthusiastic. She liked Evan—she really did—but he wasn't family. He could not be permitted to see the messy and undignified depths of her overactive emotional muscle. Anyway, she barely had to feign her hesitation, because there was one part of this otherwise unicorn-perfect notion that was giving her pause.

Living with and working for a guy like Nate Davis? Something about the idea felt… dangerous. Maybe because, even though her lamentable teenage crush on him had died, he was still undeniably attractive. But that shouldn't make her feel strange—Hannah found *lots* of people attractive. In theory. You know, to look at. Like a nice picture. So, what was the problem?

While she sorted through her usual bog of emotions— heavy and messy and capable of preserving dead things for far too long—Ruth and Evan stared at her expectantly in that way couples had, like they were the same person in two different bodies.

She huffed again—Hannah was fond of a good huff—and said, "I suppose it would be acceptable. Theoretically. If it paid well. Perhaps."

Evan grinned as if she'd just given enthusiastic consent. "Great! I'll pass on your number."

CHAPTER THREE

Hi Nate,

Not sure if you saw the emails I sent on Sunday, but I'm getting kind of nervous about this exhibition. Because everything's shit. I have produced a pile of shit. Are you out of office right now by the way????

Regards, John

John,

You said your last collection was shit and it sold for fifty grand. Relax.

Nate.

~

"YOU CALL HER YET?"

Nate gave a deep, deep sigh. So deep, it felt like it had come from his spine instead of his chest. And yet, it still was not enough to express how irritated he was by his little brother.

"No, Zach. I did not call Hannah in the thirty minutes since you arrived and gave me her number."

Zach leant against the breakfast island and grinned, early morning sun gleaming off his jet-black hair. "It's been more like an hour, mate."

"An hour I spent unpacking while you hung around looking pretty." Nate glared at his brother over the cardboard box of saucepans in his arms. "Feel free to help at any time, by the way."

Zach's grin widened. "I'm watching the kids."

Beside him, Beth perched on a stool while Josh stood beneath her. She was merrily slathering his hair with butter.

Nate ground his teeth, closed his eyes, and took another calming breath. It didn't work.

Maybe he *should* call Hannah. Right now. And hire her on the spot, regardless of references or experience, because after a week without the support network he'd built up in London, he was at the end of his fucking tether.

Aaaand his daughter was still dressing his son like a Sunday roast. He should probably focus on that, shouldn't he?

From the corner of the room, Ma looked up from her magazine and chuckled. "Are you alright, Nathaniel? You're looking a bit red, darling." She was wrapped in blankets, lounging on soft chair he'd carried in from the dining room. Her narrow cheeks plumped up a little as she smiled, and the sight was precious enough to drag him out of his growing temper.

"You understand why, though," he said. "I mean, you're

seeing this, right? You are witnessing my devil children. Correct?"

Shirley rolled her eyes. "Trust me, darling, you were far worse."

"I don't see how I could possibly—Beth! Please stop that."

Beth paused, one hand filled by a rapidly-melting ball of butter. A butterball. Fan-fucking-tastic. She had the look of a child with far too much freedom and no lack of imagination. Beneath her, Josh had the look of a boy led astray by hero-worship, one who'd go along with anything his older sister claimed was cool.

Beth raised the butterball over her brother's head with clearly threatening intent, and Nate gritted his teeth, pulling out his firmest Dad Voice. "I swear to God, kiddo, me and you are gonna fall out. No—put the butter dish down. It's too heavy. *Bethany*—"

Sometimes, reality turned into a series of photographs. Not living, breathing, moving life, but snapshots flashing and frozen, too fast to process, already set in stone. This was one of those times. It felt like everything was moving through treacle, while Nate's muscles were trapped by half-set concrete. He watched as the butter dish Beth had just picked up slid from her slippery fingers. Directly over little Josh's head.

Fuck.

Nate dumped the box of saucepans, barely hearing its ominous clatter, and did his best to vault the mammoth kitchen island. He was too slow. Way too slow. His little boy was about to be whacked on the head with a ceramic butter dish. He'd have to pack his buttery kids *and* his sick mother into the car and drive through a city he hadn't visited in over a decade to take Josh to the hospital.

Or rather, that's what *would've* happened—if Zach hadn't casually reached over and plucked the falling dish out of the air a moment before it smacked Josh on the head.

For about half a second, Nate was full of relief. Then he realised that he was still flying over the kitchen island, that he had way too much momentum, and that disaster was imminent. A moment later, he hit the tiled floor with a bruising *thud*.

This really wasn't his day. And it was barely 10:30.

Nate sighed, staring up at the kitchen ceiling. It was a lovely view, nice and plain and white. Until his brother ruined it by shoving his smug fucking face in the way.

"Everything okay?" Zach asked, his lips twitching.

"Go f—*fork* yourself," Nate muttered, standing up. He snatched the butter dish from Zach's hand and added, "Thanks."

"You look tired, man."

"I am tired." Nate dumped the dish in the sink, then went to crouch down in front of his children, who were merrily slathering each other in butter liked nothing had happened. "Guys," he said, spearing each of them with a look. Josh's deep blue gaze met Nate's without issue, open and bright. He looked just like his mother.

Whereas Beth looked just like Nate. She scowled like Nate too, her paler eyes narrowed, wild hair hanging over her face. It had been a week since they'd arrived, and he still wasn't sure which box her hair clips were in. But then, hair didn't really matter when both kids were, A. running around in their underwear, and, B. covered in fucking butter.

"Bethany," Nate said firmly, "you almost hurt your brother. If that dish hit him on the head, he would've been really sick. You get that, right?"

Beth had inherited, amongst other things, Nate's childhood reluctance to respond to criticism, so she didn't answer verbally. But he didn't need her to speak to know that she got the message. Her eyes widened and she bit her lip for a second, her gaze flitting to her beloved little brother.

"Yeah," Nate said. "That's why we have to do as we're told. Because sometimes things are dangerous, and you don't understand why, but grown-ups do. So, you listen to your grown-ups." He grasped his buttery son under the armpits and straightened up, holding the kid at arms' length. Josh giggled as his bare feet dangled in the air. "Now it's time to get cleaned up, okay? You two are gonna help me unpack today."

"Yaaaay!" Josh cheered. "Boxes boxes boxes. Can we have the boxes, Daddy?"

"Once they're empty, they're yours. Zach, grab Beth for me."

Zach rolled his eyes and picked up his niece. "Keep those hands away from me, B. I'm too beautiful to be buttered."

Beth snickered and wiped a sticky hand over her uncle's cheek.

"Ugh! Nate, control your creatures!" But Zach was already leaving the kitchen with a grin on his face, swinging Beth through the air while she squealed.

Which left Nate with a squirming, slippery Josh. He turned to his mother. "You gonna be okay?"

She gave him a look so mocking, it almost transported him back through time. For a second, he was 16 again, and she was giving him that *you-think-I-was-born-yesterday?* look while he tried to pretend he was visiting London instead of outright running away.

What a cocky little fuck he'd been. Here he was, years down the line, right back in the town he hated, with too much loss behind him and more lurking ahead. His mother's arch looks might be the same, but the rest of her was so very different. She was rail-thin instead of comfortably plump. Her curtain of black hair was gone, replaced by a bright silk headscarf. And she was shivering—*shivering*—in May, in the house, under three blankets.

But if he thought about that too hard, he might do something terrible. Like cry.

So Nate focused on the reassuring derision in her words as she replied. "I'm not one of your littlies, Nathaniel," she sniffed. "Stop checking on me."

He winced. "I worry."

"Yes. I noticed that when you sold everything you owned and moved back home in less than two months. Now go. Josh is dripping all over the floor."

Oh, fuck. Nate looked down to find gleaming yellow droplets spattered over the kitchen tiles he'd just mopped.

Business as usual, then.

"So," Zach said. "You—"

"Hold on." Nate swung around and picked up his damp, naked son, cutting off the poor boy's lap of triumph. "Joshua. Put your clothes on. We talked about this."

Josh screwed up his face. "But I don't like my pants."

"What's wrong with your pants?"

"Baby pants. I want my big boy pants."

Nate sighed. "I don't know where they are, sunshine. But if you get dressed, we can check the laundry room and find them, okay?" He put Josh down. "Does that sound good?"

"No. No pants." Josh skipped off down the hall.

Nate ran a hand over his tired eyes and checked his watch. Only... twelve more hours until he could go to sleep. Or at least, until he could lie in bed and enjoy the silence and stillness while his mind refused to rest. Wonderful.

"So," Zach repeated, leaning against the bedroom wall. "Don't take this the wrong way, but you're kind of a mess."

Nate shrugged. "I think we're doing okay."

"Mate. You're not wearing a shirt."

He wasn't? Nate looked down at his own chest. Oh. Right. He wasn't.

"Jesus," Zach snorted. "I can't believe you just had to check. You think tattoos count as clothes now?"

"Fuck off," Nate muttered, hunting down the boxed-up contents of his wardrobe. The kids' stuff was mostly unpacked, but he didn't have time to waste on his own shit.

"You're only wearing one sock," Zach said.

"Now you're just being picky."

"I think the kids are actually *trying* to torment you."

"That is correct."

"Do you even have food in the house?" Zach demanded.

Nate sighed. "I have bread, butter, beans, and frozen nuggets. The four pillars of any child's diet."

Zach arched a brow.

"Oh, fuck you. I was planning on shopping today."

Josh and Beth ran past the door, both butt-naked, screeching out a tune that Nate vaguely recognised as something from *Moana*.

Zach smirked, opening his mouth.

"Don't. Don't say a word." Nate glared. "I have it under control."

"You absolutely do not have it under control. You're going to call Hannah, right? Because Evan said she has all kinds of fancy kid-related qualifications and about a thousand years' experience. And I happen to think that she's a really nice girl."

Something about Zach's tone snatched Nate's attention. He paused in his hunt for a shirt and glared at his little brother. "You're trying to get into her pants, aren't you?"

"Obviously," Zach said. "Have you *seen* her?"

Yes, Nate had seen her. He wouldn't mind seeing her again, in fact. Repeatedly.

Which was a realisation so disturbing, he actually had to sit down.

After a second, he picked up his thread of conversation again. "I'm not about to hire her, let her live in my shitty new house and watch my hyperactive children, just so you can wheedle your way into her bed."

"I don't *wheedle*," Zach snorted. "I charm. You should try it sometime. Works a lot better than pensive brooding."

Nate stared. "How are we related?"

"I ask myself that question all the time. Will you just call her? Meet her? We're running out of time to sort this out."

Nate sighed. That much was true, at least. Isolated as it was, Ravenswood wasn't exactly brimming with live-in nanny options. Especially since most people around here would rather swallow fistfuls of their own hair than work for Nate. Small towns had long memories, and he had not been the most... *agreeable* kid.

But apparently, Hannah was willing to give it a shot. He should be rushing to call her right now, honestly. He had no idea why he wasn't, especially when he'd seen how good she was with kids. Christ, he'd even wished that some of his nanny options were more like her. Well, apparently, she *was* an option.

Why didn't he want to call her?

The question was like smoke, hard to see and harder to grasp. Nate set it aside and focused on more important things, like Ma's needs, Zach already being on thin ice at work, and his own excruciating anxiety about how very unprepared they all were for any emergencies.

Then he pulled out his phone and made the call.

CHAPTER FOUR

Ruth: Good luck btw.

Hannah: Why are you awake before midday? Are you sleeping okay? Did you get a full eight hours?

Ruth: …

Ruth: Evan says not to answer.

HANNAH STARED down at the varnished tabletop of the Unicorn's finest booth and wondered how the hell she'd ended up here.

Three hours ago, she'd been sitting in bed, staring at her blog—yes, Hannah had a blog—trying and failing to write. She'd wondered if she should Google some Oscar Wilde quotes to kickstart her creativity, because, while Oscar Wilde could be kind of a prick, he wasn't half motivational, bless him.

As she was in the midst of pondering her mental

lethargy—wondering if maybe she should take a walk to get her ideas going, or make a doctor's appointment to discuss the ever-constant threat of falling into The Pit of Mental Despair—her phone had rung.

So now, here she was, stuffed into her best skirt like a pretty little sausage, sitting in the pub waiting for...

"Here you go." Nate put the lemonade she'd asked for on the table, then sat down opposite her, pint in hand. He lifted the amber liquid and said, "I don't usually drink in the day."

She wondered why he'd bothered saying that. He was hardly the only man in the pub with a lunch larger. And the Nate Davis he'd been back in school—the one who'd given teachers heart palpitations on an hourly basis—wouldn't have bothered to explain himself. Ever.

But then, they weren't at school anymore. Hannah wondered when her still-pounding heart would remember that fact.

Ugh. Hearts. Who needed them, anyway?

"Shall we get down to business?" she asked briskly, batting away her own wayward thoughts.

He smiled. "You haven't changed much, have you?"

"I'm sorry?"

"You're still very direct. Not big on small talk."

She pursed her lips and glared at her lemonade as if it might make this whole conversation easier. "I don't like to waste time. That's all. Things are so much more efficient when everyone gets to the point, don't you think?"

Nate stretched slightly, making those impossibly broad shoulders even broader for a moment. Then his head fell back, resting against the top of the leather seat, which put his face at an angle she could only call unfortunate. Unfortunate for her, that is. It highlighted the hard line of his jaw, the softness of that wide mouth, the icy gleam of his eyes. He was unavoidably handsome. The prick.

And, to her surprise, he appeared to be actually considering her words. Good Lord. Didn't he know a polite turn of phrase when he heard one?

Finally, he said, "I think efficiency has its place. But personally, I like to take my time. Savour small moments. Life is easier to digest when you go slow."

She paused for a second, unexpectedly blindsided by his response. The words hit her hard, sinking into her skin like little hooks, and she knew—the way she instinctively did sometimes—that she'd lie in bed thinking about them tonight. They'd be top on her list of daily minutiae to agonise over, to replay again and again, courtesy of her steel-trap mind. But she couldn't quite put her finger on what made them so hypnotising.

She took a fortifying sip of lemonade and reminded herself that navel-gazing could wait until later. Right now, she had an interview to ace. It was extremely unsettling to realise that for all her hesitation, she kind of wanted this job. God, it would be good to do something that challenged *her*, instead of challenging her patience and lower back, for a change. Something that actually played to her strengths.

Now she just had to get the damn job. If she could.

The suspense of not knowing how this interview would end was already killing her. She was practically sweating her knickers off. Nathaniel Davis with his cool eyes and his cooler attitude could meander all he liked, but Hannah Kabbah was anxious, impatient, slightly obsessive, and definitely in need of some efficiency.

"I'm just going to be upfront," she said. "I know you need a live-in nanny. I, theoretically, could be a live-in nanny. But there are several pertinent facts that I should bring to your attention."

He arched a brow. "Pertinent facts?"

Oh dear. She was doing the thing. The *talk like a lawyer in a TV drama because I'm absolutely shitting myself* thing. "Well, you may be aware that I have a... slightly unsavoury reputation in Ravenswood."

Nate nodded, amusement written all over his face. "So do I. Maybe that's why I called you."

She glared. "That is not why you called me."

"It's not?"

"No. You called me because you were desperate and because your brother likes me."

"Oh, so you know that he's plotting to seduce you? That's good. I was wondering how to warn you about it without sounding like something out of a bad novel."

Oh, for fuck's sake. Zach was a lovely man, but he had the biggest mouth on planet earth. Hannah ignored her burning cheeks and said sharply, "You don't need to worry about that. Your brother's delusions are irrelevant."

"See, that's what I've been saying my whole life, but no-one listens."

"*Moving on*," Hannah said firmly. "I have decided to inform you that I suffer from depression, and if that fazes you in any way, we should likely end this discussion here."

Nate blinked. Finally, she'd managed to get that irritatingly slow, annoyingly sexy grin off his face.

That was Hannah; an expert in wiping away smiles.

She held her breath and distracted herself from the

mounting tension by examining the iridescent rainbow of her own feelings. Each shining shade represented an odd and usually inappropriate emotion.

Hannah's emotions, she had come to accept, were often inappropriate.

There was, of course, worry, a bilious green. Her lifelong companion and greatest annoyance, the one feeling that would never, *ever* leave. Worry was a bitch, but it was a bitch that Hannah knew well.

Next in the rainbow came puce, preemptive relief. Hannah realised with a jolt that part of her was hoping Nate would stop things here. That he'd count her out because she was, as people loved to put it, *mentally unstable*. That he'd think unbelievably common blips in brain chemistry made her some kind of separate species, and would therefore keep her away from his kids.

Hannah's depression had started when she was just a kid herself. She wondered how many parents without mental health experiences of their own thought to watch out for warning signs in their children. Hannah would watch, of course. And she would know. But people didn't tend to care about things like that.

Her next emotion, vivid scarlet, was resentment. Resentment that she felt the need to even disclose this information; resentment that it could bar her from a job she knew herself capable of, a job she'd always excelled at, a job she suddenly realised she really fucking wanted.

Beside resentment was bright orange rage, mostly directed at herself, because all of Ravenswood had called her crazy after she was arrested, but Hannah had been the one who'd publicly snapped in a fit of irritation that *yes*, she *was* crazy, had been for a while, and didn't give a shit.

She'd been younger then, in more ways than one.

There was self-doubt, pale and pink and private like the inside of a stranger's mouth. *You shouldn't have said anything. There's a difference between refusing to feel shame and setting yourself up for a fall.*

She was used to ignoring self-doubt. It was rather prejudiced, and a bit of a bore. If she held an emotional tea party, self-doubt would eat all the scones and call Hannah fat if she complained.

Finally, she found a familiar grey shade in her colour wheel. Disappointment. Because, during a youthful and hopeful and effervescent time in Hannah's life, Nate Davis had been the epitome of freedom to her. She had cradled a Nate-flavoured fantasy to her chest, a sweet, golden spark. She'd pulled it out when the other kids had mocked her and excluded her and ignored her, and she'd pulled it out when her moods had been low and her mind not her own and she'd known something was wrong with her but hadn't known what.

When her own ephemeral confidence had failed her, she'd always bolstered herself by thinking, *Nate wouldn't care what people thought of him. Nate wouldn't care about any of this. Nate doesn't follow all the rules that you feel chained to obey.*

And now here was Nate, proving that past, innocent version of Hannah wrong. Because he was looking at her so strangely, and he was so very silent, and now he opened his mouth to say...

"That was pretty fucking brave."

Hannah barely choked down a baffled, *What?* Clamping her back teeth together, she settled on an astonished stare.

"But also, none of my business."

She stared harder.

Nate stared back for a moment, as if they'd engaged in some kind of staring competition. Then he said, "You okay?"

Absolutely not. How dare you be so very relaxed while I study emotional rainbows in my head? How dare you pull the rug of expectation from under my feet with this complete lack of drama? How fucking dare you?

"Yes," Hannah said. She might have the most mortifying habit of speaking her mind—which, incidentally, she blamed on Ruth's corrupting influence—but even she knew when to keep her mouth shut. Most of the time. Sort of. Occasionally.

"Cool. Anything else you wanted to tell me?"

Oh, great. She'd had a vague idea that the conversation would stop here, to be honest. She hadn't planned the rest of her grand reveal. And her heart might just give out if he produced any more of those long, dramatic, thoughtful pauses in response to her colourful confessions.

Hannah cleared her throat and blurted, "I used to be a nursery nurse."

"So I hear."

"But I'm not anymore."

"So I hear."

She shoved a stray braid out of her face and gritted out, "I am legally prohibited from my former occupation."

"Are you trying to confuse me with big words?"

"No."

"Because I'm a lot smarter than I was back at school."

"...Okay?"

"I mean, I've read a thesaurus or two." He raised his hands. "I'm not trying to brag. I'm just saying."

"Are you... attempting to make me laugh?"

He gave her a crooked little smile, and that bloody dimple made an appearance. "Maybe. What is it people say? 'God loves a trier?'"

She stared, thoroughly baffled. "You do understand what I'm telling you, correct?"

"I think so." He ran a hand through his hair, pushing the silky strands off his forehead. She had no idea why, because it was an utter mess that she couldn't see being tamed any time soon.

And she did *not* find that mess beguiling in the slightest. Hannah liked tidy men. Tidy, sensible men who did not have random swallows tattooed on their hands.

Nate tapped his long, blunt fingers against his glass and said, "You.... tried to kidnap North West?"

She stared. "I beg your pardon?"

"You know. Kanye's—"

"I know who North West is. How would I ever come *close* to kidnapping North West?"

"I don't know," he said. "I truly believe you could do anything you put your mind to. Including flying to the U.S. with the intention to liberate Kim Kardashian's million-dollar child."

"Why would I possibly want to—?" Hannah shook her head sharply. "I have no idea why I'm going along with this. You're being ridiculous. I'm *trying* to tell you that I have a criminal record—"

"I know."

"Which includes—" she broke off, her brain catching up with her mouth. "You… know?"

"I know you fucked up Daniel Burne's Porsche." He wrinkled his nose. "I always hated that guy."

Hannah stared. "You *know*."

"Obviously I know. Just because I left Ravenswood, doesn't mean I was spared constant gossip via regular phone calls home."

"Your mother told you?" she squeaked, mortified.

He smirked. "Ma doesn't gossip. Zach told me."

Oh, Zach. She was so going to enjoy strangling him, when next they spoke.

"So, just to be clear," she said slowly, "you are not concerned by my numerous criminal convictions."

"Nah. I'm used to having a convicted criminal in the house."

"You… are?"

"Yeah." He leaned in close, his expression conspiratorial, and she couldn't help it—she leaned in too. Then he whispered, "It's me." And smiled.

Oh, for heaven's sake.

Hannah sat back with a huff. "You don't count."

"I don't?"

"No! You know that you're trustworthy, because you're you!"

"You think I'm trustworthy?"

"It doesn't matter if *I* think *you're* trustworthy—"

"It does," he interrupted. "It absolutely matters. If you took this job, Hannah, we'd be living together. You have to watch your own back, too, you know."

She was, for a moment, rendered speechless. Thankfully, it didn't last long. "Alright. That's... I suppose that's true."

He nodded, raising his drink to his lips. Hannah was embarrassingly distracted by the bob of his throat and the press of his mouth against glass. She wondered how strange it would seem if she closed her eyes, just to escape that hypnotic sight.

Quite strange, probably.

He finished drinking and said, "So, do you want to know what I did?"

As if she didn't know already. "You were charged with affray and grievous bodily harm on two separate occasions after taking part in supposedly non-violent protests."

He faltered. "You... appear to have memorised my criminal record."

"*Memorised* is a strong word. I heard about it. Once." Briskly, Hannah turned away from his open astonishment and picked up the planner on the booth seat beside her. She slapped it onto the table with a little *thud* and opened it up. "Anyway! Now that we've gotten the necessary disclosure out of the way—"

"What the bloody hell is that?" He stared at her lovely teal planner as if she'd just shat on the table.

"It's my planner," she said, even though that should be pretty obvious. The word PLANNER was imprinted onto the leather front cover. Honestly, people were so unobservant.

"Why is it so... *huge?*"

"Could we focus on the matter at hand?" It belatedly occurred to her that this was actually a job interview and she should be on her best behaviour. You know, polite and meek and subordinate, and all the other things she wasn't.

But it was far too late now. Somehow—maybe because he was friendly like Evan or charming like Zach or blunt like Ruth—she'd accidentally started being herself around Nate Davis. Of course, Hannah's self was generally far too abrasive to forget. And since she couldn't erase the last ten minutes, she'd just have to forge ahead and wow him with the many meaningful pieces of paper she'd collected in her life.

"This," she said, pulling out a crisp white sheet, "is my C.V. References are available on request. And this is a letter from a family I babysit for occasionally…" She laid it on the table in front of him. "I find the third paragraph especially helpful. Now, over here I have all of my qualifications—"

Nate held up a hand, using his other to turn over her C.V. "Uh… hang on. If you want me to read all of this, it'll take me a while. And I'll need digital copies."

"You will?"

He glanced up. "Oh, yeah. Turns out I'm dyslexic. Hey, since I'm back in town, I should hunt down Mr. Meyers and tell him I'm not an idiot, but he *is* a raging dick."

"Mr. Meyers died three years ago," Hannah said automatically. Retaining and relaying information was a lot easier than grappling with emotional responses.

"Hmm. Does he have a gravestone I can piss on, or anything?"

She really shouldn't laugh at such awful disrespect. She absolutely should not. But since their old Geography teacher had gained all his life's happiness through bullying the children he taught, she allowed herself a tiny snicker.

Which made Nate's wicked grin spread wider. And now that shallow dimple was visible again, barely hidden by his stubble, and she was getting heart-pounding, sense-stealing Year Ten flashbacks. *Abort mission.*

"I can definitely email these," she said briskly, sliding out a few more pages. "I mean, I can scan them, and—"

"Christ, don't bother scanning shit. Honestly, I'm not gonna read it."

She blinked. "Um... I could... read it for you?"

"I can read, love." Oh, God. Now he'd think she'd said that because he was dyslexic, rather than because she was a try-hard weirdo. Only he didn't seem particularly offended. Especially not when he said, "It's just, I'm 99% sure that I'm going to hire you."

For a moment, Hannah's jaw actually dropped. How mortifying. She clamped it shut before anything untoward could sneak out, like an embarrassing flood of gratitude or a comment about his biceps.

Finally, she managed to croak out, "You are?"

"Yeah. I mean, you should probably meet the kids again, just to make sure you all get along okay. I don't know if you noticed the other day, but they're kind of..."

"Energetic," she supplied smoothly.

His mouth tipped up into a slow, wry smile. "Yeah. That."

She knew very well that he actually wanted to see her interact with them. While she'd known Nate and his family for years, in a small town sort of way, they were technically almost strangers. People didn't take chances with their children. And she appreciated the caution. "I thought they seemed lovely, and I'm happy to meet them again."

He nodded. "Cool. Maybe tomorrow, if you're not busy. I don't want to rush you."

"But things are time-sensitive," she said. "Tomorrow is fine."

He smiled, and she thought she spied a little relief on that annoyingly handsome face. But it came and went so quickly, it might as well have been a mirage. "Cool. I do have a question for you, though."

Her heart, which had been feeling remarkably light, for once, fell. He looked very serious all of a sudden. "Oh. Okay. Well… go for it." *Please don't. Please give me the job and leave me be and never question me about anything ever. I know that may sound unreasonable, but I think you'll get used to it over time.*

"I already knew you fucked up Daniel's car," he said, "but what I don't know is why." His eyes were steady on hers, and they almost seemed soft. Gentle. But that was probably some sort of illusion. "Would you tell me?" he asked. Which was a bit of a plot twist. He had her in the palm of his hand, after all. He'd dangled a job in front of her before asking this. He could've just *demanded* an answer.

Hannah should be suspicious of his motives. She should see his careful phrasing as a front, a sly attempt to seem friendly while tearing open barely-healed wounds. But she was used to hunting out that vicious gleam in peoples' eyes. Sometimes, she was so eager to see it, she might even imagine a glint that wasn't there. So if there had been a hint of cruelty around Nate right now, she would've seen it. She *would've*.

She didn't.

All she saw was an irritatingly attractive—but otherwise

perfectly reasonable—man watching her with the same sweet reassurance he'd watched his kids with just a couple of a days ago.

So she answered. For the first time ever, actually. She answered.

"He hurt my sister," she said slowly. "I think everyone knows that, now. He hurt my sister, and I was angry. But I reacted the way I did—so recklessly—because I was angry at myself, too. He hurt her, and I didn't even notice. Years, he was fucking with her head. And in the end, she had to *tell* me. But what if she hadn't? What if she couldn't bring herself to say it? What if she'd..."

Nate reached across the table and took Hannah's hand, just as her voice wavered. She looked down sharply, and the sight of someone touching her—touching her like *that*, to give comfort—was so strange, she almost felt... dizzy? But that couldn't be right. She was getting overemotional again. What was going *on* with her right now? She could barely bring herself to look at Nate, she was suddenly so embarrassed—but she couldn't let him know that, so she looked up anyway, her expression as blank as she could make it.

She certainly wasn't ready for the look on his face. For the way his dark brows were drawn together, for the worry in his eyes or the kindness in his voice when he said quietly, "I'm sorry. I didn't know. I wouldn't have asked. I didn't know."

Hannah gave a tight shrug and pulled her hand away, mostly because she still felt dizzy. Maybe it was a blood sugar thing. She took another sip of lemonade, and a moment of silence passed.

Then Nate leaned back, his posture casual, arms resting

on the back of the booth in that way men had—always taking up space. Usually, it irritated her. But right now, the way his T-shirt stretched across his broad chest was distracting her from annoyance.

"You know," he said, his tone lighter, "you haven't asked about pay yet."

"Oh. Well." Hannah cleared her throat and pulled herself together. "I require the equivalent of at least nine pounds an hour. Which is quite reasonable, I think. And you seem a reasonable sort."

He barked out a laugh. "Ah, I see. So, you tell me what I'm paying?"

"Evidently. Can you manage it?"

Nate pretended to think for a moment, cocking his head dramatically. Finally, though, he said, "Sure. I can manage that. Might even throw in some benefits."

And that was the moment Hannah realised she was a terrible, wicked, and ungodly woman. Because when he said *benefits*, she thought of something other than the friendly joke he'd probably intended. Something deliciously inappropriate and alarmingly appealing.

This did not bode well.

DREAMING, for Hannah, was a little bit like being drunk. In both states, she felt removed from herself—but not in a negative way, not like disassociating. It was lighter, a giddy, reckless experience that usually felt delicious. The cautious voices that typically tied her up in knots disappeared, sucked away like cobwebs through a vacuum cleaner.

Hannah's experience of drunkenness and dreaming were enough to convince her that she didn't have only a single self. Maybe no-one did. Certain basics of identity might remain the same, but people could change significantly depending on their circumstances.

For example, Sober Hannah would rather die than let some random girl give her head in a club bathroom, because 1. germs and 2. germs and 3. dignity and 4. germs. But Drunk Hannah had happily let precisely that scenario come to pass on a hazy summer night in 2009, and had been rewarded for it with a rare orgasm. She hadn't thought about the prevalence of the herpes virus or the amount of faecal matter in the average toilet cubicle, not even once. And she'd been rewarded with the best sex of her life, while her sober encounters tended to result in awkward disappointment and general disillusionment, no matter what she did.

Drunk Hannah, clearly, was not Sober Hannah. That was okay.

And Dream Hannah was not Awake Hannah, either. That was okay, too.

This was what Hannah told herself as Nate Davis sank his teeth into her shoulder.

She gasped, stretching out on the enormous bed they shared, arching back against his erection. He was perfectly sized—big enough to make her sigh, not big enough to require gallons of lube—because she had made it so. That was the beauty of dreams, you see. He spread her arse slightly with one hand, until his rigid cock nestled between her cheeks—which would be scandalous enough to send Awake Hannah into fits, but only managed to drag a purr of satisfaction from Dream Hannah. She rocked against that thick shaft as Nate ran his tongue over the tingling bite marks on her shoulder.

He stroked her hip, trailing silken whispers of arousal over her skin, and Hannah realised they were completely naked. Maybe they hadn't been a second ago, but they were now. Also, their enormous bed appeared to be floating in a tropical ocean. Weird, but she'd go with it.

"Stop thinking," he whispered in her ear. "Look at me."

"No, thank you."

She felt him smile. His lips were pressed against her throat, soft and warm. Then he reached between her thighs with one steady, tattooed hand and touched her. Actually, *touched* might be too feeble a word: he ran the blunt tip of his middle finger over her folds, teasing her slick, swollen flesh. When he nudged her clit, Hannah moaned.

His finger circled her stiffening bud, the contact too much and too little, delicate and delicious. His mouth, hot and wet and wanting, sucked at a spot just beneath her ear. She melted against him like warm chocolate and he rocked his hard dick against her arse in a rhythm that echoed her pounding heart. "Look at me," he said again.

"You're very demanding," she managed to gasp, "for a figment of my imagination."

"That's not what I am," he murmured. Before she could beg for more of the dizzying sensations he produced between her thighs, Nate's teasing touch became a firm, fast rhythm. He flattened his fingers and massaged her clit, distributing that perfect pressure, heating her blood into molten lust.

Hannah moaned, then rocked her hips back and spread her legs wider. "You're not demanding?"

"I'm not a figment of your imagination." He pushed her onto her stomach, then dragged her hips up into the air and spread her thighs.

"You are," she insisted. "If you were real, I wouldn't feel like this."

"Like what?"

"Good. I wouldn't feel good."

"I'm real, Hannah." He parted her folds, the fat head of his cock sliding over her slick entrance. "You know me."

"I don't know you. I haven't seen you in years."

"You remember me."

"I never knew you. No-one knew you."

He leaned over her, his chest covering her back, his body caging hers as his length nudged at her entrance. She felt his breath against her ear as he whispered, "You knew me. Of course you knew me. That's why you wanted me so bad."

"Nate…" She closed her eyes, shuddered at the promise of satisfaction, at the kiss of his hard dick spreading her wider and threatening to fill her up. Fuck, that slick glide would be so *good* if he would just—

"Look at me," he said again.

"*No.*"

He sighed, pulling back. Away from her. What the fuck? This was her dream, for Christ's sake!

"Come back here," she snapped.

"You know what I want."

"What is this, a subconscious revolt?" she demanded. What the hell was going on? She had no idea—and she couldn't ask her mother to interpret this particular dream, since it involved fucking a local hot dad on a floating bed. What was she supposed to do, Google it?

"You know me, Hannah. You know me because we're the same. Admit it."

"Oh, piss off. Jesus. I can't even get a decent shag inside my own fucking head. Why haven't I replaced the batteries in my vibrator yet?"

"Because you don't masturbate. You just have dreams like this and wake up wondering what happened. But you don't remember, because you sleep too deeply."

"Great," she said dryly. And then, a second later: "Wait, so I won't remember this? That *is* pretty great."

"You want to forget me?" Nate asked, sounding a little offended.

"Of course I do. This is atrocious. I don't know what my subconscious was playing at, bringing you here. Frankly, I only allowed it because I like your tattoos."

"But you don't like *me*."

"Not like that. I'm not fifteen anymore."

"Are you sure?" he asked, his voice unnervingly dark.

"That I'm not fifteen?"

"*Hannah,*" he growled.

Oh, fine. She knew what he meant. "Yes! Okay? Yes, I'm sure. I'm very sure." While sitting on a dreamy, floating bed, butt-naked, with her own arousal sliding down her thighs and a desperate need for Nate's phantom dick, she said firmly: "Nathaniel Davis, I am *not* into you."

"In that case," he said, "you'd better wake up."

NATE'S HOUSE, Hannah discovered the next day, was east of the train tracks, close to the town centre, and on the smaller side. It was also painfully charming—or at least it looked that way from the pavement. Instead of brick, it was made of those old cobble stones, and the front garden was alive with… flowers. Yellow ones and purple ones. That was the best Hannah could do in terms of identifying plant life. The whole thing was adorable.

She approached it with as much trepidation as she would Dracula's mansion.

"You've got this," she murmured under her breath. "You are in control. Base emotions do *not* rule you. Attraction does not necessitate action."

The positive affirmations didn't help.

She didn't know why, exactly, but Hannah had woken up that morning convinced that she was being haunted by the ghost of her old crush. Except it had turned poltergeist, and it would not give her a minute to breathe. This was all Nate's fault, obviously, for running around looking like a modern-day Danny Zuko, but the consequences of that irresponsible sexiness would inevitably be heaped on Hannah's shoulders.

A crush, she knew, was a powerful thing. A dangerous thing. Her crush on Nate had been the first she'd ever had, and she'd hated every damned minute of it. The inappropriate thoughts, the inappropriate dreams (which probably more puberty-related than Nate-related, but whatever), the sweaty palms and pounding heart…

Good Lord, it had all been quite sickening. And the threat of sliding back into that messy existence was making Hannah teeter on the edge of hysteria. She was slightly concerned that, if he opened the door looking a little too handsome, she might do something disturbing. Like slap him. And slapping the poor man wouldn't help her plot to secure employment, now, would it?

Hannah cleared her throat, adjusted her braids, and smoothed down her floor-length skirt. Although she'd ironed it twice before leaving the house, she checked studiously for any embarrassing creases. Really, you could never be too careful. Once, she'd wandered about for hours in a skirt that had an odd V-shaped furrow right over her vulva. She'd gotten so many strange looks that day.

Satisfied that all was in order, she stepped through the pretty little gate, strode up the pretty garden path, and rapped smartly on Nate's pretty front door.

Almost immediately, a shadow fell behind its frosted glass. A very large shadow. Hannah swallowed as she heard locks and latches clatter, and then the door swung slowly, ominously open... to reveal *Zach's* smiling face.

The anti-climax almost killed her.

"Hey," he grinned. "You're here."

Hannah winced. "Am I early? Am I late?" She couldn't be late, could she? She'd timed it so perfectly—

"Stop that. You're completely, precisely on time." Zach grabbed her arm and dragged her into the house, as if he somehow knew she needed the extra push. "We're in the garden."

"*We* being..."

"Me and Nate and the kids. And Ma. Literally all of us. Surprise!"

"Oh," Hannah said faintly. "Great, that's... that's great..." She tapped her palms against her legs. Christ, it was hot.

Why had she worn a skirt? Her thighs were chafing. Chafing was not conducive to social perfection. The skirt had definitely been a miscalculation, but—

"Nervous?"

She looked up to find Zach giving her the kind of arch, cocky look that had made him Ravenswood's most successful man-slut. "No," she said. It wasn't a lie; it was positive self-talk. "Stop trying to psych me out."

"I'm not! I swear. I've just never seen you like this before. You're always so cool. Which I like, by the way." He flashed one of his trademark, lazy-sexy smiles.

"Not now, Zachary."

"But later?"

"Put your head in the freezer or something." She ignored his answering burst of laughter, casting a sharp eye over the hall. There were boxes stacked precariously by the stairs, and the living room she saw through a nearby doorway looked disorganised, to say the least.

But her mind was distracted from its mental tidying as childish shouts danced on the air. The sound filled her chest with a familiar peace, a feeling she'd sorely missed over the years. All at once, her nerves faded like the last bright sparks of a firework, until she was cool and composed, a blank night sky again. There was no need to panic.

Yes, she might be rusty after two years, and yes, Nate triggered some sort of minor nostalgic lust in her, but that didn't matter. She was here to work, and work was one thing Hannah could do, no matter what. She had skills and experience and qualifications coming out of her ears, and most importantly...

Kids loved her. Kids really, really loved her. They were

the only people who did, and that was her superpower. So, she'd re-meet Bethany and Joshua, and they'd have fun playing in the garden, and everything would be fine, and then—*then*—she'd actually, finally, be working in childcare again. For now.

That was enough to make her heart sing.

She took a deep breath and gave Zach her best smile. "Lead the way."

CHAPTER FIVE

"When you're fatter than complete strangers with boundary issues prefer, those complete strangers with boundary issues make sure to tell you so. In *explicit* detail. They do this because they hate happiness."

— HANNAH KABBAH, *THE KABBAH CODE*

"Grandma, would you like an apple smoothie?"

"Oh, yes, please!" Nate watched as his mother widened her eyes and licked her lips, holding out one eager hand for a cup of pond scum and mushed-up leaves.

Beth passed it over with a giggle, then turned to Josh and ordered, "Another one! For Uncle Zach!"

Josh nodded so hard, Nate was surprised he didn't fall over. Smoothie making in the garden was clearly a serious business.

It was nice, having a garden. Very nice. He'd forgotten that part of living in Ravenswood; all the greenery. The kids were having the time of their lives. Maybe they'd forgive him for the move soon.

He raised his camera and lined up a shot of Beth, mud smudged over her snub little nose, kneeling by their shallow pond. She looked up, caught him, and gave a glare more suited to a teenager than a seven-year-old.

"Don't take pictures of me, Daddy," she commanded.

He didn't blame the poor kid. He'd been photographing her nonstop from the minute she was born. "Don't worry, I won't. I'm just looking at you."

She sniffed dubiously. Nate chuckled and turned the camera elsewhere, zooming in on Josh's chubby fingers snatching at leaves on a rhododendron bush; then on Ma, who was lounging on the quilted garden swing, 'apple smoothie' in hand. She winked at him, lifting her plastic cup, and he snapped a picture.

Finally, as if by instinct, he looked toward the patio doors, camera still raised to his face...

And saw Hannah.

He'd been expecting her. Of course he had. But the sight of her still felt like a surprise. Maybe it was because of her smile—the kind of breathtaking, sunshine-bright grin he could never have predicted from a woman so tightly contained. Of course, she was aiming that elusive expression at his little brother, since they were friends. And she was *talking* to him, too, without any of the self-consciousness she'd shown Nate.

Because she had been self-conscious, during their odd little interview, despite how bold she seemed. He could sense it, somehow, every time she hesitated, every time she bit back words or swallowed feelings. It made him want to bring all the shadowy parts of her into the light. He'd had this odd certainty that she needed it, like she was a plant that could do with re-potting and a sprinkle of water. But it turned out that she didn't need that at all, from him or anyone, because she had no trouble shining with Zach.

Which would teach Nate to think about adults the way he thought about his kids.

Nate lowered the camera and called, "Josh. Beth. Come over here, please." For once, they did as he asked. Reluctantly, sure, but he'd take what he could get.

When they drew closer, Nate crouched down in the grass and put a hand on both their shoulders. "Okay; you remember I said someone would start living with us soon, to watch you guys while I'm not here?"

They stared like beady-eyed birds, which he decided to take as a yes.

"Do you also remember the lady we bumped into in the meadow that one night? The one who gave you marshmallows?"

"Yeeeees," Beth sighed. "That was only the other day, Dad."

And Josh, taking his cue from his older sister, echoed, "Yeaaaah, Daddy." He tried to roll his eyes, but it looked more like he was being momentarily possessed.

Nate bit back a smile. He didn't want to disrupt the gravity of their disdain. "Right. Well, she's here, and her name is Hannah, and we're gonna go and say hello to her. Very politely. Okay?"

"Okay," Beth huffed.

Josh bit his lip.

"She's really nice," Nate said. "I promise. Look, she's just over there. She's your Uncle Zach's friend."

Both kids turned to stare at Hannah, who was currently saying hi to Shirley. Hopefully the fact that she was standing by their idol and hero, Cool Uncle Zach, giver of sweets and toys, would get Hannah points.

Nate straightened and led his kids over the grass. His heart swelled when he felt first Josh, and then Beth, take his hand, their palms soft and plump and sweaty. Never got old.

Hannah smiled as they approached, all soft and closed-lipped and oddly sweet. Her lipstick was kind of red today, kind of orange. Like she'd painted her mouth with pure heat. "Hello," she said, all her focus on the kids.

"Hannah," he said, "this is Beth and Josh. Kids, this is Hannah. Say hello."

Beth did a little wiggle on the spot, which meant she was nervous. But she still lifted her chin and said, "Hello Hannah." He squeezed her hand and smiled down at her—and, miracle of miracles, she actually smiled back, sticking her tongue through the hole left by her missing front tooth.

Then he heard Josh say hello too, just like his sister. Always, just like his sister.

And then Hannah shocked Nate completely by kneeling down on the grass in her pristine white skirt. She folded her hands on her lap, posture perfect as always, and said, "Your grandmother tells me that the two of you have a very important secret." Her voice dropped to a whisper on *secret* in a way that somehow seemed perfectly natural and genuine. Her expression was grave, lips pursed, brows slightly raised.

Both kids leaned toward her. "Secret?" Beth echoed.

Hannah nodded, looking at one child, then the other, very slowly. Somehow, the same earthy gaze that tore people down so effortlessly became a spotlight, a round of applause, and a gold star, all at once. She looked so thoroughly *interested* in the kids, he could see them blooming before her like flowers before the sun.

"She says," Hannah murmured, "that you have a top-secret recipe for the best apple smoothies in the world. Is that true? Or is she mistaken?"

"It's true!" Josh whispered back.

Beth glared at him. "Shh!" Then, looking at Hannah, she muttered. "It's not a *secret*. It's just *leaves*."

Hannah cocked her head to the side. Just like she used to, in class, when she was listening. She nodded toward the swing, where his mum was watching them all with a smile on her face. "If it's not a secret, will you show me how you did it? You see, I would like to make someone as happy as you made your grandmother."

Beth blinked. She puffed up her cheeks. Then she shrugged and said, "If you reeeally want…"

That space was supposed to be filled by more eager requests, but Hannah simply sat back and watched, pure interest all over her face.

And finally, Beth said, "Okay. Okay. You can come and look."

Hannah smiled. "Wonderful." Then she stood, far too gracefully in his opinion, and held out both her hands.

To Nate's utter astonishment, his children released him without hesitation and took hold of Hannah like a pair of limpets. They skirted around him as if he were a particularly inconvenient garden gnome, heading for the pond and chattering over each other. He stood alone and slightly alarmed, blinking rapidly.

Zach came over to him with a grin. "See? She's great. She's like magic. You just accidentally love her."

Nate decided not to answer that. He turned away from his brother just in time to watch his son spill a cup of algae all over Hannah's skirt. Oh, shit. Josh and Beth both had their little hands over their mouths in the universal child expression for *Oops*.

"Sorry!" Josh squeaked.

Nate wasn't surprised when Hannah said, "It's okay, Josh. Accidents happen." He'd expected that, actually. Despite her pristine exterior, she had years of experience working with kids. She wouldn't have gotten far if she got upset over dirty clothes.

But he *was* surprised by the look on her face. By the expression that crept over her features after Josh had calmed, after the kids had turned back to the pond and started chatting away, after the other adults in the garden stopped paying attention.

She stared down at the sodden, green-tinged fabric, running her hand over the stain. And she looked…

She looked fucking delighted.

"Caitlin from my class said that nowhere is as good as London because London is where the queen is, but Daddy says the queen is not important anyway so I should like it here. But I don't like it here." Bethany Davis had been giving

Hannah a calm and detailed monologue on the benefits of London versus Nottingham for at least ten minutes, and she didn't seem to be running out of steam. Hannah almost regretted asking.

Except not really, because she loved hearing kids talk.

"I don't like Caitlin that much anyway—Caitlin W., I mean. I like Caitlin G., even though she's not in my class." Bethany—Beth—hesitated. Her little bottom lip pushed out a bit as she frowned. "Oh. I am not in my class either."

Beside her, the mostly-silent Josh shredded leaves diligently.

"That's okay," Hannah said. "I think you'll enjoy your new school, once you get settled in."

Beth scowled. "Why? I don't like it now."

"That's because you're new. When you're new, everything stands out too much, and it makes you feel strange. But once you get used to things, you won't feel strange anymore."

Wide, blue eyes blinked slowly. Beth appeared to be considering those words. She looked slightly mollified, to Hannah. But she still asked, suspicion in her voice, "How do *you* know?"

Nate's sudden arrival saved Hannah from replying. He'd hung back for a while now, letting her play with the kids—who, it turned out, she adored. Zach had called them demons, but he clearly didn't have much experience with children. Beth and Josh were smart, funny, creative, and headstrong. As far as Hannah was concerned, those were all excellent qualities in a child—even if they did demand a little extra effort from the adults around said children.

As she'd been drawing that conclusion, she'd also been

conscious of Nate's presence in the garden. She felt him like the ocean felt the moon, she supposed. Those pale, piercing eyes tracked her every move. It was sweet how protective he was over his kids. When he finally approached them, it was with an apologetic smile that brought out that damned dimple and made her heart lurch awfully. *Ugh.* Feelings were so very excessive, and uncomfortable, too. In fact, emotions were the psychological equivalent of walking on a blister.

"Hannah," Nate said in that smoke-and-gravel voice. He hadn't sounded like *that* all those years ago. "Can I drag you away for a second?"

She turned to Beth. "What do you think? Can you and Josh do without me?"

"No," Josh piped up. The word wasn't even a whine; he just said it in this calm, reasonable tone, as if he sadly could not spare her and his dad would have to cope with the loss.

Nate's lips twitched. "Sorry, kiddo. I'll bring her back soon."

"Daddy—"

"Soon! Promise!"

Josh huffed and passed his sister another handful of leaves. Nate smoothed a hand over his sullen son's hair before looking up at Hannah. "I thought you might want to look around."

He thought right.

They wandered into the kitchen through the open patio doors, and he quipped, "So. Is it too soon to ask you to move in?"

She allowed herself a smile. "I don't know. You're coming on kind of strong."

"Haven't heard that in a while," he said wryly. But as they moved deeper into the house, the kids' high voices fading behind them, he grew serious. In the shadows of the hallway, he paused, and Hannah stopped too.

"Listen," he said, "this all feels kind of weird—hiring someone to look after my kids. *I* look after my kids. But I've been thinking about it from every angle and I really…" He sighed, rubbing a hand over his face, and Hannah noticed for the first time how achingly tired he looked. Beyond the striking handsomeness of his strong bone structure and soft smile, beyond the impact of his dark hair and bright eyes. Those eyes were cradled by plum shadows so deep they almost looked like bruises.

"There's nothing wrong with needing help," she said.

He arched a brow. "Right. I bet you ask for help all the time."

She felt her cheeks heat. He had her there. More than he knew.

"Sorry," Nate said, squeezing his eyes shut for a second, shaking his head. "I'm kind of all over the place right now. The point is, I have no idea what Ma's gonna need from day to day, and Zach works full-time. My job is flexible, but it's not easy. I know this is the right thing to do."

And she knew exactly why he was saying these words out loud, why he was letting them spill out like some absent stream of consciousness instead of keeping them all bottled up. She'd seen how his gaze flew to Shirley every time she coughed or shivered—and how it slid away again a second later, weighed down with the thick, sticky slime that was guilt.

Yeah; Hannah knew guilt. For some reason, Nate had a lot of it. And it seemed to be fucking with his head.

"I'm just going to be honest," he said. "I really want to give you this job. You know what you're doing, the kids like you, I like you, my mother goes to church with your mother... it all seems very neat." He barely managed a playful smile, but even his weakest effort made her want to smile right back.

Which Hannah didn't like. She preferred to be in complete control of her own smiles; life was unpredictable enough without bringing errant facial muscles into the equation. But she wouldn't hold his compelling handsome-ness against him. Much.

"I'd love to take the job," she admitted. "As long as you're not about to show me a rat-infested attic room with a single-paned window."

"Oh, no, Hannah. This is Ravenswood. The attic room is riddled with genteel field mice."

She might've laughed at that, if it weren't for the way he'd said her name. Or rather, how it hit her—as if she'd never heard it from his lips before. Which was ridiculous, because she most definitely had. She knew she had.

But as he flashed her a grin and led the way, she couldn't shake the feeling that she'd never heard it quite like that.

Hannah put that thought aside for later and followed him up the stairs, trying her best not to look at his arse. But really, it was right *there*. Directly in front of her face. Taunting her like a smug, juicy peach in black shorts. And holy shit, had she really just used the phrase *smug, juicy peach*? What the fuck? The force of her own astonished horror smacked Hannah so hard, she almost fell back down the carpeted steps.

"I don't know if this is a reasonable request," he said, "but I was hoping you could move in by the end of the week. I mean, I'm not sure where you live—"

"On the other side of the park," she replied, brushing off the last of her baffled self-disgust. Maybe if she ignored these strange, Nate-related thoughts, they'd go away. "You know, the new flats? I'm in my sister's, so I don't have a lease or anything." She followed him past what looked to be the kids' bedrooms, stepping over unpacked boxes and strewn-about Lego in the hall. The urge to tidy everything in sight was practically suffocating her, but like the valiant soldier she was, Hannah squashed it. Common sense dictated that she leave all presumptuous cleaning until it was too late for him to get rid of her.

"You live with your sister?" he asked.

"She's dating her next-door neighbour. Suffice it to say, she's not exactly using her flat right now."

She trailed off as he reached a door at the end of the landing and pushed it open to reveal the neatest, blandest, most minimalist little room she'd ever seen in her life. The walls were cream. The floors were pale wood. The furniture was cream *and* wooden. It held a no-frills double bed, a wardrobe, a desk, and a set of beside drawers.

"It's not great," he said ruefully, "but you'd be the only one using this bathroom over here, and I can—"

"It's perfect," she said. And meant it. She was quite thoroughly in love.

Nate stared at her for a moment, as if trying to read her.

Which, of course, made Hannah so uncomfortable she might actually crawl out of her skin. Whatever. No big deal.

Then he said, "You're serious."

"I usually am."

"You actually like this room."

She looked over the neutral space again. There was nothing overwhelming or excessive or dark or distracting. This little room looked the way Hannah wished, more than anything, the inside of her head could be. Of course, she'd have to add the colours—always, she needed colours. But that was fine. Because nothing would *clash*, you see.

"It's perfect," she repeated firmly. Despite her commitment to polite distance and tamped-down enthusiasm, Hannah found herself smiling. She was vaguely conscious of Nate watching her with a quiet smile of his own, a sort of pleased disbelief that seemed to say, *I don't understand you one bit, but I still like you.*

Which was ridiculous. People didn't like Hannah. *Nate* didn't like Hannah, despite claiming to. He was just… naturally… lovely. Even though, throughout their years growing up together, he'd been almost as antisocial as her prickly little sister. Oh, whatever. Clearly, people changed.

She wandered over to the room's wide window and looked down into the garden below. The trees at its border made a sort of canopy, so she could barely see the grass—but she saw Shirley swinging on the patio, and Zach chasing a laughing Beth, and Josh carefully plopping grapes into the birdbath.

"Just to check," she said absently, "are grapes allowed in the birdbath?"

"What?" She heard Nate come up behind her—but it

seemed more accurate to say that she felt it. He frowned out of the window, leaning over her shoulder, then sighed. "That kid. How did he even get those out of the fridge? You know what? Never mind." Nate shook his head.

She turned to look at him fully, because the fond exasperation in his voice was just... it was sweet. Sweet and soft like marshmallows, and she wanted to see it reflected in his eyes. Only, just as she turned her head, he looked down at her, and all of a sudden—

Well. All of a sudden, their faces were much closer than she'd planned. Much, much closer. And she could see the tiny, moon-pale scars that littered his skin. There was one over the bridge of his nose, plus a few scattered across his temple in short, sharp slashes. And then there were little circular ones over his eyebrow, and a crease through his lower lip that made her think he'd had some... interesting piercings at one point. Which wouldn't surprise her.

What *did* surprise her was the way she felt—as if all the oxygen had been sucked out of the room. As if something hung between them, too heavy and tense to turn away from. As if tearing her eyes from his would shatter it.

So, embarrassingly, it was Nate who broke the silence. Nate who cleared his throat, and blinked a little too slowly —more like a quick squeeze-shut of the eyes—and shook his head. He stepped back once, and then again. For a second, she worried he'd smack into the wall behind him. But he stopped just in time and said, "Well. Well, then. Shall we—I mean, if you like it, let's..."

"Yes," she said quickly. "Let's." And then she turned and left the room.

FOR SOME REASON, as he followed her downstairs, Nate's mind latched on to the fact that earlier—in the garden—Zach had called Hannah *Han*.

He supposed that was a decent nickname for Hannah. The kids at school used to call her Bunny, or some shit like that. Those same guys were probably kicking themselves, these days, but that was none of his concern. He couldn't stop thinking about that nickname. Han.

Nate wondered when, exactly, his little brother had grown close enough to a woman like Hannah Kabbah to casually shorten her name. He had this idea that if *he* ever shortened Hannah's name, she'd short-circuit like a robot under the sheer weight of all her horrified disgust. Around Nate, she seemed to vacillate between painfully uptight and reluctantly open; like any smiles or jokes or laughs she threw at him were a charitable endeavour she regretted almost immediately. But she'd spent the afternoon smiling at *Zach* without hesitation.

Yes; this was what his mind chose to focus on. Not that odd moment upstairs when, for a second, he'd looked at her and found himself unable to move. Unable to pull away from the soft, vanilla scent that hovered around her, from the velvet texture of her skin or the amber flecks in her dark eyes. He saw no reason to think about that incident at all.

She waited for him by the front door, standing arrow straight, mouth set in a plastic smile. Her skirt was covered in grass stains and there were little white ovals that *might* be daisy petals caught in her hair. But none of that mattered when she held herself so stiffly and watched him so distantly. She seemed almost alien in her perfection, removed from his reality, as bright and untouchable as a star in the sky.

And lonely, too. He didn't mind the perfection, but he didn't like that loneliness. He'd been lonely before.

"So," he said, clearing his throat. "I'll be in touch, I suppose? About moving."

She nodded politely.

"I know it's kind of fast, but obviously I can help, so—"

She gave a little huff that might've been a snort. "If you don't think I can organise moving house within a week, I've severely misrepresented myself."

"Fair enough," he said wryly.

"Wonderful." She clapped her hands together like a judge banging a gavel, and that, he supposed, was that.

Except he didn't want it to be. Because something about her still seemed so... *sad*. He had no idea what, or why; he just wanted it to stop.

Maybe he was losing his mind. That would explain why, instead of saying something sensible like *Goodbye*, he blurted out, "You're kind of bossy, you know that?"

She arched a brow. "I am thirty years old. If I had gone this long without identifying my key character traits, I would be suffering from a sad lack of self-awareness."

He grinned, leaning back against the hallway wall. "So you do know that you're bossy."

"Of course." She cocked her head. "Are you waiting for me to apologise?"

"Now why would I want that?" he murmured. He was

genuinely confused, actually. "Is that what people usually want? For you to apologise?"

She sucked in her cheeks for a moment, her jaw shifting, eyes narrowed, suspicion clear. She was so electric, so brimming with energy, and yet she seemed so determined to contain it. He wondered if she realised how utterly she failed. It was kind of cute.

He arched a brow and waited.

She arched two brows, as if they were in some sort of eyebrow-raising competition. If they were, she'd just won. Nate did not have three eyebrows.

"Hannah," he said, his voice almost sing-song. He was enjoying this far too much. "Are you going to answer me?"

She flicked him a disgusted look. She was damned good at it, too, and she really took her time. Her dark gaze raked over every inch of him—twice, as if to be sure—before turning away dismissively. It reminded him of the way she'd been at school, sitting alone at the front of every class and glaring at anyone who mocked her. Had it always been so intoxicating, that look?

No. No it fucking hadn't.

"I don't know what you're *leaning* for," she finally muttered.

"Leaning?"

"Against the wall." She glared at him again, or maybe at the wall. "You look like an oversized teenager."

Why was he so very pleased to hear her insult him?

Nate grinned and shoved his hands in his pockets. He was almost tempted to slouch, just to piss her off even more. "I had no idea you cared so much about posture." Lie.

Anyone who'd ever set eyes on her would know she cared about posture.

She snorted as if to say the same thing. But her lips twitched, just a bit, like she was actually fighting a smile. "You haven't changed at all."

"Oh, I haven't?"

"No," she said dryly. "You always did strut around in your black clothes thinking you were cool—"

"I was cool."

This time she actually smiled outright, even as she ignored his interruption. "—with your cigarettes and your dyed hair—"

Nate rolled his eyes. "I have never dyed my hair. I don't know who started that rumour."

"People just assumed," she smirked. "Because it's rather…"

"I think the word you're looking for is *black*."

"Thank you so much," she said dryly. "I would've been lost without you."

"Ah, don't sell yourself short. You'd get there eventually."

She smirked. Everything about her was relaxing inch by inch, and that sharp little smile grew wider. He was really, really glad he'd pushed. Needling her produced excellent results. He'd have to bear that in mind.

Bear that in mind for what? Your longstanding professional relationship?

For a moment, Nate came to his senses and asked himself what the hell he was doing, trying to make Hannah Kabbah smile. Then she spoke again, and his brain put up a *Do Not Disturb* sign and went off for a nap.

"You don't still smoke, do you?" she asked.

"Nah. Ellie hated it. My wife, I mean."

She wouldn't ask about Ellie. No-one in Ravenswood asked about Ellie. He'd be relieved about that fact, if it didn't make him wonder what they thought they knew.

It wasn't like his wife's death was some big secret: it had been nothing more scandalous than a car accident. The problem was that, his whole life, he'd felt this gut-wrenching disgust at the thought of anyone thinking they knew him. The thought of people watching him, discussing him, making assumptions about him—he felt it like spiders' legs creeping over his face in the dark. It was why he'd left this town in the first place.

But he didn't feel it now. Not exactly. Because even though Hannah didn't ask about Ellie, she sort of leaned in as if to say…

As if to say that he should keep going?

So, after a moment's hesitation, Nate went on. "The first time I asked her out—it wasn't long after I left Ravenswood. I was sixteen, maybe seventeen, and I still thought I was hot shit. But I asked her out, and she turned me down because she didn't do smokers." Usually, the memory made him grin. Right now, though… well, he was already grinning. Wider than he had in a while, actually. And it felt good.

Hannah was smiling back, too. "Is that why you quit?"

"Yeah," he laughed. "That's why."

"And then you asked her out again?"

"Yep." He ran a hand through his hair, suddenly embarrassed.

She let out this little puff of air that might've been a highly buttoned-up laugh, and said, "Good gracious me. That's almost romantic. I'm shocked."

Nate could feel his cheeks burning even as he rolled his eyes. "I wouldn't call it romantic."

"You gave up an addiction to get the girl. They write books about men like you." She spoke sagely as a grandmother, her eyes dancing. She didn't seem sad anymore. Which was why he didn't mind, this time, when she edged toward the door and said, "Well. As illuminating as this conversation has been, I should really get going."

"Oh, right." He unlocked the door and held it open for her, and she nodded regally as she passed—but then, just before she stepped over the threshold, she paused.

And then she reach out and touched him. Actually *touched* him. She put her hand on his forearm, and looked up into his eyes, and said, "I'm quite fond of your mother, you know. I'm... I'm glad that I can do something to help."

He swallowed and nodded slowly.

She gave him a smile so impish, he almost forgot the dread lying heavy in his gut. "Also, I will be unpacking all these bloody boxes you've got lying around. I absolutely cannot cope with clutter."

With that, she sailed out of the house and down the garden path. He stood in the doorway for far too long—not watching her leave, but staring down at his own arm. At the place where she'd touched him.

The earth hadn't moved, when her skin had brushed his. The stars hadn't aligned, and his heart hadn't pounded its way right out of his chest.

It only felt that way.

CHAPTER SIX

Zach: Told you I was right about Hannah.

Nate: Whatever. You do realise, now that she watches the kids, she's off-limits?

Zach: Those are your kids, man. Not mine.

A FEW DAYS LATER, Hannah sat on her neat little bed in her neat little room and took a deep, lemon-scented breath. She may have gone overboard, after moving in, when she'd mopped the floors. And scrubbed the skirting boards. And wiped the drawers inside and out. Cleaning helped her feel settled. But the window was open, letting the night air in and the potentially dangerous chemical fumes out, so, God willing, she would not accidentally kill herself via Domestos tonight.

She might just die of satisfaction, though. Hannah smiled to herself as she cast a pleased look over her books and laptop arranged neatly on the desk, and her clothes hanging—organised by colour and season, of course—in the wardrobe. Then she opened her planner to the current week and pulled out a few fine liners from her 20-colour pack. Specifically: teal for medication and self-care, forest green for work, and raspberry for social commitments.

Hannah preferred to organise her weeks in advance—typically every Sunday—but she'd been thrown off her routine, what with recent events. *Recent events* being a euphemism for her rampant recklessness, as demonstrated by marshmallow-based attacks on authority figures and her alarmingly quick decision to move into the house of a man with tattooed hands.

She still wasn't sure how she felt about those tattoos. She didn't *mind* them, not at all. She just couldn't understand what it was about the ink on Nate's hands, especially, that made her stomach dip like a swallow swooping through blue skies. They triggered this odd fizzing in the centre of her chest that felt like something long-dormant awakening.

And now she was thinking far too hard about feelings and tattoos and *Nate* when she should be carefully planning the days ahead.

"Come on, bitch," she muttered, uncapping the forest green pen. "Get it together."

Hannah's professional responsibilities were remarkably light. She was starting to feel bad about the amount Nate was paying her, not to mention the free food and board. She'd only really be with the kids in the evenings and on Saturdays. Plus, she'd tidy the house, organise the weekly food shop, things like that.

Frankly, she would've done that for free if it meant she got to check out Nate's arse every so often.

The quiet hummed with crisp possibility as she finally filled in her planner. Since she was alone, she allowed herself the luxury of smiling at nothing like an utter loon. She couldn't help it. This felt like the night before the first day back at school. This felt like a brand new opportunity to conquer the world. This felt like getting back to herself, like returning to the life she'd thrown away when she'd let her temper get the better of her years ago.

Starting tomorrow, Hannah Kabbah would be working in childcare again.

And she'd be damned good at it, too. By the time she was done with the Davis family, every yummy mummy who'd ever sneered at her would want to know what her secret was.

Hannah would take the most inordinate pleasure in telling them to go fuck themselves.

She woke up before her alarm, which shouldn't have been possible.

Hannah's anti-depressants doubled as knock-out pills. She loved her tiny lilac tablets, not only because they kept her from petrifying into a frigid grey ball, but also because they ensured she got a solid eight hours' sleep every night.

Or nine. Or ten. Or eleven.

She had to be really careful about setting that alarm.

But when Hannah woke up to birds tweeting outside her window, it was still drowsy-dark outside. Countryside, summer morning dark, when the sun's rising somewhere in the distance and the farmers are up and about, but the Hannahs should be safely wrapped up in bed.

Hannah was not safely wrapped up in bed. The minute her eyes slid open, she got up. Lying in bed was an activity she reserved for sleep or depressive episodes. Otherwise, physical inertia led to the kind of mental overactivity that had once caused her to reimagine the entire cast of *Legally Blonde* as *Twilight* vampires, and then play the new version of the film in her head.

She'd given it three stars, which had been generous.

So she was up. Up, annoyed, and confused as to what had woken her at—she checked her phone—four-fucking-thirty in the morning. A few minutes of intense listening answered the question well enough: someone was moving around downstairs. Quietly, so quietly that she strained to hear them.

Maybe she had special senses, like in those comics Ruth loved to read, and her mutant brain had psychically alerted her to a very respectful burglar. Or, more likely, to an errant child pouring their own cereal and making a mess of the kitchen.

Hannah threw on an enormous, wooly cardigan—to match her enormous, wooly sleep socks—and went downstairs.

NATE'S INSOMNIA had absolutely nothing to do with Hannah Kabbah.

He knew this because he'd been suffering with insomnia

on and off his whole life, and for the past few weeks, it had been quite firmly *on*. So his inability to sleep tonight—the way he'd lain in bed staring at the ceiling for hours before thirst and boredom and irritation beat out bone-deep exhaustion—was nothing new. Nothing to do with her.

Which, Nate supposed, begged the question: why the hell couldn't he get her out of his head?

He was sitting in the living room, surrounded by left-over boxes, taking sips from a glass of ice-cold water because it was way too fucking stuffy in this house. Weren't older builds meant to be poorly insulated? Why did it feel dry as the bloody Sahara in here? These were the trivialities he chose to focus on, because they helped him ignore other thoughts.

Thoughts like, *Hannah sleeps just down the hall from you now.* And, *Hannah's sleeping in your house. Isn't that weird? Doesn't that feel weird? You should think about why it feels weird.*

Those questions, Nate knew, were a trap. The minute he examined the deeper workings of his own brain, he'd run head-first into all the disturbing shit he kept locked up in there. Like his secret love of N-Sync and his obvious attraction to the woman he'd just hired as his nanny.

Oh. Fuck.

There was a chance that Nate could've put that thought back where he'd found it—maybe hidden it beneath a few rocks, some tree branches and a bit of moss, for good measure—if Hannah herself hadn't appeared in front of him at that moment.

Huh. It had been a long time since he'd gotten tired enough to actually hallucinate.

"Are you okay?" she was asking, and a little arrow

formed between her eyebrows as she frowned. That was cute. It was such a central arrow, so neat, like someone had drawn it. Apparently, even Hannah's face obeyed her need for order. Or at least, it did in his pre-dawn hallucinations.

He stared at her, drinking in the creation of his over-worked brain. She was dressed for bed, of course. His hallu-cinations were nothing if not sensible. Her hair was up, and she had some kind of silky scarf on her head like a girl from the 1950s. She was all wrapped up in an enormous cardi-gan, which was very respectful of his brain. He was proud of himself for not imagining her naked or something. That would have been awful. Terrible. *Horrible.* Wonderfully evil. Mostly evil.

God, he needed a shag. That was it. That was the only reason why he felt so fucking horny all of a sudden. He wasn't really getting hard over a fantasy version of Hannah's bare knees, peaking out from beneath the hem of her huge cardigan. That would just be *odd.*

"Nate?" Dream Hannah said. "Could you speak or some-thing? Just so I can be sure you're not having a stroke."

He grunted.

"Oh, lovely. Thanks."

She was even funny in his head.

And then she, Dream Hannah, a figment of his imagina-tion who was absolutely *not* real, reached out and flicked him on the forehead.

"Ow," he yelped. *Wait.* "Fuck. Hannah?"

"Yes," she said dryly. "That's me. Hannah. I moved in today, if you recall. I'm your—"

"Sorry," Nate said quickly. "I was tired." Because he really couldn't allow her to finish that sentence. If she said some-

89

thing like *I'm your nanny/employee/brand-new and vulnerable household dependent*, the urge to throw himself off a cliff would grow even stronger than it already was. Had he really just been thinking about Hannah—*Hannah*, of all people—like *that*? Seriously?

Sleep deprivation was a dangerous thing.

She cocked her head, a slight smile on her lips. "Jesus, you must be knackered. Were you just, like, asleep? With your eyes open?"

Oh, perfect. That sounded way better than *I thought I was hallucinating so I took the opportunity to stare at you like a pervert.* "Yep," he said cheerfully. "I was asleep. Well, dozing, you know."

"Why aren't you in bed?" She sat down beside him, curling up like a cat, leaving a good metre between his right knee and her tucked-up feet. Why did that huge space feel more like a particularly tension-filled inch?

"I won't sleep tonight," he said. "No point lying there in the dark."

"Ah. You thought you'd come down and *sit* in the dark, instead?"

He shot her a wry look. "Works sometimes. Why are you up, anyway?"

She shrugged. "I don't know. First night in a new house, I suppose."

"Ah. And, um… why are you wearing that?" He nodded at her cardigan.

She arched a brow. Somehow, that single, tiny movement was powerful enough to make him feel like a misbehaving toddler. It was as if she'd peered into his mind, seen every filthy thought he'd *accidentally* had tonight, and found them all mildly amusing.

Cheeks burning, Nate clarified. "I meant, aren't you hot? Is that wool?"

Hannah looked down at herself for a moment, as if hesitating. Then she said, "I'm fine."

He opened his mouth to ask, *well what the bloody hell have you got on under there, to be fine in this heat?*

Which is when it occurred to him, like a punch to the face, that she might actually be naked.

Time for a change of subject.

She seemed to agree, because she said suddenly, "I thought you were one of the kids, to be honest. When I heard you moving around, I mean."

"The kids sleep like it's their job. They'll go twelve hours straight if you let them. Have since they were born."

She cocked her head. "That's impressive."

"Ellie had grand ideas about the effects of routine."

"She sounds like a sensible woman. What are your thoughts on routine?"

"Excellent for children," he hedged.

Of course, Hannah's all-seeing eyes wouldn't let him get away with that. "And for you...?"

Nate winced. "Not so much."

"You haven't been sleeping for a while, have you?"

Busted. His lips twisted into a rueful smile as he sank deeper into the cushions. He ran a hand through his hair and asked, "Do I look that bad?"

And she looked. She really, really *looked*. At him.

Sometimes it felt like Hannah saw straight through him.

Her gaze would skate over Nate like he was a smudge or a typo, like she was allergic to actually seeing him, and the sensation was… strange. But it was even stranger now, to have her studying him in that way of hers—like he was something under a microscope, something she could conquer if only she could understand it. Something she *would* conquer, if she wanted to.

Her gaze focused on his face first, and really, she could've stopped there. He looked like shit, and he knew it. But apparently, the signs of exhaustion in his features weren't enough. She moved on to the rest of him, and Nate remembered abruptly that he wasn't wearing a shirt. Or, you know, trousers.

Would it be really fucking obvious if he crossed his legs right now? Would it make her more or less uncomfortable if he held a pillow over his underwear like a modest maiden? He wasn't sure. But his mental gymnastics were interrupted by the realisation that Hannah appeared to have gotten… stuck. She was in no danger of ever seeing his barely-clothed groin because her gaze had snagged on something around his chest area.

Nate looked down at himself, trying to figure out what had made Hannah so very expressionless. Her face was so impassive, even for her, that he suspected she was actually screaming inside her own head. But when he examined himself, all he saw was his own supremely average chest. Oh, and…

"It's my wedding ring," he said, running a finger over the cord around his neck—the one that held a plain gold band, hanging just above his heart.

She blinked a few times as if she were mentally rebooting. "What? Oh. Right. Yes. The, er…"

She was being weird. The fact nudged at Nate, but it wasn't forceful enough to break through the mental fog of his exhaustion. His sluggish mind didn't have enough energy to analyse things further, so he didn't bother trying.

"That's sweet," she said finally. "That you wear it, I mean. Are you..." She paused. "I mean, do you miss her a lot?"

"Are you asking if I stay up every night thinking about her, and that's why I'm always tired?" he asked dryly.

She let out a little puff of air that *might* be a laugh. Like she was amused, but didn't know if she should be or not. So he forced his weary face into a smile, just to let her know it was okay.

"I've always suffered from insomnia," he said. "Gets worse when I'm stressed. I don't... I mean, I miss Ellie. I wish she was here. But I'm okay. I'm not still grieving, or anything."

Hannah nodded, but she had that look on her face—the one that seemed to encourage more. The one that said, *I'm here and I'm listening, if you're into that, but we could also go our separate ways and pretend this never happened. Whatever you want.*

So he added, "She died four years ago. Car accident. It was... well, it was the worst thing that ever happened to me, but, you know. I had the kids. Josh was so little. I had to be okay. And I think I'm lucky, because for me, faking it helped make it real."

"I see," she murmured. "That *is* lucky. And kind of badass."

The smile he'd forced turned real. Funny, really, how she managed that, when her own smiles were so hard to draw out. "I bet you're one of those people who has strangers telling you their deepest darkest secrets."

"I am," she admitted. "Apparently it's something about my face."

"I think I'd agree with that. Sometimes you look kind of… friendly?"

The alarm in her expression was so intense, he almost laughed out loud. "Friendly?" she choked out. "I am *not* friendly."

"Only sometimes," he said again. "I think when you're feeling sympathetic, you forget to do the thing."

"The thing?"

"You know." He scowled stiffly in his best Hannah impression. "The thing."

She closed her eyes and put a hand over her face. "Please tell me I don't look like that. And if I *do* look like that, lie to me. I beg of you."

"You don't look like that," he said obediently. "You're prettier. And there's more lipstick involved."

She was still covering her face, but he saw the corner of her mouth twitch. Which was great, actually, since it meant she wasn't freaked out that he'd accidentally called her pretty. It also reminded him that she wasn't wearing lipstick right *now*. He was so used to those bold shades, she should've looked naked without it.

And she did. But not in a bad way, like she was vulnerable or lacking. No, this was more the *get your arse in my bed* kind of naked. The kind of naked he really shouldn't be thinking about, because what the fuck, Nate? The state of his head right now was reminding him of his little brother. And Zach's head, he assumed, was a hellscape of misremembered porn, constant arousal, and generally inappropriate behaviour.

Which was fine, because that was Zach, and he had a right to be as filthy as he wanted. He even had a right to be mentally filthy about Hannah because thoughts never hurt anyone. But Nate... Nate needed to get control of whatever this weird attraction was, fast. Because he did *not* have a right to be mentally filthy about his fucking nanny. He wasn't that kind of guy.

Hannah moved the hand from her face and snuggled deeper into her enormous cardigan, as if the house wasn't hotter than the devil's arsehole, and he was struck again by the need to take her picture. The shadows clung to her but she stood out like a beacon. Her skin drank in scraps of light and elevated them to sunshine. The softness of her body and the strength of her *self...*

Yeah, he wanted to take her picture. And he'd focus on that want above all others, since it was the least shameful.

He wouldn't mention it, though. Frankly, *all* his wants were a little bit much, when it came to Hannah.

"I should go to bed," he said. "Have to be up with the kids soon."

She nodded. "Are you sure you don't need me in the mornings, by the way?"

"Nah. I want to spend as much time as possible with them. Don't worry about getting up."

"Okay. Well, I guess I'll go up, too."

Great. Now he'd have to walk beside Hannah, with her bare legs and her bare mouth and her... fuck.

"I'll just put this in the kitchen," he said, raising his glass. "See you later on?"

"Right. Later." She gave him a bright sort of smile, like she was trying to reassure him, and then she stood and padded out of the room.

Nate waited until he heard her climbing the stairs. Then he went to the kitchen. But he didn't drink the rest of his water, or even pour it away; instead, he bent over the sink and emptied the glass on his own damned head.

CHAPTER SEVEN

"I like to keep things simple. It's all so much neater that way."

— HANNAH KABBAH, *THE KABBAH CODE*

As TIME PASSED, Hannah fell into a routine so relaxing and so thoroughly enjoyable that she began to question her own moral fibre. She was supposedly working, and certainly being paid for it—but all she ever seemed to do was clean to her obsessive heart's content, play with two adorable (if slightly unruly) children, and blog.

Her first week with the Davises passed rather uneventfully. When Nate wasn't driving Shirley around town or to appointments, he came home and shut himself in his office. Hannah had no idea what he actually did in there—photography stuff, she assumed. Apparently, that was Nate's job.

Although she'd thought photography required more space than an office and more participants than a single man, but... maybe not?

Aside from that particular mystery, living with Nate was easy. The kids were sweet. He was sweet to the kids. He was sweet to her, damn him, and it made her feel constantly on edge. Because no-one could be that pleasant forever, right? Surely it wasn't a normal, natural thing? The kind of people who toasted bagels for everyone in the morning and cleaned up after themselves without issue and asked about your day as if they really gave a shit didn't actually exist. It was just a front they put up for nefarious reasons.

Except she couldn't imagine what nefarious reasons Nate might have to smile at her with such kindness, or joke with her even when she was prickly, or otherwise mind his damned business 24/7. Oh, and *pay* her on top of that. She didn't get it. At all. And when she'd asked Ruth about the matter, all her nightmare of a sister had said was *Evan's nice all the time. Maybe Nate's just one of those people.*

Honestly, Hannah had far preferred it when Ruth could be trusted to support her cynicism.

The following Tuesday night—or rather, Wednesday morning—she woke up inexplicably early again. It didn't make any sense, and it certainly didn't ease her suspicions that this whole situation was some kind of elaborate twilight zone trap. Still, just like last time, she dragged a cardigan on over her scant pyjamas and wandered downstairs.

And, just like last time, she found Nate.

He was sitting in the dark again, head bowed over his phone like a supplicant. The little glowing rectangle lit up his face, and for a moment she stood there in the doorway and watched him.

He sighed as he tapped at the phone. The exhalation seemed to hold a century's-worth of sheer exhaustion. Beyond the strong lines of his jaw, his cheekbones, and his hawkish nose, his face looked drawn and strained. Indigo bloomed beneath his eyes like bruises. He ran a hand through his too-long hair, and she tried not to stare at the tattoo on the inside of his elbow. But really, who had tattoos *there?* Surely that had to hurt.

Then again, she remembered darkly, he had a nipple piercing, too. The nipple piercing that, when she'd seen it last week in the dark, had made all of her thoughts fall clean out of her head. So clearly, he didn't mind pain.

"Hey," she called softly from the doorway. She'd been trying not to startle him, but he still jumped a little. She'd noticed, over the past week, that once he was focused on something, the rest of his world melted away. He didn't see anything else, hear anything else...

Hannah imagined that sort of focus could be put to use in a lot of interesting ways.

Actually, Hannah tried to imagine very little, because her imagination was a wild and reckless creature that could not be tamed. Dear Lord.

"Hi," he said finally. "Fancy meeting you here." And then he smiled.

She had a slight problem with Nate's smiles. Especially this one, the slightly teasing one that was wry and sharp-edged and uneven. *Zach's* sexy grin was the one that had achieved seductive infamy in Ravenswood, but she was starting to think of his as the knock-off version. Because

Nate hadn't smiled much back when they were young, but now? Now, he was the king of smiling. Smiling was his bitch. He *owned* smiling.

And she clearly needed more sleep, if the loopy train of her thoughts was anything to go by.

Stepping into the room, she nodded at the phone in Nate's hand and asked, "Everything okay?"

He gave a negative sort of grunt as she settled down beside him on the sofa. Usually, Nate employed full sentences, probably for the kids' benefit. To set a good example. But she'd started to notice that when they were alone, he didn't bother—and she wasn't sure if she should find that insulting. Of course, the mortifying truth was that she actually quite liked it, because it made her feel like he was comfortable with her.

Ridiculous. Ridiculous, ridiculous, ridiculous.

He held up the phone and said, "I've been reading about lung cancer."

Her internal ramblings came grinding to a halt. "Oh, Nate. Don't do that. You shouldn't do that."

He gave her a look. "Would you? If it was your mother?"

And really, what could she say? She already knew the answer.

He locked his phone with a click, extinguishing its light. Still, she saw the shadowy outline of his head as he shook it, visible in the low moonlight. "Maybe I'm reading a load of Google bullshit, but everything seems off to me. Her symptoms are...weird. Different. Worse than they should be."

"Don't stress yourself out," she said firmly. "It won't help anything. Not a single thing."

"I'm already stressed out. Always. My heart rate seems to think life is the grand fucking derby."

And now *her* heart was kind of breaking. "I'm sorry," she whispered.

"I know," he whispered back.

But it didn't seem like enough. What *would* be enough?

Nothing, she realised. Pain wasn't neat like that. It wasn't about checks and balances, and there was no spell that would make it disappear. Maybe that was why she felt so impotent, sitting here beside him, knowing he was suffering in a way she couldn't comprehend. Maybe that was why she ached with the urge to hold his hand. She couldn't remember the last time she'd held an adult's hand. But she wanted to comfort him, and hand-holding was comfort, wasn't it?

It didn't matter, in the end, because she wasn't going to do it.

Instead of reaching out, she nodded toward the vast, ghostly shape standing just a few feet in front of them and said conversationally, "How about that fort, huh?"

She could almost feel the relief radiating from him. Nate didn't like heavy subjects. He liked to keep things light. She understood why.

"It's a feat of engineering," he said. "I'm very proud."

The kids had built the mammoth structure of blankets, pillows and furniture just yesterday. Apparently, it was a castle. No-one was permitted to take down the castle, on pain of death—which was a direct quote from the lovely Beth.

"They did it alone, too," Hannah said. "I was making dinner. I didn't help at all."

"You didn't?" he asked, disbelief colouring his voice. He'd been with his mother.

"Nope. I came in and they were done. Have you been inside yet?"

"I have not. Which is very poor parenting, I know." Without hesitation, Nate went to crouch beside the fort's shadowy entrance. He looked over at her, his eyes catching the low light, gleaming like something celestial. "Are you coming?"

"*Me?*"

"No, the household ghost. Yes, you. Have you been in here?"

She huffed out a breath. "I've had a look."

"A look?"

"You know, poked my head in."

"Oh, that won't do. Come on, Hannah. That's not very supportive, now is it?"

"I beg your pardon?"

"The kids put their hearts and souls into this majestic architecture, and you haven't even nipped in for tea? I'm shocked." He clicked his tongue. And then, as she squinted at him through the darkness, Nate began squeezing his broad shoulders through the fort's narrow entryway.

"Careful," she murmured. "You're a lot bigger than the kids."

"I am? I had no idea."

She snorted.

"You're coming in here too, you know."

"I most certainly am not."

"You most certainly are," he said calmly. As if it was perfectly ordinary for them to have a conversation about a fort while he crawled deeper and deeper into said fort. "You're very uptight, you know, Hannah."

"Uptight?" she spluttered in outrage, as if it wasn't true. Which it was. But good *lord*, he didn't have to *say* it.

"Yep. Not that I mind."

"How very gracious of you," she drawled.

"I mean, it works to my advantage. And it's cute."

Hannah almost choked on her own tongue. Cute? *Cute?* What the fuck was that supposed to mean?

"But I'm getting worried about the amount of work you do," he said casually, as if he hadn't just thrown her into a minor internal crisis. "I'm in, by the way." A glow that she could only assume was his phone lit up the fort from within, and she saw the dark silhouette of his body, half-sitting, half-lying in the crouched space.

Jesus. She hadn't been this into a shadow since she'd watched *Peter Pan* as a kid.

"Are you coming?" he called.

"No. What do you mean, you're getting worried?"

"Let me rephrase that," he said. "You *are* coming." Why did he have to say *coming* like that? Why did his voice have to be so deep and rich and ugh, this fucking man. Irritating, he was. Beyond irritating. "And what I mean," he added, "is that you never stop. You must've cleaned the house a thousand times in the last week. You and the kids play the kind of games that even *I* can't be arsed with, and I'm their dad. And when there's nothing else to do, you're in your room typing... well, whatever it is you're always typing."

My blog, her mind supplied. *Yes, I have a blog. I have a lot of feelings and I am a millennial cliché. It'd be really cool if you could read it and love it and tell me how fabulous I am and feed me Chocolate Fingers.*

Then, somehow, her treacherous tongue actually allowed an ounce of that drivel to run free. "My blog," her mouth said, without any permission whatsoever.

Hannah wondered if 30 was too late in life to apply for a brain transplant. Just a complete and total brain transplant. Was that a thing? No? Okay, never mind.

"You have a blog?" he repeated. "Really? Huh. Would you show me?"

Calmly, Hannah replied, "I would rather die."

He burst into laughter. "And she calls *me* dramatic. Can't you tell me something small? Like… what's it called?"

"You want me to tell you the name of my blog?" she snorted. "What, so you can Google it and read everything? Okay."

"I wouldn't read it if you didn't want me to."

"Sure."

"I really wouldn't," he insisted.

"Could we move back to the original point?" she asked. "*Please?*"

"Oh, fine. Party pooper. Basically, I don't want you to take on too much. Just because I'm paying you doesn't mean you should work your fingers to the bone."

The irony of him saying that when he wandered around with eyes cradled by painful shadows was almost too much to bear. Ruth always described Hannah as *mothering*. Well, she had the most intense urge to mother Nate Davis all the way into bed.

Not like *that*, obviously.

He just looked really fucking tired, was all.

"Noted," she said finally. "I will, ah… relax."

"I'm not saying you should, or you have to. I'm saying you can. You definitely, definitely can. But I will say you *have* to have some fun every so often."

"Oh, I do?"

"Yes. Like right now. Get in here."

Could he hear the smile that curved her lips without permission? "No."

She could definitely hear the laughter in his voice. "Hannah. Get in the fucking fort."

"Fine," she huffed, as though it were a great trial. As though she didn't really want to, even though, of course, she did. She'd wanted to since the minute she'd seen it. But Hannah was a grown-up, a sensible and mature adult. Sensible and mature adults did not crawl into pillow castles.

And yet, here she was, doing it anyway. Because Nate had pretended to make her. She kind of loved him for that— in the general sense of the word, obviously. Not the… well, never mind. The meaning was clear. *Totally* clear. And since this was her head, and *she* knew how she'd meant it, she really didn't need to have this argument with herself anyway, so there.

She knew she'd made it when she bumped into Nate in the dark. The light of his phone had gone off again, so she had zero warning before her head knocked into something that might have been his shoulder. Or his knee. No, probably his shoulder. Whatever it was, the skin was bare, and even though her bloody forehead was hardly an erogenous zone, she found herself shivering anyway.

These odd physical reactions she kept having were getting out of hand. She never had them around Zach or

Evan, and they were both just as handsome as Nate. Theoretically. Objectively.

But, Hannah realised with a jolt, Nate wasn't just *objectively* handsome anymore. He was actually handsome. Really handsome. As in, she would *really* like to find his mouth in the darkness and kiss it.

Oh, dear God.

"So," he said grandly. "Here we are. In the lap of my children's brilliance. What do you think?"

"It's… beautiful," she squeaked.

He laughed. "But we can't see anything!"

Pull yourself together, woman. "Right," she said, her voice closer to human than dolphin this time. "I just meant, you know, the experience. Beautiful. Ten out of ten."

Nate snorted. "Are you feeling okay?"

"Oh, you know. Tired," she said.

Never coming down here again, she thought. *You awful, attractive bastard. What on earth have you done to me?*

EVERY NIGHT, Nate sat in the dark and pored over medical websites until his eyes swam and the words danced way more than usual.

Every few nights, if he was lucky, Hannah came to rescue him.

It felt like being rescued, anyway, when she showed up in her enormous cardigan and gave him someone to needle and a goal to work toward. When he was alone, Nate thought about the fact that he'd run away from home, that he'd stayed in London even after Ellie's death, that he'd rarely come back to visit, and now his mum might be... dying. And he'd wasted time thinking she'd last forever.

But when Hannah was around, all he thought about was making her laugh and smile and fucking relax for once, because she so desperately needed it and so obviously couldn't manage it without encouragement. Extreme encouragement. The kind that was pushy and obnoxious enough to make her feel as though she *had* to join in, she *had* to laugh—it wasn't her fault, she wasn't being weak, she could blame it all on him.

Yeah, he had her down by now. It had only been—what, two weeks, since she moved in? But he had her down. At least in that regard. The rest of her was still a mystery.

A mystery that was none of his concern. Teaching an employee how to have fun couldn't be called unethical, but wondering too deeply about her life goals and her hobbies and the things that made her wary... that was heading into dangerous waters.

So when she showed up that night, a blessed distraction from an article that was making his brain vibrate in his skull, Nate kept things upbeat. It wasn't hard, really. Not once he noticed her feet.

"Jesus, woman." He winced as she curled up like a kitten beside him. "Are those *socks*?"

She looked down, as if to check. "I think it's quite clear that they are."

"*Please* tell me you don't wear socks to bed."

"Not all the time," she said. "But usually. I'm surprised you never noticed before."

It didn't seem polite to explain that his focus was usually somewhere higher than her feet. "Oh, dear God," Nate grimaced. He wasn't even feigning horror, at this point. But really, this was a good thing: he'd found a flaw in a seemingly perfect woman. She wore socks to bed, which was demonic behaviour. He should be happy about it. "Hannah, you do realise that only cursed people sleep in socks. Don't you?

She rolled her eyes, letting her head fall back against the cushions as she sighed. She always managed to straddle this odd line between stiffness and grace…

And now he was thinking about Hannah straddling. Nate turned his mind to safer things, like the 2D shapes in Josh's latest homework project.

Ah. Much better.

"So you're one of those anti-sock people," she said dryly. "How disappointing."

"Only at night. Sleeping in socks is unnatural." His tone was solemn. "It's okay. I won't judge. But I will offer help and support in this difficult time."

"I like socks," she sniffed. "They make me feel secure."

"Secure?"

"Feet are very private."

"The absurdity of that statement aside, why is privacy a concern when you're in bed?" Nate demanded, with barely-contained laughter colouring his voice.

Her lips twitched, then actually managed to smile. "Privacy is always a concern, Nate."

She really was unbelievable. And the worst part was, he liked it. Especially right now, when she relaxed and joked while still being her usual buttoned-up self. When she was like this with him, he felt as if he'd done something right—and, strangely, as if he'd gotten a gift in return. He wasn't sure why. Maybe because she was so beautiful, especially when she smiled, and Nate liked looking at beautiful things.

Yep. That was probably it.

"Are you okay?" she asked, and he realised that for the past few seconds he'd actually been staring, in complete silence, at Hannah's mouth. Fuck, that was weird.

And what did he say, to make it less weird? Why, he said, out of nowhere, "I'm not staring at your mouth."

Because, really, what was more reasonable and non-threatening and *totally* unsuspicious than a sentence like that?

She blinked. "Um... oh. I mean—"

"I'm really tired," he added quickly. "So fucking tired. I was just, you know, staring. At nothing. But your face was in the way of the nothing, so..."

She was still blinking. She looked, in a word, baffled. But then her expression changed, and she said, "It's fine. I'm used to people looking."

And now *he* was baffled. "You're used to people looking at your mouth?" It was an excellent mouth, to be fair. But he'd have thought most people would have better manners and more functioning brain cells than him.

"At my teeth."

"Your teeth?" He frowned. "Why would anyone stare at your *teeth*?"

"Because they're enormous," she said slowly. "I'm assuming you noticed. Since we went to school together, so you were there when everyone—"

"Oh, right."

"—called me Bugs Bunny." She steamrollered right over his polite attempt to cut the conversation off there. Judging by her narrowed eyes and pursed lips, she wasn't in the mood for politeness.

"Hannah," he said, "I wasn't staring at your teeth."

"Okay."

"I really wasn't," he insisted.

"Oh my God, will you shut up about my teeth?"

"Will *I* shut up about your teeth?"

"Well, you're the one who was staring at them."

"Hannah! I wasn't…" Common sense finally broke through his panic. "Are you taking the piss?"

She sniffed and looked away. But not quite fast enough to hide her smirk.

"Oh, Jesus Christ, woman." He slapped a hand to his chest. "Don't *do* that."

Her huff of laughter was *almost* a genuine, honest-to-God chuckle. "Don't make it so easy, then."

"I thought you were actually upset! I thought you were going to murder me in my sleep or—or *cry*."

"Don't be ridiculous," she said. "I'd never cry."

Which is how Nate learned that he could go from agonising over his mother and battling a migraine to pissing himself with laughter in under half an hour. The key, it turned out, was Hannah Kabbah.

CHAPTER EIGHT

Zach: Want to get a drink?

Hannah: No.

Zach: Want to eat cookies and bitch about people?

Hannah: Meet you at the park in twenty minutes.

"ORANGE."

"No. Yellow."

"Orange."

"*Yellow!*"

"Guys," Nate sighed, looking up from his coffee. "No arguing before 8 a.m. please."

Josh apparently took that as a challenge. "But the *sun,*" he growled, "is *yellow!*"

"It is not!" Beth snapped. "Because *I* saw a picture of the sun on the board yesterday, and Mrs. Clarke said astronauts took it, and the sun was on fire and it was *orange!*"

"I HAVE SEEN THE SUN!" Josh bellowed. "AND IT IS YELLOW!"

"The sun," Hannah said firmly, "is a ball of burning gas." As always, the sound of her low, steady voice made the kids magically shut up.

Nate sipped his coffee and decided that, since he hadn't slept in two days, she could take this one. Why she was up at all, he had no idea, but he wasn't about to complain. He suspected she was awake just to help him, because she knew he was tired. But she'd certainly never say that, and he was grateful for it.

"Since it's burning," Hannah said, "that essentially makes it a ball of fire. I propose, therefore, that to solve this argument, we set something on fire."

It was a mark of Hannah's all-round brilliance that he didn't automatically spit out his coffee. Also, that his kids had apparently learned the definitions of *essentially*, *propose*, and *therefore* some time in the last few weeks. Because he certainly hadn't taught them.

The kids burst into predictable cheers, their bad humour forgotten. But Nate, despite his pretty extensive trust in Hannah, couldn't stop himself from catching her eye and croaking, "Fire?"

"After school," she said calmly, "and under controlled conditions."

He snorted. "I'm assuming that's my job."

"Obviously that's your job. Something tells me you have plenty of experience setting things alight." While he tried to figure out if that was an insult, she added primly, "*I* will supervise."

"Supervise, huh?"

"Yes. The kids can draw the flames. We'll make it a science project. They can write a letter about it, and we'll send the whole thing into school. The teachers will be so impressed, they'll decide that the Davis children are hardworking, intelligent, and come from a nice family. So next time Beth loses her temper and kicks someone, or Josh zones out on a whole afternoon of classes, they'll be treated sympathetically."

Nate stared. Blinked. Stared some more. "Your mind is…"

"Terrifying," she finished, rifling through one of the cupboards. "So I've been told."

"Actually, I was going to say brilliant."

She looked over at him sharply, as if to catch him smirking behind her back or something. But Nate was just drinking his coffee and thanking God for her existence, and she must've seen that on his face. Slowly, the suspicion in her eyes fading, she turned back to the cupboard.

And then, a moment later, she screamed.

It was a very *Hannah* scream, of course. More of a tiny, muted screech, actually. The kids didn't even notice it over their back-and-forth about the best flavour of jam to put in porridge. But Nate heard it as if she'd screamed right into his ear, and not just because his head was pounding like an anvil.

He was next to her in seconds, moving so fast he poured half his coffee onto the floor. "What? What is it?"

She was staring into the cupboard like she'd just found a corpse in there. But when he looked over her shoulder, all he could see were cereal boxes, a few of which had fallen over, and…

Oh. She'd found his money. Some of it, anyway.

"Nate," she hissed, "why the hell do you have..." She poked the stack of cash gingerly, as if it might bite. "Jesus. Are those fifties? What is that, like, ten grand?"

"Relax," he said, because her voice was getting dangerously squeaky. "It's just money."

"What the hell does *that* mean? Where—"

"Hannah!" Beth piped up. "I finished."

Smooth as silk, Hannah spun around with a smile and said, "Wonderful. Good girl."

"Did I eat enough?"

"I'm done too!" Josh said around a mouthful of porridge. "Did *I* eat enough?"

Nate couldn't even be offended by the fact that his kids apparently considered Hannah the highest authority in the household. Frankly, at this point, so did he. "You both ate enough," he said. "Go upstairs and get dressed. Neatest uniform gets a sticker on their chart."

"Yay!" Josh scrambled down from his seat, closely followed by Beth, and they ran off as if it was some kind of race. Like they hadn't *both* gotten a sticker every morning, ever since Hannah had put those charts up. Ah, the spirit of competition.

The minute they left the room, the inquisition began.

"Are you a drug dealer?" she demanded.

"Are you serious?"

"Are you an arms dealer?"

He sighed and put down his coffee. "You're serious."

"It doesn't seem *likely* that you're managing exotic and illegal operations from the heart of a countryside small town, but I wouldn't put it past you. I still have no idea what it is you do all day."

"Hannah. I'm a photographer."

"Photographers don't sit in offices all the time!" she insisted. "And they don't make any money! According to my calculations, and assuming you make the bulk of your profit via works rather than events, your annual income shouldn't exceed £30,000! And that's me being generous, Nate. Generous!"

Considering the time, and his headache, and the fact that he'd been feeling shit about his work—or rather, his lack of work—recently, Nate should've found this conversation irritating. *Should've.*

Instead, talking to Hannah felt like recharging his batteries. That narrow look she gave him, the way she folded her arms like a scolding parent, made a smile creep onto his face. And the fact that she'd be outraged if he laughed only made the urge even harder to fight.

"If I confess," he said, "will you call CrimeLine with an anonymous tip?

Her mouth opened, then closed, then opened again. Her lipstick was a sort of deep rose today, so her lips looked like a flower blooming over and over. Finally, she spluttered, "Well, no. Of course not."

Now, that *did* surprise him. He arched a brow. "Really? You don't think it's your duty as an upstanding citizen?"

"I'm not an upstanding citizen. While I disapprove of nefarious but lucrative activities—"

Why did she have to say things like that just as he took a sip of coffee? She was going to make him choke.

"—it's really none of my concern if you're choosing to

fill the city's sky-high cocaine demand," she said calmly. Apparently, some of her shock had faded now, because she pulled a box of cereal from the cupboard with only a single suspicious look at the money. "My concern is the children. And your imprisonment, while potentially deserved, would not be good for them."

He was simultaneously pleased and offended. "It's nice to hear that you'd put the kids' happiness above law and order, but I can't believe you think I deserve prison."

"Oh for goodness sake, Nate," she snapped, waving the cornflakes around. "Just tell me where you got all that money!"

"Now you're auditing me?"

She glared. "I know you're winding me up. I can see it all over your face."

"Fine, fine! I don't work much now, but I did okay when I was younger. I did great, actually. I'm a fine art photographer. So, I made a lot of money, Ellie invested it, blah blah."

She appeared to think on that as she made her breakfast. "Fine art like... Cindy Sherman?"

For a second, he was surprised—but then he remembered that Hannah Kabbah's magnificent mind knew at least a little bit about every topic on earth. "You like Cindy Sherman?"

"God, no," she said. "But I know who she is. So, if you don't work much, what is it you do all day?"

"Creative consultancy. Pays well."

"Right. And you just keep all your money... in the kitchen?"

"No," he corrected. "I keep fifty grand cash throughout the house."

She gaped. "Why?"

"You know." Nate shrugged, turning to get a spoon out of the drawer for her. "In case."

"In case of what? Global banking collapse? Alien apocalypse? Full-scale identity theft? *What?*"

"Just… in case." She gave him a baffled look, and he sighed. "I can't just *believe* that I have money and we're safe and everything's okay. I have to see it. I have to touch it. Haven't you ever been poor before?"

"No," she said promptly. Then, wincing: "I'm sorry. That was insensitive, wasn't it? Oh dear. Am I being awful? Am I being an enormous snob?"

"What? No." But she still looked worried; so worried that he finally slipped up. After almost a month of avoiding it successfully, Nate reached out and touched her.

He couldn't even feel bad about it, because the minute his hand settled on her hip, she calmed down. Just a little bit, but still. It was only the lightest pressure, a comfort, he told himself firmly. A reassurance. He wasn't thinking about the curve of her body or how soft she seemed, or the fact that they were closer right now than they'd been in a while —closer even than the nights they sat together in the dark. He wasn't thinking about that at all.

"Listen," he said, dragging his mind away from those thoughts that didn't exist. "I know this is easier said than done, and you can definitely tell me to go fuck myself, but I wish you wouldn't worry so much. About the way you are, I mean. I know you second-guess yourself all the time, but I *like* the way you are."

She shook her head once, as if to clear it. Slower than

he'd ever heard her speak before, she asked, "What does that mean?"

Good fucking question. "Well… Obviously, when we were at school, you didn't have many friends." Which was the polite way of putting it. "But I didn't have friends either. And I know people say things about you, but they used to say things about me too. Doesn't mean they were right. There's nothing wrong with you, Hannah. I like you. I like how blunt you can be, and how serious you are, and how passionate you get. It's honest. Everything about you is honest. That's not a bad thing."

She stared up at him, and something in his head… shifted. Or slotted into place, maybe. For the first time, he looked at her upturned face and didn't force himself to see it objectively. For the first time, he let himself notice that she was beautiful. She was beautiful in a way that had nothing to do with the symmetry of her features and everything to do with the odd, burning weight she created in his chest. She was so beautiful that, if he'd walked into a bar and seen her, he'd have walked right the fuck back out.

Nate didn't go for women who made him feel this much, this easily. He didn't want that kind of connection. But he was starting to realise that he accidentally—*inconveniently*—wanted her anyway.

Fuck. He shouldn't have hired her, should he? Even if she *was* amazing with the kids, even if she *did* make his life a thousand times easier and he could trust her with shit like his weird habit of collecting cash…

He should've hired someone who didn't make him smile without trying, or inspire his mouth to talk without permission from his brain. He should've hired a nice, ordinary, very *bland* nanny. Maybe a twenty-year-old who vaguely got on his nerves. Not a woman he was currently fighting the urge to kiss.

"I like you too," she said, so suddenly and simply and *honestly* that he almost couldn't take it. Luckily for him, she added, "The kids are suspiciously quiet. I'll check on them." And, abruptly, she left.

It took him longer than it should have to realise that she hadn't touched her breakfast.

HANNAH, unsurprisingly, was cleaning. It was the most productive way to burn off energy when she felt jittery.

Two days had passed since Nate had, rather suspiciously, claimed to like her. She still wasn't quite sure what to make of it. Well, no; that wasn't true. She knew exactly what to make of it: he was a nice man, who, like his brother, found her pleasant to be around.

It must be some sort of family deficiency, the way they laughed at her sharpness and softened at her irritation. Unlike his brother, however, Nate didn't *like*-like her. Which was a good thing, because, though they'd become friendly over the last month, their relationship was still professional.

So why did the fact that he liked her—could, in fact, list *specific traits* that he liked!—fill Hannah with a bright, zinging sort of pleasure? Because she was far too fond of him, that was why.

But, she reminded herself as she dusted the living room blinds, it was only natural to develop certain sympathies toward a man when one ate dinner with him most evenings and watched him kiss his children goodnight. Wasn't it?

Thankfully, Hannah was saved from answering her own question by the upbeat chirp of her phone. She abandoned her duster and trusty can of furniture polish, wiping her hands off on her old skirt and pulling her phone out of her bra pocket.

Yes, Hannah had bra pockets. She sewed them in herself. Ruth teased Hannah quite mercilessly for it, but then, Ruth didn't wear bras at all—because, unlike Hannah, she was not in possession of a cleavage that bounced like frolicking puppies.

Ruth: Hi. This is me checking on you.

Well. How unusually thoughtful.

Hannah: Checking on me?

Ruth: You know. Making sure you haven't been crucified by devil children or added to Nate's secret basement collection of kidnapped women.

Hannah wondered briefly if this basement situation would involve being tied up by Nate. Then she wondered extensively if she had somehow poured crack on her cereal that morning instead of sugar.

Hannah: You saw me at Sunday dinner last week. And every week since I moved in. You do remember that, correct?

Ruth: Yeah. But I don't see you any other time. And you've stopped bugging me to socialise. Not that I'm complaining.

Hannah: You socialise with Evan.

Ruth: I think you really like this job. I think you're busy being an overachieving nanny. Either that or you really have been kidnapped and we've been eating dinner with Nate-Wearing-Hannah's-Skin.

Was it strange to laugh at the thought of her boss in her skin suit? Almost definitely.

Hannah: Really, I'm good. The devil children are actually a lot of fun, and all Nate does is worry about his mother, his children, global warming, Brexit, the dying bee population, and possibly the appropriate elastic-to-cotton ratio in a pair of socks.

Ruth: ...

Ruth: ...

Hannah: He worries a lot, is what I'm saying here. Arguably too much to risk kidnapping anyone.

Ruth: Cool? I suppose? Do you like the job, or...?

Hannah: I love the job. It's too easy. I feel like I'm taking advantage. All I do is play with the kids and post on my blog.

Oops. She hadn't meant to say that blog part, but now the message was sent, and delivered, and read, and Ruth was replying, and oh dear God what had she done.

Ruth: Wait, you have a blog???? Can I see??

Hannah: Absolutely not.

Ruth: PLEASE

Hannah: I would literally rather eat one of my braids than show you my blog.

Ruth: Wowwww. You're rejecting your own sister like this?

Hannah: Can I see your webcomic?

Ruth: That's different. My webcomic has sex.

Hannah: IT DOES???

Ruth: Mind your business.

Hannah: YOU DRAW SEX???

Ruth: What's your blog about?

Hannah: ISN'T YOUR WEBCOMIC ABOUT ALIENS?

Ruth: Don't make me hunt down your secret blog.

Hannah: RUTH

Hannah: DO YOU DRAW ALIEN SEX

Hannah: I NEED TO KNOW

Ruth: …Only sometimes. Very occasionally.

Hannah: I'm telling mother.

Ruth: I propose a deal. Keep your mouth shut about my alien sex and I'll stop asking about your blog.

Hannah: I accept.

Ruth: …You have bamboozled me again, haven't you?

Hannah: <3

Hannah slid her phone back into her bra pocket, a silly smile taking over her face. Then she picked up a duster and set her sights on the cabinet by the door. It was probably filthy up there, right at the very top, where no-one could see. But she was nowhere near tall enough to reach it. She'd need a boost. Now, if she could just drag the armchair a little closer…

LIKE THE EXCELLENT son he was trying to become, Nate had gone straight to his mother's house after taking the kids to school. And had promptly been told, in no uncertain terms, to bugger off.

Apparently, Shirley's bookclub met first thing in the bloody morning and discussed romance novels over tea and biscuits. Why they didn't meet at night to discuss romance novels while chugging wine like *normal* middle-aged women, Nate had no idea.

But he was grateful to know that his mother would be surrounded by friends within the hour.

He arrived home to find his front hall disturbingly shiny and clutter-free. Hannah, quite clearly, had been here. At least twice a week, she stormed through the house, cleaning every inch with an attention to detail that was both alarming and somehow arousing. Nate had considered bleaching his own brain after it started producing images of Hannah brandishing a highly impractical feather duster, wearing an even more impractical French maid outfit.

Apparently, he had the erotic imagination of a sexless and slightly misogynistic old man.

He could hear her singing in the living room, which meant she was quite firmly in the flow of things. While *nanny* did not mean *cleaner* in Nate's mind, Hannah seemed to love this task above all else. Her cheeks got all bright and shiny, and she smiled more, and sang when she thought no-one could hear. Her voice was terrible. He loved it.

So he went into the living room, hoping to catch her in the act. He certainly wasn't expecting to find her right by the door, balanced precariously on the back of an armchair.

"What the hell are you doing up there?" he demanded, which turned out to be a bad idea. Because apparently, she hadn't noticed he was there—so when he spoke, she yelped, and wobbled, and fell.

Of course, he caught her.

She fell hard, and she certainly wasn't as light as Josh or Beth, so Nate ended up stumbling back against the wall. But, since he stumbled with Hannah safely in his grasp, that was alright. Then he registered the softness of her body in his arms, and the fact that he was basically grabbing her arse, his other hand grazing the underside of her breast. *Fuck.* Ever since he'd messed up the other day, he'd been trying so hard not to touch her. Because whenever he did, a flash-flood of attraction struck him without mercy, and he was left dazed and confused.

Kind of like right now, in fact.

His skin tingled in that electrifying way it had whenever they came into contact. For one tense, yearning moment, he imagined holding her the way he wanted to, close and intimate. He pictured her clinging to him just as desperately, then fantasised about throwing her down into the chair she'd fallen off and licking his way into that lush, taunting mouth.

Then he crushed the image ruthlessly and with no little self-disgust. He was back in the real world, where his utterly untouchable nanny was staring at him as though his head had fallen off of his shoulders. He wondered if she was about to ask him why the fuck he was still holding her. Hopefully not, because he didn't think his answer—*"Sorry, you just feel really good"*—would cut it.

So, before she could speak, he asked, "You okay?"

She nodded slowly, her eyes still pinned to his, that baffled surprise still written all over her face. When she said, "Thank you," her voice seemed lower and huskier than usual, the sound intoxicating.

"I'm sorry," he said. "I didn't mean to scare you."

"Doesn't matter. You saved me." The words were teasing, her slow smile electrifying. Most of the time, when she smiled, she kept her lips together—like she didn't want to seem too enthusiastic, or maybe because she didn't like her teeth. *He* liked her teeth. So when she gave him a rare, full grin, the sight did something to him that was almost violent. It was like taking a shot of pure joy.

And then she made it a thousand times worse by reaching up and running a hand through his hair. "You're covered in pollen, you know." Her fingers ghosted over his skull, the pressure sweet and barely there. He wanted to close his eyes and lean into her touch. He wanted to carry her with him everywhere he went, like his own personal sunshine. She showed him her yellow-stained fingertips and gave him a smile that seemed to say, *What are you like?*

"I took the back way home. By the rapeseed."

"Poor planning," she murmured.

"But I like the colour." He liked holding on to her, too. And Nate believed in doing things he enjoyed. She seemed comfortable enough, cradled in his arms, and her nearness —her warmth, the perfume of her skin—made him reckless. So he didn't put her down yet. Five more minutes.

"That's one thing I admire about you," she said, her hands sliding up to his shoulders. "You do what you want to do. I mean, you don't deny yourself without good reason."

He didn't, did he? "You shouldn't deny yourself either."

"I can't help it," she whispered.

Nate knew that. It was what she needed him for, after all. To push.

But right now, with his mind swimming in heady lust and his cock swelling uncomfortably in his jeans, he couldn't be trusted to push responsibly. So, reluctantly, he finally put her down. The action forced her body to slide against his, and he wondered if she could feel his pounding heart. He *hoped* she couldn't feel his rigid dick—but when her hands tightened on his shoulders and she gave the softest, smallest gasp, he suspected that she had.

Fuck.

Their eyes met, hers wide and fathomless, his doubtless guilty. To his surprise, she didn't look away. Instead, she bit her lip. His hand must have been under someone else's control, because before Nate knew it he was sliding his thumb over the curve of her mouth, smoothing away the line she'd left in her earthy lipstick. His palm cradled her face, the evidence of his bad behaviour staining the pad of his thumb cinnamon.

This was what happened when he crossed mental lines; physical lines followed. He'd let himself acknowledge this attraction instead of folding it up and shoving it into a box, and now she knew. He'd sell his soul just to put his mouth on her, and now she knew. Or at least, he thought she did.

"Nate?" Hannah frowned. She didn't sound horrified. Or terrified. Or happy. She sounded completely and utterly confused.

Which was both unexpected and extremely convenient. If Hannah somehow didn't understand what was going through his mind right now… well, maybe he could make it so that she never would. Because it was one thing to want her, but it was another thing entirely to burden her with the knowledge.

So, with worryingly little effort, Nate shut down. He pulled up his old mask of casual mocking, the one that convinced everyone he was too cool to care and too wild to be cared for. He stepped back abruptly, practically jerking away from her touch. She wobbled for a moment, losing the support of his shoulders, and his heart clenched. But then he reminded himself that she was perfectly capable of standing alone—that she would *want* to stand alone, if she knew what he was thinking.

"You should be more careful," he said, trying not to wince at the coldness in his own voice.

Her brows rose, and her cheeks hollowed as if she'd sucked them in. "With what?"

"That." He nodded sharply toward the chair she'd been standing on. "You'll break your bloody neck. Don't do it again." *Don't trust me again. Don't touch me again. And don't ever, ever let me touch you.*

Her nostrils flared slightly, her eyes narrowing, but for some reason she held back her irritation. No; not *some reason.* She held it back because they weren't at school, and she wasn't just some woman he watched with interest from afar. She was his employee, and she was cautious around him.

He had power over her, and she remembered that, even if he didn't.

What the fuck had he been thinking?

Guilt flooded him, every inch of his body tensing, his mind a screaming hive of pressure and pain and that infuriating lust. "What?" he asked tightly, even though she hadn't said a word. He *wanted* her to say something. He wanted her to lose her temper and snap at him, because he deserved it even more than she knew.

Instead, after a long, heavy breath, she gritted out, "I'm going to the supermarket."

Her shoulders were stiff as she left. The fact that she'd abandoned a chair out of place and left her sunshine yellow duster on the cabinet told him, better than anything else, that she was furious.

But at least she was angry because he'd been awful, not scared because he wanted her. At least she hadn't noticed the lust ripping through him like a forest fire. At least she'd never know that he'd come perilously close to kissing her nose or burying his face between her legs, or something else —the urges were all wildly divergent, as well as horribly impossible.

And she hadn't detected a single one.

He'd gotten away with it. Thank fuck.

CHAPTER NINE

NATE HAD NOT GOTTEN AWAY with it. Twenty minutes later, Hannah pushed her trolley through Ravenswood's tiny, overpriced supermarket and pondered the undeniable fact that Nathaniel Davis wanted to fuck her.

She didn't think she was being presumptuous. It was obvious that he wanted to sleep with her, and *painfully* obvious that he was horrified by the fact—which Hannah was used to. She'd had many people recoil from her as they realised that, through some twisted miscommunication between mind and body, they'd developed lust toward a woman they didn't even like.

But Nate does *like me.*

Obviously not enough. No-one you want ever does.

Hannah squashed that second, pitiful voice grimly. She reminded it in stern and unyielding tones that she was attractive, occasionally amusing, and undeniably useful. Eventually, someone would want her. They wouldn't stumble into a grey and plodding relationship with her;

they wouldn't sleep with her on a semi-regular basis until her personality became too much to bear; they'd *want* her.

That person just wouldn't be Nate.

More's the pity.

Oh, would you stop *that?*

Hannah tossed a loaf of bread into her shopping trolley and moved on to the next important issue: her own undeniable attraction to the man who paid her wages.

Which appeared to be getting out of hand.

But she had a theory. A theory that explained why his presence flooded her body with sultry, languid heat, why his touch felt like the spark before a fire, why his smile wiped her brain like she was a computer rebooting.

It was her crush, that was all. Her old, sad, teenage crush. It *should* be long dead, but somehow, the dregs remained— maybe because Nate had left town before her affliction could come to its natural end? Whatever the reason, it had survived like a frozen pathogen. She wasn't worried, though. Eventually, her body would kill it off, and everything would be fine again.

Hopefully sooner rather than later, because romantic attraction never ended well for Hannah. It was a tragic but bearable flaw, likely designed to counteract the effects of her intellectual brilliance, general competence, and excellent bone structure.

She was perusing the instant porridge and considering ways to speed up the death of her crush when she heard it. The stage-whispers. Those faux-hushed, gleeful tones she'd trained herself to identify from a mile away, because they signified Ravenswood's foremost currency: gossip.

Hannah did not like gossip. She hated it, in fact. But she

needed power, and she needed control, and in this town, those things required an ear to the grapevine. So, quietly, Hannah eased her trolley deeper into the aisle and thanked the Almighty for its well-oiled wheels.

Keeping her movements casual—because she would never risk being caught *skulking*—Hannah glided toward the siren call of those vicious murmurs. When she reached the bagels in their little plastic bags, all printed with the Statue of Liberty, she paused. This was the perfect position, she decided. From here, she could hear all.

Hannah chose a bag of bagels and frowned intently at the ingredients list. And listened.

"…frightful flash she is, Mam. Dripping with jewels, you know." The first woman had a smoker's voice, raw and scratchy. The combination of upper-crust accent and humbler dialect marked her as a type Hannah had labelled 'Horsey Women'. Horsey Women were fabulously wealthy, tended to have enormous, elegant noses and pink, wind-whipped cheeks, lived on ancestral farms, and neglected their children for the sake of their prize mares.

Hannah's mode of categorisation wasn't a precise science, but she happened to know that this particular Horsey Woman fit the mould to a T. It was Kathleen Grey who stood gossiping on the other side of the shelf—and Christ, how horribly depressing that Hannah could discern the voice of a woman she despised through a wall of American bread.

"Oh, Kath," said the second woman, older and far more delicate in her speech. "I don't know how you find these people."

"I know, I know. But that ain't the worst," Kathleen murmured, words blade-sharp with excitement.

"I can see by your face that you're dying to shock me. Wicked girl. Go on, then."

"She's *divorced* if you'd believe—that's why she's come here, ain't it? Reckons she's getting a fresh start."

My, Hannah thought acidly. *Divorce. What a scandal.*

"And a fresh man?" the second woman theorised.

"Not likely," Kathleen snorted. "Now, I don't like to make judgements on people—you know me, Mam, I mind my business."

Hannah barely choked back a snort.

"But it's clear as day why the husband left. On the one side of her face, she's quite pretty. But on the other side, gosh, she's got the most awful scars."

"Scars?"

"Scars! On her face!"

"How uncouth."

"I know. I'm so sorry for her. And on top of that—I mean, I don't really like to say. You know these things don't matter to me. But on top of it all, she's, you know..." Kathleen said the next word in hushed tones, as if it were a grievous slur. "*Black.*" Then, sounding thoughtful: "Or should I say coloured?"

Hannah resisted the urge to shout, *No, you most certainly should not.*

"Oh," the second woman sighed. She sounded genuinely put out by this poor, scarred woman's misfortune. Black, on top of it all!

Hannah realised that she was crushing the bag of bagels

in her hand. Well, bugger. Now she'd have to buy the damned things.

"I know," Kathleen murmured. "The poor cow. She's probably had a right time of it..."

Further commiserations occurred, but Hannah was saved from hearing them by a spark of searing awareness that thrilled along her spine. Somehow she sensed the presence of his body beside hers, even before she saw him from the corner of her eye. She shouldn't know him without looking. But she did.

Nate leaned on the side of Hannah's trolley, his face perilously close to hers, his breath ghosting over her cheek as he whispered, "What are we staring at?"

"Not staring," she corrected, her voice equally hushed. "We're listening." Her brain had clearly malfunctioned, because it took a whole ten seconds for her to remember that there was no *we* about it, and a further three to realise that she'd just admitted to eavesdropping. Another three, and she collected her wits enough to scowl at his awful, handsome face and demand, "What on earth are you doing here?"

He'd had a playful glint in his eye, along with a sweet little smile that reminded her of Beth. But at her question he grew sombre—or maybe it was the edge of hard suspicion in her voice that wiped away his cheerfulness. Either way, he released the trolley and stood up straight, until a damned mile of height separated them again.

She'd spoken loud enough to blow her cover, which was fine, because she'd had enough of gossip for one day. When Nate replied, though, he kept his voice low. "I was looking for you."

"Well, you found me." She threw the crushed bagels into the trolley. "Which can't have been hard, since I told you exactly where I'd be."

"I don't know." He shrugged, wrinkling his nose. "I had to wander through the dairy aisle for a bit, and those fridges are fucking freezing."

"Watch your mouth."

"Watch *your*—" his words cut off like brittle wood, that lazy-sexy grin fading. Nate's pale brow creased in a rather ferocious frown, and he rammed his hands into his pockets. He seemed trapped between two opposing forces, bobbing along on a current of charm only to be tugged into frustration by a riptide.

"Watch my what?" Hannah arched a brow.

"Nothing. Absolutely nothing." He flashed her an expression that was 50% wince, 50% sheepish smile, and 100% adorable.

And you, Hannah Kabbah, must be 100% deranged.

"I came to apologise," he said. "I'm sorry."

She stared. "For?"

"I was rude. At the house. I mean, I was in a bad mood, and I worry about you climbing all over the furniture, and —" he shrugged his broad shoulders. Hannah put a tight leash on the sensations that said shoulders inspired in her. "Sorry," he finished simply. "That's all. I just wanted to say sorry."

She continued to stare. Even though she'd been furious, half an hour ago, she was now struggling to remember why. "So… less than an hour after speaking to me in a manner that was slightly less than friendly—"

"It was rude."

"It was brisk, at worst."

"It was… curt," he said grimly.

"Less than an hour after speaking to me rather curtly," she allowed, "you felt the need to hunt me down in the middle of the supermarket and apologise?"

He sighed, running a hand through his hair. "Looks like it."

She stared at him in silence a moment longer. Just enough to make him nervous, his wide mouth tightening the way it did when Josh and Beth got a little too quiet. Just long enough to get her ridiculous heart, which wanted to melt at his hesitance, under control.

Then she said crisply, "You need a haircut." And pushed the trolley away.

For a moment, she walked alone, Nate standing behind her as if frozen. But then he jerked into movement, catching up with those long, loping strides. He put a hand on her shoulder, only to snatch it away a second later as if he'd been burned.

Ah, yes. *That* was why she'd been furious with Nate; because he had the temerity not to want her even though he desired her.

Which, now she considered it, seemed rather unreasonable. On her part, not his.

But also his.

"I'll do that," he said, pulling the trolley from her grip— careful not to let their hands touch, she noticed.

"Oh, will you?"

The corner of his mouth twitched. "Evidently."

"Are you staying, then?"

"Might as well. Who were you listening to?"

Oh, crap. She'd really hoped they'd move smoothly past that. "No-one," she lied abominably.

"Okay. *What* were you listening to?"

"Nothing."

He squinted down at her as he pushed the trolley. "Hannah. You're a horrible liar."

"Take the hint, then." She paused by the store's little bakery and grabbed a few plastic bags and a pair of tongs. "Clearly, I don't want to tell the truth."

"Which makes *me* more determined to find out."

"That shows very poor character."

"Unsurprising, since I am a man of very poor character."

She frowned over at him. "No, you're not. You're absolutely not." Oh dear. That sounded far too earnest. She cleared her throat. "I was just thinking how nice it is that you spend so much time with your mother."

He snorted. "Seriously? Don't start thinking I'm son of the year. I ran off like a spoiled brat and left my family behind so I could deal with my own bullshit. When they wanted to see me or the kids, they had to come to London because I was too pathetic to come back here like a man. I robbed my children of time with their grandma just because this place used to make my skin crawl." He scowled, his voice flat and hard. "I don't even remember why I hated it so much. I mean, I remember why I hated it, but the anxiety…"

She bit her lip, studying the baked goods in front of them because it was better than staring at him. "Sometimes bad feelings don't make sense."

"Well, that's true. Bad feelings never make sense."

"Don't beat yourself up," she said softly. "You're here now. That's all you can do."

He didn't answer. She didn't push. Instead, she checked her shopping list and went about collecting pastries, until finally he said, "Jesus, woman, how many bloody croissants do you want?"

"These are for your permanently ravenous children, thank you very much."

"A likely story," he muttered. But humour danced through his words again, lighting them up. As if that dark, self-flagellating speech hadn't even happened. Before she could think about that too hard, he asked mockingly, "You alright there?"

It was quite obvious that she was not *alright there*, since she was currently making a fool of herself, jumping up and down to reach the highest shelf. But Hannah paused in her indignities, pulled herself up to her full and majestic height —which was actually rather negligible—and said, "Fine, thank you."

Nate rolled his eyes, plucked the tongs from her hand, and got her a Danish.

Reluctantly, she muttered, "Cheers."

"So, the shopping list was a cool idea," he said, as they wandered toward the next aisle.

Hannah tried not to smile. "I can't claim credit. I believe they've been popular for centuries at least."

"You know, you could just take the compliment."

"Oh, was that a compliment?" she asked innocently. While internally she screamed *It better* not *have been a compliment, because I'm too high-strung to deal with attractive*

men who occasionally devour me with their eyes and infrequently
compliment me with their... mouths.

"Yeah," he said. "I'm glad you're mostly in charge of food now. You actually make real meals."

"*You* make real meals."

"I plonk as many of the necessary food groups on a plate as I can," he corrected. "You cook shit that makes sense, like... like curry."

"It's true," she said mildly. "I am an eminently sensible cook."

Hannah was used to her sense of humour going completely unnoticed. She constantly made what *she* thought of as jokes, only to have those around her take each word completely seriously. She had decided long ago that her comedic delivery was simply too atrocious to save.

So when Nate laughed, she thought that she must be hallucinating or something.

But she wasn't.

NATE HAD no idea why Hannah seemed to think that he would let her carry the shopping. But she did get strange ideas in her head, sometimes, bless her.

Still, once he made his position on bag-carrying clear, she didn't argue. Instead, she took great satisfaction in ordering him about, telling him exactly how to unpack everything in his own bloody kitchen. And he took even greater satisfaction in her casual bossiness and easy smiles and the way she rolled her eyes at his teasing, because it meant he hadn't ruined anything. She didn't know he was currently suffering through a mortifyingly creepy attraction to the woman he paid to watch his kids. In her mind, the two of them were... friends, maybe. Close enough to talk and joke like this, anyway.

And that felt fucking fantastic.

"It's amazing how much more smoothly things go," she mused from the kitchen island, "when I have someone large and obedient to hand."

"I am not obedient," he grumbled, as he arranged the fruit juice in the precise order she'd asked for.

"Obedient," Hannah repeated. "Like a well-behaved child—"

Nate growled. It was an excellent way to hide how much fun he was having, and also how much he'd like to put her over his knee.

"—with unusual strength," she finished. "Are you *growling* at me?"

"If I were, would you shut up?"

"Nothing can shut me up." She grinned, then ran her tongue over the edge of her teeth. Which he had never seen her do before. He had no idea what it even meant, but the sight of that smiling mouth and that curling tongue and the gleam in her dark gaze...

He was standing in front of her, shopping abandoned, before his brain fully grasped that his body was moving.

She looked at him, her smile nowhere to be found. Now her laughing eyes were wide, her lips slightly parted, and he could see the soft, pink inside of her mouth beyond the armour of her lipstick. He wanted to taste that mouth.

But he wouldn't. He shouldn't. He *couldn't*. It was just kind of unbelievable how much he needed to. How he felt fucking desperate to, as if he'd give anything to kiss her, including his damn principles.

It's not about you. It's about her. And even though she smiles for you, and laughs with you, and whispers in the dark with you, that doesn't mean she feels anything like the shit you feel. So back away. Now.

He stepped back.

"Nate," she whispered.

Another step.

"Nate, you—"

"Let me know," he said casually—as if he hadn't just stood there staring at her mouth—"if I can help you with anything else."

She stared for a moment, the slow rise of her chest visible as she dragged in a breath. Then she said, "Like what?"

He cleared his throat. "Like dusting places you can't reach. I feel bad about you risking your neck to clean the house."

She nodded slowly. And then the tension in her body dissolved, the heat in her gaze fading, until he could almost forget the last thirty seconds had even happened.

Almost.

"Don't be ridiculous," she said, refolding a tea towel that looked perfectly fine to his mortal gaze. "I barely do anything. I'm beginning to feel as if I'm swindling you."

"You do plenty," he said. "You get the kids from school. You scrub my house to within an inch of its life. You cook, and you got us a..." He grimaced. "A family calendar. Seriously, you have no idea how much peace of mind it gives me to know that you're here. That if there's any kind of emergency, I won't be caught between looking after the kids and looking after Ma." He rubbed his eyes, suddenly tired. He still wasn't sleeping well. And he couldn't stop reading medical articles, even though they made his head throb like a motherfucker.

Something just wasn't sitting right with him.

Hannah distracted him from that familiar tangent when she said, "I meant to ask you, actually, about the boxes in the dining room. I wanted to unpack, but I don't want to go through private things—"

"Nothing's private," he said. Which was true. He'd had a single box of items that might be labelled private, and that had long since been unpacked in his room—but he had the oddest feeling that he wouldn't mind Hannah seeing any of it anyway. "It's just shit we don't necessarily need, so I didn't get around to it yet. I've been lazy. I'll do it."

She gave him a wry look. "*Lazy* is not the word I would use to describe you."

"Maybe you don't really know me," he winked.

She didn't smile back. Instead, her eyes sliced him open and examined him from the inside out. She opened her mouth to say something that he knew, instinctively, would ruin him.

So he was relieved when his phone rang, interrupting her.

But he wasn't relieved for long.

CHAPTER TEN

"My body is not my enemy. My body is me."

— HANNAH KABBAH, *THE KABBAH CODE*

WAITING rooms were the ninth circle of hell. Especially when you were sitting in the Respiratory Department with your mother, trying to wipe your sweaty palms against your jeans while she flicked serenely through a magazine.

They need me to come in, she'd said. *They have something to tell me,* she'd said. And then, her calm voice wavering just a little: *Apparently, it's urgent.*

And that was all they'd said. *Urgent.* No details, no explanations, no reassurances.

It was a good thing, Nate decided, that they were at a hospital right now. Because he could feel himself creeping closer to a fucking heart attack with every passing second.

Nate had been telling himself for a while now that his mother was going to die. Not because he believed it; he didn't. But when Ellie had died so suddenly, it had felt like the moment a brawl turns bad, when you're drowning in kicks and punches from every direction. Like, *bam*, your wife's dead, and you weren't expecting it at all, so here's the dress she ordered last week—and here's her favourite food in the fridge, chocolate pudding, because you picked some up to surprise her yesterday—and here's an email about the holiday you booked for next year, and…

Hit after hit after hit.

If he was prepared for his mum's death, even a little bit, maybe it wouldn't hurt so much. Because Nate couldn't fucking cope with that again. The threat of loss hovered on the surface of his mind, slick like oil over clear water, and he was stuck in that greasy pool trying not to drown.

You thought that she would live forever and now she has cancer and you're waiting for a last-minute appointment in a healthcare system that doesn't do last-minute appointments, and Jesus fucking Christ, maybe you were right—maybe she's going to die.

Beside him, Shirley huffed out a little laugh at something she'd read. The tail of her silk headscarf lay over her gaunt shoulder. He stared at the paisley pattern for a second or an infinity, and then it occurred to him that his mind was turning dangerously blank and heavy, and he should think of something else. He glanced up at the clock on the wall and realised it was almost four. Hannah would've picked up the kids by now.

Hannah, who'd turned grey as the dust she loved to vanquish when he'd told her where he was going, and why. For a moment, she'd looked almost as terrified as he'd felt. But then she'd cleared her throat and stiffened her spine and told him in that cool, calm voice that he mustn't worry, and that everything would be fine, and that he was to go right now and do whatever was needed and not think about the kids for even a second.

Nate wondered what he'd done in a previous life that had led him to meet so many wonderful women.

And then, finally, a nurse appeared and called his mother's name.

THEY ENTERED a clinical little room occupied by no less than four strangers. His heart plummeted like a ten-ton weight, tearing through every inch of flesh and bone in its way.

A woman with enormous brown eyes behind gold-rimmed glasses stepped forward to shake his mother's hand, then his. Which was not usual doctor behaviour, in Nate's experience. So what the fuck was going on?

She wore a smile that could only be described as politely grim. The other inhabitants were men, two scruffy-haired and tired-eyed, one razor-sharp in a well-cut suit. That suit alarmed Nate more than anything else about the situation. It was an indisputable truth that once corporate fuckers got involved, shit was heading rapidly downhill.

"Ms. Davis," the woman murmured. She must be a consultant. The consultants in this department all spoke like that—as if their patients were inches from death, so loud-ness wouldn't be appropriate. "I'm Doctor Yaszia Irshad. With me are my colleagues Dr. Brown, Dr. Law, and Mr.

Young, who is a member of the hospital's board. Please, take a seat."

Shirley actually smiled at the murder of crows before them, then toddled off to her chair as if they were all taking tea together. But not before shooting Nate a look that quite clearly said, *Don't you dare make a fuss.*

So Nate didn't make a fuss. He kept his mouth locked tight, so his fear and his fury and his rising nausea couldn't escape. He sat beside his mother and clutched the arms of the chair until his knuckles ached. He absolutely did not make a fuss.

For now.

"We called you here urgently because there has been a re-examination of your scans and symptoms. Dr. Brown is a specialist consultant in respiratory diseases, and Dr. Law specialises in a condition called sarcoidosis. They are of the opinion that you have been misdiagnosed, Ms. Davis. That, rather than suffering from lung cancer, you are suffering from sarcoidosis."

Somehow, despite the fact that he was suffocating, Nate managed to croak out, "Pardon?"

"We made a mistake," said Dr. Irshad.

Shirley stared. Nate stared. The consultant offered a smile that looked more like a wince.

Finally, Nate said through lips that felt frozen stiff, "You made… a mistake?"

The doctor cleared her throat. "Unfortunately, yes."

And then the suit slimed into the conversation with a sharklike smile and a soothing tone. "This sort of thing is unbelievably rare, and highly unfortunate. Human error, you understand. Of course, you have our utmost apologies—"

"I don't give a shit about apologies. What, exactly, was the mistake? What the fuck is going on? Explain. Now."

"Nate," his mother said, her voice severe, her glare pointed. That was the *Behave yourself* look. The *Don't lose your temper* look.

Well, it was too late for that. He was about thirty seconds from throwing his chair through the nearest window. Or through Mr. Young's expensive teeth.

Dr. Irshad adjusted her glasses and said, "Ms. Davis, you don't have lung cancer."

"Well," Shirley said cheerfully, "that's a relief."

Nate couldn't quite share the sentiment. "If she doesn't have cancer," he gritted out, "why the *fuck* has she been going through *fucking chemotherapy?*"

"Oh, well, that's the good news," the doctor said brightly. "Some of the medication has actually been treating her, so—"

"Treating her *what?*" he snapped. "What's wrong with her? And how the fuck do you make a mistake about fucking *cancer?*"

"Please," Mr. Young said reasonably. As if Nate were interested in *reasonable* right now. "I understand that you must be very upset—"

"Upset?" Nate spat. "*Upset?* Are you taking the *piss?*"

"Nathaniel," his mother snapped. "Sit down!"

Nate hadn't even realised he was standing. He took a breath and sat. Did oxygen always burn his lungs like this? He was pretty sure it shouldn't. Could sheer fury spawn fire-breathing abilities? At this point, he kind of hoped so.

The doctor pushed her hair out of her face and, after a moment's hesitation, started again. "What you're suffering from, Ms. Davis, is a relatively rare condition called sarcoidosis. You *do* have tumours in your lungs and wind-pipe, which are a concern. But they aren't cancerous. Sarcoidosis actually mimics cancer—hence the confusion with your diagnosis—and treatment plans are often quite similar. The methotrexate you've been taking has reduced your tumours, which is good, but the bad news is, sarcoidosis doesn't really go away. Tumours can appear anywhere in your body, at any time." She collected a little pile of pamphlets and handed them to Shirley. "We'll need to carry out more tests urgently, to make sure that you aren't suffering from neurological or cardio sarcoid—"

"Hold on," Nate said, keeping his voice low this time. He almost ground his teeth into dust with the effort, but he managed. "Are you saying that she... she's not..." His voice cracked slightly.

"Am I going to die?" Shirley demanded.

Doctor Irshad blinked. "Well, sarcoidosis is a very serious illness. It's incurable, and it *can* cause disability or death. As I mentioned, we still have to scan your mother's brain in particular. But well-managed *respiratory* sarcoidosis only reduces life expectancy by 2 to 5 percent, which is far better than the statistics around lung cancer."

Nate's entire body sagged. Was it possible to feel sick with relief? *Was* this relief, or was it thwarted adrenaline and disbelief making his stomach churn and his hands shake?

She's not *going to die. Probably. Hopefully.*

He pushed down the tumult of emotions rising in his

chest and looked at his mother. Her mouth was slightly open, and she'd wrapped a finger around the edge of her head scarf as she stared blankly at the floor.

He reached across the space between their seats, which moments ago had felt like a gulf of mortality. "Are you okay?"

She blinked at nothing for a moment, then turned to look at him. "I'm not sure. I… I should just be happy, shouldn't I? But I thought…" Her face crumpled like a sheet of paper, and he realised that the cheerful calm she'd radiated over these months had been a front. He watched as her wall collapsed, brick by brick.

"I thought I was going to die," she whispered. "I was dying. I was dead. Now I'm not. What do I?"

He shook his head slowly, mind racing. "From this moment on? I'd say whatever the fuck you want."

O‍H, what a joy it was to be drunk.

Nate sat in his mother's living room while she slept like the dead—the *not* dead—upstairs. He had his seventh shot of Jack in his hand and his little brother by his side. Which was, to Nate's mind, the perfect way to handle the revelation that months of dread had been a lie.

This strange, new lack of fear was making him afraid all over again. There was a huge gap in his mind where a dragon named Terror had once stood, and he was telling himself to walk through it—while fighting the certainty that he'd be hit with invisible claws and burned by invisible fire.

"You're overthinking again," Zach accused, his voice slightly slurred. "Shot."

Ordinarily, fraternal pride demanded that Nate contradict his brother's every word. But tonight, he downed the fucking shot.

"Now you," he croaked out, letting the sickly-sweet burn sting his throat.

"I'm not overthinking. I never overthink."

"Take a fucking shot before I pour it down your fucking throat."

"You're in a smashing mood tonight," Zach muttered. But he took a shot.

The little glasses were piling up on Ma's doily-covered coffee table, surrounding the central plate of left-over Celebrations from Christmas. Nate had the oddest urge to pull out his phone and take a picture—and an even odder desire to start carrying his camera around with him again. But that must be the alcohol talking, because he only really photographed people, and he wasn't even managing that, these days.

So instead, he looked at his brother, finding eyes that mirrored his own: a bright, clear blue dragged down by the dark shadows beneath and the exhaustion dulling their shine.

He'd never wanted his brother to look like him. Not like this. Not his Zach.

"We're fucked up," Nate said. "All of us."

"Why's that?" At least Zach's tone was light as ever, even if his hands shook as he put down his shot glass.

Nate reached for one of the pamphlets they'd been given hours earlier and sneered at its minimalist cover. "This…

this *thing*, it can be life-threatening. But it's not fucking lung cancer. We should be happy. But we're here getting pissed out of our minds, and Ma looks like she's seen her own damn ghost."

"Because she has," Zach said softly. "Nate... do you have any idea how much I've cried in the last few months? I fucking *cried*. Because I thought—I thought she was dying. Do you know I asked Hannah to take me to church? I went to church, and I prayed to..." He sighed, raking a hand through his hair. "I just wanted to take the pain. To take it for her. And I couldn't. And it made me want to die." Something thick and brutal curled around Zach's voice, like suffocating smoke.

Nate understood every single word his brother had just said. He'd felt it all himself. But he wished, more than anything, that he hadn't understood that last part. That he wasn't the kind of man who could hear those words and know instinctively that Zach wasn't just being figurative.

His heart squeezed as he laid a hand on his brother's shoulder. "Why didn't you tell me?"

Zach's lips twisted into a smile. "Are you really asking me that? Like you don't get it?"

Because he did, of course. Nate had been wondering, ever since that day when Hannah had said so simply, "I suffer from depression," if he should say... something. Something like, *Hey, I kind of get it, because for about six months, so did I!* He hadn't wanted to, in the end, because it didn't feel the same. His wife had died and he'd fallen into a bad place, but he was better now. And he got the impression that Hannah would never quite be 'better'. The last thing he wanted was to be insensitive.

Which is why he didn't push for further explanations from Zach. Instead, he pulled his brother into a clumsy sort of sideways hug, pressing his face into the other man's silky hair. It was like hugging Josh. A very *big* Josh.

"I'm sorry," Nate said.

"Not your fault," Zach mumbled.

"I mean I'm sorry that I left. I'm sorry I left you." Because he shouldn't have. Even as Nate learned to conquer his rage and like himself, even as he'd found photography and met Ellie, even as he'd built a new life... he'd felt like a traitor. Because he'd been building it all without his family.

They broke the hug. Looking at Zach was like seeing a younger, cockier, pretty-boy version of himself. Sometimes he wondered how his geeky little brother had become a man. Then he remembered that he'd missed that, too. Because he'd left.

"I can see your brain moving a mile a minute," Zach said. "You really are an angsty motherfucker."

Nate huffed out a laugh. "Shut up."

"You didn't leave me. You didn't leave us. You were suffocating here so you did what you had to do. You don't need to apologise to me, Nate. Because, when we need you, you're here. That's what matters."

It was exactly what Hannah had said—and Hannah was the smartest person Nate knew, so he'd almost let himself believe her. But it was only now, hearing the same sentiment in his little brother's voice, that he really accepted it.

"And while I'm fixing all those fucked-up ideas of yours," Zach said, "let me tell you this." He lowered his voice slightly, his eyes gentler now. "Ma's not okay. She's still as sick as she was yesterday, whether they call it cancer or sarco-whatever-the-fuck. And she's still taking the same awful drugs. She might have to take them forever, Nate. So just because she's not terminal, doesn't mean you can't feel like you're falling apart right now. And I said the same thing to her. Don't think you have to feel better. You don't *have* to feel anything. Let yourself hurt sometimes."

Nate blinked blearily at the pile of shot glasses stacked in front of them. "When did you get so smart?"

Zach laughed. "I don't know. Maybe when I started hanging out with Hannah?"

Hannah. The tenuous peace Nate had found in the last few minutes was disturbed by the way his brother said her name. "What's going on with you guys, anyway? Are you still trying to…"

Zach sighed. "Want to know a secret?"

If that secret concerns you, Hannah, and anything other than extremely innocent and platonic friendship, absolutely not.

Unfortunately, Zach seemed to take Nate's silence as a *Yes.* "I'm not into Hannah."

Nate jolted. The words took a moment to fully sink in. His first, ridiculous instinct was to say, *Why the hell not? Are you high?*

But he managed to choke that down in favour of a non-committal, "Oh?"

"I *should* be," Zach said. "I really like her. She's funny. And she's hot. *So* hot. I mean, she's got that—"

"Alright, I get it." *Please don't make me hit you when we're getting on so well.* "So what's the problem?"

Zach sighed. "I don't know. I think something's wrong with me. I just can't get *into* anyone, you know? I see people, and I think *Yeah, you're cute. You'll do.* In theory, anyway. But then in reality, I just don't want to. Christ, I haven't had sex in about six months."

Nate didn't point out that he regularly went without sex for six months. It didn't seem tactful. Instead, he said firmly, "There's nothing wrong with you. Okay?"

"Whatever," Zach mumbled.

"I'm serious. Whatever it is, doesn't mean there's something wrong with you." Nate paused as he figured out how to ask his next question politely. "When you say you haven't had sex, do you mean that you... can't..."

It took a second for his meaning to filter into Zach's tipsy brain. "Oh, no, I can. Everything's, you know, working. I just don't want to."

"Huh." Nate sat back, thinking on everything he knew about his little brother. "That *is* unusual, for you."

"I know," Zach said glumly.

"How do you feel otherwise? Is anything else different?"

He shrugged. "Not really."

"Hm." Nate was honestly at a loss. He might be biased, but he was of the opinion that if Hannah Kabbah couldn't inspire proper lust in Zach, no-one could. "Sorry, man. I don't know. Should we drink some more?"

"It's okay," Zach sighed. "And yeah. Yeah, we should."

So they did.

CHAPTER ELEVEN

HANNAH SAT in the dimly-lit living room, the kids' fort—still going strong—casting strange shadows on the walls. When she heard the front door creak open, she almost leapt out of her skin. But by the time Nate appeared in the doorway, she was composed, her oversized cardigan pulled tight over her chest.

"You're up." He didn't sound surprised.

"Are you okay?" she asked. It was a ridiculous question, when he was standing there swaying on his feet. He seemed small, somehow, even though his broad shoulders filled the doorframe. Nate definitely *wasn't* okay. But she couldn't say *What the hell happened? Tell me everything*, the way she wanted to, so silly questions would have to do.

After a moment's hesitation, he came closer. Hannah realised he was drunk after his second step, and by the time he sprawled onto the sofa beside her, she decided that he was actually wrecked. That didn't do much to ease the frantic pounding in her heart, the pounding that hadn't stopped since he'd disappeared earlier that day.

But then he said, "Ma doesn't even *have* cancer."

And she was too astonished to feel anything but numb. Somehow, she managed to say, *"What?"*

So, in meandering, rambling, bitter tones, he told her everything. It didn't take her long to realise why his words were so slurred and his eyes so hazy.

"Fuck," she breathed. *"Fuck.* Wow. What? Wow. I've never even *heard* of that. What's it called? Sarco—"

"Sarcoidosis," he said, only stumbling over the word slightly. "I Googled it a few hours ago. The results weren't great. I have decided to save further research for another day." He sounded so controlled, she wondered if she'd been wrong to assume he was drunk.

But then he turned his head and looked at her, and she saw… everything. He was fucked. He was absolutely fucked. And she wasn't just talking about the sweet scent of whiskey on his breath.

"You should go to bed," she whispered.

The corner of his mouth twitched up into a zombie of a smile, one with a dangerous edge. "You know I won't sleep."

"You can take things for that."

"I," he said grandly, "am generally resistant to sedatives and hypnotic agents."

"Oh," she replied. "Well… that's…"

"Irritating," he finished. "It's very fucking irritating. Do you take sleeping pills, Hannah?"

She swallowed. "Not really."

"I'm just asking because, you know, the kitchen's right under your room, and the other night I dropped a Wok on my foot and swore for ten minutes straight. But you didn't wake up."

She tried, rather unsuccessfully, to hide her laughter. "I see."

"Sometimes you sleep hard. Like the kids. But other times you come down here and see me. So I thought, maybe sometimes you take something."

Every night, she took something. She still had no idea what it was that made her wake up sometimes. But all she said, tentatively, was, "I don't know if we should talk about my…"

"Your private medical history?" he suggested. "Mmm. Yeah. You're right. Because, you know, technically, I am your employer. Do you ever forget that? I forget that."

He'd thrown his arm over the back of the sofa at some point, and she was conscious of it like a burning flame, just behind her neck. She'd have been lying if she said anything other than, "Yeah. Sometimes I do forget." *Mostly because I want to.*

"I think we forget in different ways. I feel bad about it—I really do. But I didn't know, when I hired you."

She frowned, partly in response to his odd words and partly because his expression had just turned dark and stormy. He looked… troubled. And he sounded baffling. "Know what?"

In the shadows, his eyes were like twin black holes. "Maybe I did know, and I was just being an oblivious prick. But your face, you know, is perfect. Perfectly *imperfect* in the way that's actually perfect. I think that blurs the lines. Don't you? How was I supposed to know, when I thought it was just… just about your face?"

Hannah blinked. "Are you always such a rambling drunk?"

His tense expression melted into a half-smile, that harsh gaze softening. "I'm never drunk. When Ellie died, that's the last time I was drunk."

Oh, dear. "And when did Ellie die?" she asked softly.

"Tuesday the 7th of February 2014 at 11:57 a.m.," he said. "Hey, I sounded like you for a second there. Queen of details. Hannah Kabbah, Her Royal Highness, Queen of Details." He sounded... disarmingly cheerful. He sounded oddly like his son. She could even see him smiling through the darkness, that single dimple sending an arrow of unwilling affection to her chest. He settled deeper into the cushions, and the heat his arm gave off, so close to her neck, increased. As if he were closer, now. As if, in a minute, she might feel the fine hairs on his arm whispering against her skin.

"Nate..."

"What?" he asked, propping up one of his legs. His knee, covered in denim, grazed her bare calf. Suddenly, that arrow of affection in her chest didn't seem so innocent— because one glancing, accidental touch sparked another, hotter arrow, and another, and another. They slammed into her so hard, she barely remembered to breathe.

Focus.

"Are you..." She frowned, pursed her lips, wrestled with the awkward words. "I mean—do you think you're over Ellie's death?"

He'd told her before that he was. But they hadn't been close then. He could've lied. There were family pictures all over the house that included the woman who must've been his wife, a woman with cropped, brown hair and dark eyes and a broad smile. If he was still hurting, would he keep the pictures up? She wasn't sure. Because occasionally he'd say something—like the precise minute that his wife had died—and she'd worry that despite his cheerfulness and his casual attitude, he was secretly crumbling inside.

He looked at her now, his expression thoughtful. "I ask myself that sometimes," he said calmly, as if they were planning the week's dinners. "You know, I talk about Ellie a lot. I mean, *a lot*. I think it's important for the kids. Don't you think that's important for the kids?"

She would've said yes, but his words stumbled on without pause.

"I do, I think it's important," he decided. "I want them to feel like they know her. But the thing is, talking about her, and the way *they* talk about her—it's good. I think if it weren't for them, I wouldn't have the balls to mention her name. Because at first, it hurt so much to even *think* about her, and I had to force myself. But now I'm used to it."

He reached beneath the neckline of his T-shirt and drew out the cord he always wore around his neck. She saw his wedding ring flash in the hint of moonlight through the window, and then its gleam was hidden by his fingers as he toyed with the gold band. "I didn't take off my ring for a while. Maybe a year. I couldn't. I tried to take it off one day and I thought I was going to be sick. But then, after a while, I tried again, and I felt okay.

"I think I've been fine for a couple of years, and I didn't even notice the change. Until now, I mean. When Ma was diagnosed…" He grunted, corrected himself. "*Misdiagnosed*. It felt like this huge hole ripped open inside me. And that was when I realised: I used to have a hole like that for Ellie, but it's gone now. I can feel the scar, but it's healed."

He fell silent, his thoughtful gaze settling on her. It didn't feel like the kind of scrutiny that made her skin crawl. When their eyes met, it felt like touching him, like putting a hand on his shoulder. It made Hannah suddenly sleepy after hours of being too worried to relax. She found herself simultaneously glad that he'd recovered and furious with the world for giving him another hole to deal with.

But he *would* deal with it. She suspected he could deal with anything.

"You took Zach to church," he said abruptly.

Hannah blinked, yanked from the mire of her thoughts. "I did. A little while before you arrived."

He nodded. "Do you know why he asked?"

"I thought it must be to do with your mum," she said carefully.

Nate grunted. Then, after a pause, he said, "Is that where you go on Sundays?"

"Yes. And then I have dinner with my mother and sister, and sometimes Evan."

"That's cute."

Hannah had decided to forget that his arm was resting on the back of the sofa, right behind her. She'd told herself firmly that she was imagining its warmth, imagining the comfort it seemed to radiate. So of course, he chose now, when her tension had eased, to touch her.

He slid a hand under the curtain of her braids and ran a slow, absent finger over the indent of her spine, stopping just above the neckline of her shirt. Every part of her, every inch of her body and thought in her head, focused on that contact like it was the centre of the fucking universe. But Nate wasn't even looking at her. He was staring into the shadows, frowning hard, his teeth sunk into his lower lip.

"I think Zach was depressed," he said.

She almost forgot about his fingers resting against her skin. "You do?"

"Actually, I know he was. He kind of told me. He told me lots of things. I'm worried about him, but he says I shouldn't be. He reckons he's been working on it and he's better now."

Her heart thudded against her ribcage, but Hannah forced herself to breathe deeply. She hadn't realised exactly how much Zach meant to her until... well, apparently, right this second. Somehow, though, she managed to focus on Nate. "Do you believe him?"

There was a heavy pause. Then Nate shifted, as if his body was fidgeting along with his thoughts. "I don't know. Is it that easy, to just... make yourself better?"

"I understand why you're worried," she said. "But some people are really good at managing their health. You know, once you get used to it—taking your medication and forcing yourself to go outside, keeping journals so you can watch your own thoughts..."

"Is that what you do?" he asked, his voice barely above a whisper, as gentle as the way he'd touched her.

She managed to say, "Yes. I had a therapist. I learned things. I force myself to remember those things. It works out okay."

"So, you don't struggle? You never slip?"

Although it pained her to admit it, she refused to lie. Not about this. "I do. I do slip." Even when everything was fine, when she *should* be great, unease stalked her like a predator.

Because she knew that at any moment, things might change. Her own fucking brain chemistry, the traitor, might drag her out of her body again.

So often, she was afraid. It was exhausting.

"When you slip," he said carefully, "do you ever think of reaching out? Asking someone for help?"

"Think about it? Yes."

"Do you do it?"

"Absolutely not." She'd said that too emphatically, hadn't she? She'd shown him too much of her fear. Too much of the gnawing voice that said, *No-one would care if you did, anyway, and that would just make everything worse.*

There was a pause before he replied. "That's okay. I'll watch you. In case."

The layers of meaning in that statement hit her like wave after wave of cool ocean under a hot sun. *That's okay. I'll watch you. If you ever fall, you won't have to drag yourself up and find me for help. I'll be ready. I'll pick you up off the ground.*

I'll watch you.

"When I'm depressed," Nate said casually, "I always know what I *should* be doing. I know exactly. I just don't do it."

The words jolted Hannah out of her thoughts. They were the last thing she'd expected to hear, for more reasons than one. But the most unsettling thing was how familiar they seemed; how he could've plucked those sentences right out of her head.

"I should take care of myself," Nate said. "I should talk to someone. I should laugh with the kids and really mean it. I should take a minute to breathe and feel the air moving inside my lungs. I know these things, and that just makes it worse, because I also know that I'm not going to do it. It's like sitting in front of a wall—one you can see right through —and on the other side is the person you should be. And it's so clear, it seems so close, and so much *better*. So you think, 'Hey, maybe I could climb the wall. Maybe I could knock it down. Maybe, if I walked far enough, I'd find the end and just… step around it.'

"But you never do," he murmured, his voice hoarse. "You just keep staring through the wall and thinking about it, because making plans is so much easier than acting, and you're so fucking tired. You don't know if you've ever truly been awake; you can't remember the feeling anymore. And after a while, watching that other you do the things you should be doing—it feels good enough. Knowing what you *should* do takes as much energy as doing it, so why push yourself? Taking the extra step, actually *living*—it just seems so excessive, all of a sudden. So unnecessary. Why cause yourself so much trouble, so much pain, chasing after something you barely remember… when you can sit and watch it through the wall?"

Nate spoke as if in a distant trance, his eyes unfocused— but after a second, he finally looked at Hannah. If she'd been looking back at him, she'd have noticed that he seemed suddenly sober. She'd have seen him sit up straighter and blink rapidly, seen his cheeks flush a little. Seen him pull his fingers from the back of her neck and stare, astonished, at his own hand.

But she wasn't paying attention to Nate. She was figuring out how to keep breathing when it felt like he'd just ripped out her insides.

"Hannah," he whispered. "I'm sorry." She tried to ask

what he was sorry for, but she couldn't speak. Emotion clogged her throat like a cork in a bottle. And then he said, "I didn't mean to make you cry."

Oh. *That* was why she couldn't speak. Tears were to blame for the hot prickling of her eyes and the wetness gliding down her cheeks. Of course they were. Of course.

She was absolutely furious with herself. What a ridiculous time to start crying. Well, *any* time was a ridiculous time to start crying, but this just took the cake. And the worst part was, she couldn't stop. Her body was not obeying. She pressed her hands over her eyes and ordered herself to behave, but the tears kept coming and the sobs kept burning through her chest, and for some reason she couldn't knock it off.

Then, suddenly, she was caught in Nate's arms as he dragged her onto his lap like she was one of the kids. He wrapped her up in what could only be described as the best hug ever: warm and dark and safe, smelling faintly of whiskey and Nate. It was as if a little world of its own existed in his arms. A world where she could press her face against his chest and cry very, very hard without feeling like an absolute ninny.

Which is exactly what she did.

Until, finally, her sobs quieted, leaving her head aching and her eyes puffy. Of course, with the ability to stop crying came the ability to feel embarrassment like never before. Hannah promptly descended, therefore, into the deepest pit of mortification known to humankind.

"Oh, God," she mumbled, pulling away. "I am so sorry."

"Don't be sorry." Nate let her escape the soft little haven he'd created, but he didn't release her completely. She was still sort of sitting in his lap, and frankly, she didn't feel inclined to move.

Even though she absolutely should.

"It's good to cry," he said. "When you told me you never cry, I was worried."

She huffed out a snotty sort of laugh. "Worried."

"Yeah. Crying is important. But I know you're shy."

"I am *not* shy."

"You are. You can only cry in secret." He put an arm around her and settled deeper into the sofa cushions. Somehow, Hannah's treacherous head allowed itself to rest on his shoulder. Oh, the shame. The indignity. The betrayal!

"Next time you need to cry," Nate said calmly, "tell me. And we'll do that again. That was okay, wasn't it?"

"You are being absolutely nonsensical."

"I'll take that as a yes." His head had fallen back against the sofa and his eyes were closed. She made out the solid line of his jaw, the broad softness of his mouth, those impossibly black lashes resting against his too-pale skin. He'd always been white as a sheet, but she was starting to worry he might be anaemic.

Although, if he were anaemic, he wouldn't have so much… muscle. Would he? Hannah wasn't sure. She'd have to Google it. And make lots of steak for dinner.

"Hey," he said suddenly, as if a thought had struck him. "You're not naked!" His hand had somehow wound up under her cardigan, resting against her pyjama-clad hip.

She blinked. "Did you think I *was*?"

"Under the cardigan. Yeah."

"Seriously? All this time, you thought I was naked?"

"I mean, I tried *not* to think about it," he said wryly.

"Oh, dear God."

"Don't fuss. How the hell do you wear this thing *and* pyjamas? It's hot as fuck in this house."

"I run kind of cold," she said. "And even if I didn't, I couldn't just roam around in *shorts*."

"God forbid," he muttered. "I, for one, have never seen a thigh before. If I did, I might go mad with lust."

She snorted. "Not likely."

For a moment, his eyes opened. The moonlight filtering through the window gleamed off of his pale gaze, and she thought she saw something... inconvenient.

Electrifying.

"You know," she forced herself to say, "you should probably put me down."

"It's okay," he said. "It's dark. And it's nighttime. And I'm drunk. So it doesn't count."

"What doesn't count?"

His eyes slid shut again, freeing her from that icy, exhilarating trap. "Wanting," he said softly. Too softly.

She waited for a moment, assuming that he'd finish his sentence. Or, you know, say something that made the least bit of sense. Something that didn't make her pulse rush heavily in her ears and pound tauntingly between her thighs.

But he didn't. And the minutes stretched into true silence. Just as she was telling herself he couldn't possibly have fallen asleep, Nate snored. It was more like a little snuffle, really, one that reminded her of a dreaming dog, but she felt better calling it a snore. She nudged him gently, and he snored again. Apparently, he was not waking up.

So, with an embarrassing level of reluctance, Hannah

clambered off his lap. Then she pulled the curtains shut, shoved his massive body into a vaguely horizontal position, and draped her huge cardigan over him like a blanket.

A half-blanket, perhaps.

When she left, she closed the door behind her very gently, and definitely didn't look back.

CHAPTER TWELVE

Zach: Glad u exist
Nate: Same.

~

NATE WOKE up the way people did in nightmares. Those realistic, emotional nightmares that revolved around some sort of anxiety; like he was fifteen again, and he actually gave a shit about school, and he'd overslept on exam day.

But as he bolted up into a sitting position and squinted, bleary-eyed, at his surroundings, several facts became painfully apparent.

1. He was no longer fifteen, or young enough to binge drink without facing the consequences.
2. Those consequences were fucking vile. They included a headache so sharp that his vision was

blurred and a tongue that felt like a dead rat had invaded his mouth.

3. Despite not being fifteen and no longer having exams, he'd still overslept for school.

"Fuck," he muttered, then winced as the sound of his own voice sent a bite of pain through his skull.

At which point, realisation number 4 hit him: the house was deathly silent.

Where the hell were his children? The sunlight sneaking through the living room curtains told him that it was most definitely morning. Which meant that Beth should be bellowing in his ear and Josh should be sprawled across his chest. The lack of child limpets attached to Nate's person was cause for concern.

He stood up, gritting his teeth as his vision darkened and his head spun. When the dizzy spell passed, he looked down to find that he was clutching something soft and cream-coloured against his chest. It was woollen. It was knitted. It was…

Hannah's?

Nate held up the cardigan and stared at it. The movement released a burst of familiar fragrance: sweet pastries, the soft perfume of lipstick, and the way-too-real hint of skin and soap.

Definitely Hannah's.

Which made him feel a hell of a lot better. Mostly because it reminded him that his children almost certainly hadn't been kidnapped while he slept off a drunken stupor. Hannah wouldn't *let* them be kidnapped. He wondered briefly if she could be kidnapped herself. Then he decided she would scold any would-be abductors so thoroughly, they'd run off to the nearest church to… confess. Or whatever it was people did in church.

Was Hannah Catholic? He had no idea. He'd ask, only he was uncomfortably aware that he probably asked her way too much about herself already.

And with that thought came a memory of last night. Of him running his mouth and making her cry and *letting* her cry, and generally being way too fucking obvious about the fact that she made him…

Well. There was no point dwelling on all that. He had children to locate.

She should've heard him coming up the stairs, but she'd been struck by lightning.

That was how it felt when Hannah managed to carry out an idea—not just to fulfil a task, but execute a vision, however pretentious that sounded. She'd been wasting her copious free time for days now, prettifying her blog to hide the fact that she wasn't writing jack shit.

And then, this morning, she'd opened her laptop and done nothing *but* write. Now she couldn't stop, and it was electrifying, and yes: it felt like being struck by lightning. Hearing Nate say her name was the accompanying thunderclap.

Hannah stifled a rather embarrassing scream and slapped a hand over her chest. She looked up to find him hovering in the doorway of her bedroom. He had her cardigan in one hand, his fingers tangled in the fabric, and he looked…

Well, he looked a thousand times better, actually. But he probably felt like shit.

"You're awake," she said, displaying her razor-sharp intellect and sparkling wit.

He grimaced as if he deeply regretted his conscious state. "Where are the kids?"

"I took them to school."

Nate sighed, rubbing a hand over his jaw. The dark shadow of his stubble was startling against his skin. Hannah reminded herself to pump him full of steak as soon as possible.

"I," he said wryly, "am a terrible father."

She stared. "I beg your pardon?" Surely, he must be joking. Except he looked painfully serious, standing there, the slight smile on his face not enough to hide the worry in his eyes.

"They haven't even seen me since yesterday," he said. "They must be—"

"They're absolutely fine. I let them peek at you through the door and they thought your snoring was hilarious. I told them you weren't very well, and you'd see them at dinner. Easy."

"Thank you," he said, far too seriously for her comfort. As if she'd just saved his life or something, instead of doing her job. "Thank you. Jesus. I don't know what I'd…" He trailed off, shaking his head. "This is exactly the kind of dad I never wanted to be."

Very carefully, Hannah shut her laptop and set it aside. "Nate. When I was seven my father came to visit us for the last time. He bought me a doll and gave me a speech about how babies were the most important thing in the world. If you had one, you must give up everything to protect it. I haven't seen or spoken to him since. Because his wife was pregnant, so he couldn't risk visiting us anymore. He was having a *real* baby. And he gave up everything to protect it."

Nate's self-flagellating expression was replaced by shock and sympathy. Lord, she hated sympathy.

"Hannah—"

She held up a hand. "I don't need you to say anything. In fact, I'd rather you didn't. Platitudes are wasted on people who don't need them. What I want is for you to get your head out of your arse and think about fathers like mine. Better yet, think about fathers like *yours*, Nate." Because Jacob Davis had run off years ago with a bloody bee keeper, of all things. "Are you doing better than them? Fuck yes. Could you ever become them? No. Because you actually care about your children. You put them first. You'd die before you let anything hurt them. That's your job, and you're doing it. Don't ever think you're not."

He appeared speechless. Frankly, Hannah had almost rendered herself speechless. She had no idea she was capable of giving emotional pep talks to anyone outside her family.

It's because you care about him. Because you're comfortable with him. Because he doesn't make you feel like a caricature instead of a human being.

Hannah shoved those thoughts ruthlessly into her Do Not Touch vault. That was quite enough sentimentality for one day.

Nate frowned, running a hand through his wild hair. "Hannah. You're so—"

She had to cut him off, of course. Unless that sentence ended with *repugnant*, it couldn't possibly do the choppy waters of her mind any good.

"You really do need a haircut," she said briskly, opening her laptop again. "I've had quite enough of watching you run around like an abandoned sheep. You have two hours to pull yourself together, after which I will be attacking you with a pair of scissors."

She'd wanted—*needed*—to wipe that gentle look off his face, and it worked. Nate's lips tipped up into a smile, and he drawled, "Is that an order?"

"It's a firm instruction."

"Do you know how to cut hair?"

She cocked her head. "What do you think?"

Nate folded his arms and leant against the doorframe, that lazy-sexy smirk on his face. "I think there's absolutely no reason why you *should* know, but somehow I don't doubt that you do."

He looked quite despicably handsome, standing there, and it was making her think about terrible things—like whether or not she could reach his mouth just by standing on tip-toe. She needed him to leave, immediately, before the force of all that sexiness sucked anymore oxygen out of the room.

So she said crisply, "Two hours. I recommend you down a litre of water, at least."

He huffed out a laugh and gave her a mock salute.

And then, thank baby Jesus and all the bloody angels, he left.

∽

TWO HOURS LATER, Nate was sitting on a chair he'd dragged into the garden while Hannah loomed over him like an avenging angel. An avenging angel with ladybird-printed kitchen scissors, fire-engine-red lipstick, and a mean stare.

"Why are you glaring at me?" he finally asked, after a few minutes of gentle outdoor silence.

"I'm visualising," she murmured, cocking her head to the left.

"Are you sure you know how to do this?"

"It's a trim, Nate. Relax."

"*You're* telling *me* to relax? Now I'm worried."

To his surprise, she flashed him one of her rare, wicked grins. It warmed him from the inside out. Hell, it might even have pushed away the last vestiges of his headache. The smooth glide of Hannah's painted lips over white teeth was apparently more powerful than aspirin. Good to know.

"Okay," she said suddenly. "My artistic process is complete. I am ready to begin."

He tried, and tragically failed, to hold back a snort of laughter. She rolled her eyes as she moved to stand behind him, but she was still smiling.

It felt strange, sitting outside in the grass, listening to birds sing, feeling Hannah push his head gently this way and that. They fell into silence as the sharp *snip* of her scissors filled the air, and every so often she made a thoughtful little humming sound in the back of her throat. But she didn't speak. She was probably concentrating.

And that would've been fine, except the quiet let Nate's mind wander to dangerous places. He thought about his mother, who he still worried about—even though he'd called earlier, and she'd insisted that she was fine. Oh, and told him to stop calling. Whatever. He forced himself to move on from that pointless avenue and fell headfirst into another forbidden well. One that was far more enjoyable.

Hannah. He could smell her. He could *feel* her, almost as if she were pressing her body against his, when really, she was just standing particularly close. Occasionally, he felt her breath against the back of his neck, or his ear, or his jaw, and each time he worked hard not to betray himself. Not to reveal the way his muscles ached with the effort of keeping still, or the fact that his hands itched to touch her.

He'd thought often—usually in the dark—about dragging up those long skirts she wore and running his hands over her thighs. He'd thought about pulling her into his arms and sliding his palms down her back until he reached the lush curve of her arse. He'd thought about trailing his fingers over her breasts, circling her nipples just to see what sound she made... But he wouldn't have to touch her like that. He'd be happy to hold her hand. He'd be happy to hug her again, because sometimes she seemed too small and sweet to stand alone all the time. She was like one of those tiny dogs who defended themselves with vicious fervour, but could, realistically, still be crushed by a toddler on a scooter.

Regardless of how crushable she seemed, though, he couldn't touch her. Ever. Nate was just reminding himself of this depressing fact when she said, "So. You're a photographer."

He cleared his throat, but his reply still came out a little too raw. "Yep. Yeah. That's me."

Her words flirted with laughter as she murmured, "Oh that's you?"

"Shut up," he muttered.

"Are you a *good* photographer?"

"You tell me. You've seen my pictures."

"I have?"

"Any picture in this house that doesn't include me, I took it."

"Oh." She paused. He found himself almost anxious to hear what she thought. But in the end, all she said was, "They don't look like Cindy Sherman's." From the tone of her voice, he felt like that might be a compliment.

"Ah, well. I like natural portraiture for the family, but my popular stuff is all conceptual. It's like… fantasy."

"Conceptual? Like Rosie Hardy?"

"You've heard of Rosie Hardy, too?"

"Maybe," she said. "But I'll tell you now, I know nothing about photography. Don't think you can start using fancy words and I'll understand." He saw her from the corner of his eye as she focused on the front of his hair. For a second, he let himself sink into the ripe curve of her mouth, the velvet texture of her lipstick, the way her eyes tilted up slightly at the outer corners. Then he forced himself to look down at the grass.

"I won't use any fancy words," he promised. "What do you like about her?"

For a moment, she was quiet. Then she said softly, "The magic."

"That's what I like too. Making magic."

He wasn't supposed to be watching her. So why did he see her smile?

And why did he hear himself say, as if listening to another man speak: "I want to photograph you, you know."

There was a pause as the steady snip of her scissors stopped. Nate used that pause to ask his mouth what the fuck it thought it was doing. When, precisely, had it decided to stop being a team player? His mouth did not respond.

Finally, Hannah said, "Me?"

So he added to the excruciating awkwardness by confirming: "Yeah."

After another pause, her scissors started up again. Well, that was a relief. At least she hadn't, you know, stabbed him in alarm.

"I'm aware," he added, "that this is usually something guys say to get innocent, unsuspecting women out of their clothes—"

"You want to photograph me *naked*?"

"*No*," he said. Actually, he kind of shouted it. Then, clearing his throat, added much more calmly, "That's not really my thing. Usually. But what I'm trying to say is, I'm not telling you any of this in a weird way—"

"I didn't think you were," she said. Which made him feel a hell of a lot better. "But I don't really understand why you'd want to take my picture. I'm not very photogenic."

"Really? Because you have an unusually symmetrical face, so I'd think you would be."

She ran a hand through his hair, sending a dart of sensation down his spine. It didn't seem fair that at any moment she could just touch him and make him burn like this. As if it was nothing. He short-circuited and caught fire while she stood there looking pristine as ever.

"Thank you," she said, "but I'm not. I'm too self-conscious. I'm awkward, when people are watching. Your hair's done."

"Right," he murmured absently. "I mean, thanks."

"Do you want to see it?"

"I'm sure you did a great job."

He was sure he didn't give a shit, because even if she'd completely fucked up his hair it would be worth it. Worth it to sit there for a while and have the full force of her exhilarating focus. Worth it to feel that electric thrill when she ran her fingers through his hair...

"What if I could take your picture without you knowing?" he asked suddenly. His mouth had decided to run away again. He'd be giving the thing a stern talking to. *There is no I in team, mouth. And talking shit like this is not going to result in the outcome you so clearly want. Give it up.*

He had a feeling his mouth would never listen, though. It did, after all, belong to him.

She arched her brows, standing in front of him with those scissors still in hand. "Like... when I'm not looking?"

"So you wouldn't be uncomfortable. That helps people, sometimes."

She shrugged. "I think I'd know, even if I couldn't see you. I feel it when—when people look at me." Hannah faltered for a moment, but her next words were smooth as silk. "You're welcome to try, though. Don't blame me if you end up disappointed."

He stood, an odd sort of anticipation spreading through his body like low heat. He had permission. His rogue mouth had actually done something useful. Unbelievable. "We'll see," he said. "I might surprise you."

She gave him a wry look over her shoulder as she walked towards the house. "I am rarely surprised."

And he, after grabbing the chair they'd dragged outside, followed like the obsessed mess that he was. "Then I'll definitely surprise you. Someone has to."

She snorted. "Good luck. You're covered in hair, so brush it off before you come into the kitchen."

Nate shrugged and put the chair down on the patio, pulling off his T-shirt. He probably should've done that before, to be honest, but he hadn't been thinking. Or rather, he'd been too busy thinking about Hannah. He shook the shirt out on the concrete, then followed her inside.

And found her leaning against the kitchen island, staring at him as if she'd been frozen.

"What?" he asked.

She continued to stare.

"Hannah. *What?*"

Her name seemed to snap her out of whatever trance she was in. Her lips pressed into a tight line, and he watched her throat shift as she swallowed. "Nothing!" she said brightly, and turned to hurry off.

Which struck him as exactly the sort of thing Hannah would do if, say, the apocalypse was nigh, but she didn't want to worry anyone.

So Nate reached out to take her hand, tugging her gently to a stop. "Are you okay?"

"I'm fine."

He reeled her in closer, frowning at the odd expression on her face. "No, you're not."

"*Yes* I *am.*" Her eyes narrowed. "I'm just worried about

you running around half-naked all the time. You'll catch your death."

"…It's at least twenty degrees outside."

"But it's about to rain!"

"Hannah, we're in the house."

She spluttered for a moment, looking completely un-Hannah-like and thoroughly adorable. Finally, she burst out, "I think you might be anaemic."

"Why would I be anaemic?" *And what does that have to do with my shirt?*

"You're so pale!"

He laughed. "Ouch."

"Oh, stop it. I didn't mean it like that. You look…"

Nate arched a brow. "Terrible? I feel like we've covered this before."

"What? No. You don't think that, do you?" The strange expression on Hannah's face turned to worry, that little arrow appearing between her brows as she frowned. "You're gorgeous."

He almost collapsed in shock. The words were unbelievable enough, coming from Hannah of all people. But even better was the way she slapped her hands to her cheeks after she said it, like a character in a play. She spun away from him, her hair whipping through the air.

"Oh *dear*," she muttered to herself. "Why, Hannah, *why*?"

Good fucking question. Because he really didn't think Hannah came out with statements like that very often. Especially not accidentally. An impossible explanation flashed into his head, bright enough to leave him blinking rapidly. Really, it was more of a fantasy—maybe a side-effect of excessive shower masturbation—than an explana-

179

tion. Yet something wicked and hopeful coiled inside him, urging him to ask… "Hannah, do you—?"

"There is really no need to finish that sentence," she said. Her voice wasn't cool and calm as usual. It was clipped in a way that told him, loud and clear, how nervous she was.

Which made Nate actually consider that the impossible explanation he'd dreamt up was more than just wishful thinking. And then she turned to face him, her expression somewhere between irritation and embarrassment, and he was sure. Impossibly, he was sure.

"It's really nothing personal," she scowled. "It's just, you know. You look like *that*. And you can't keep a bloody shirt on for more than five minutes!"

His mouth, previously so very active, was now having trouble forming words. "I… look… like…"

"You look like—have you ever read those books about Hades and Persephone where Hades is inexplicably hot and… okay, you know what? You have definitely never read one of those books."

Nate resolved to memorise every word she'd just said and Google random combinations of them all until he found the books she was talking about.

"This really has nothing to do with you," she said.

Finally, his mouth started working again. Maybe because he'd finally absorbed the fact that Hannah appeared to be saying she was… *attracted* to him? "What has nothing to do with me?"

She didn't seem to hear. "I'm pretty sure I'm ovulating," she went on, as if talking to herself. Then she squeezed her eyes shut and whispered, "Oh, why the fuck did you *say* that, Hannah?"

"Why don't you say *more*, Hannah?"

"No thanks," she squeaked.

Her eyes opened slowly, as if she was afraid of what she might see. And, in the end, she was. Because the moment she realised that Nate was walking steadily toward her, she stepped back.

And again.

And again.

But he didn't stop walking. He couldn't. Instead, he said, "Let me make sure I'm understanding this correctly."

"Or," she interjected, "you could forget I ever said anything at all."

He decided to ignore that suggestion. "You're saying that I shouldn't take my shirt off—"

"I don't think I said *that*—"

"Because I'm..." his lips twitched. "Gorgeous."

"You are so fucking smug. Why do I even like you?"

"And also because you're ovulating."

"Oh, Jesus Christ, please don't sack me—"

"Hannah. I'm not going to sack you. You could set fire to the dining room curtains and I wouldn't sack you."

She paused for a moment in her steady retreat. "That seems oddly specific."

"You did set fire to my dustbin the other day."

Her back came into contact with the fridge, bringing her retreat to a sudden stop. "That... that was for the kids. It was science."

"I know. You're big on experimentation, right?"

"Um... right?"

He put his hands against the fridge on either side of her head, caging her in. The appliance felt more like a freezer

181

against his heated palms. Nate leaned down until he was as close to eye-level with Hannah as he was likely to get. It helped that she rose up on her toes to meet him. He wondered if she knew that she was doing it.

Probably not. Her pupils were so blown that, if he didn't know any better, he'd think she'd taken something. Her tongue slid out to glide over her scarlet lower lip, and then she said, "You don't seem very upset about this."

"Guess why."

"I'd rather not."

"Oh, yeah. I forgot. You're not interested in me at all, are you? You're just…" he bit back a laugh. "Ovulating."

CHAPTER THIRTEEN

Hannah: I think your lack of filter is rubbing off on me.
Ruth: Nah. You've always had a big mouth.

HANNAH WASN'T sure what would kill her first: abject mortification, the way her heart was ricocheting around her chest (which couldn't be healthy), or the rather concerning fever she seemed to have developed some time in the last thirty seconds.

Actually, that fever had started when Nate had whipped off his T-shirt like it was nothing—like he didn't have a despicably broad chest covered in tattoos she shouldn't like so much, with that little silver bar winking through one nipple. And her temperature had increased to truly dangerous levels when he started smiling like... like he wanted to *eat* her.

Which he was still doing right this minute, at worryingly close quarters.

She could see swirls of frost in his blue eyes, see the tiny, rough hairs that made up the shadow on his jaw—see the softness of that generous mouth. She wished she couldn't. She should close her eyes. Things were bad enough right now without a close-up view of the handsomeness that had been turning her brain to mush for the last few weeks.

He buried his face in her hair and she felt him take slow, deep breaths. For a few precious seconds, she was enveloped in the shadows of his body and the sweet, smoky scent of him, and she felt incongruously safe. As if she could let down her own exhausting shields and allow him to take over for a while.

Then his lips brushed her forehead. It could barely be called a kiss, she knew that. Still, arousal sparked at the chaste press of his mouth, shimmering through her body until it landed between her legs. Fuck.

Nate pulled back, looking at her with a rueful expression. "I shouldn't be doing this," he said.

She should be happy at this sign that he was beginning to see sense, but all she felt was that delicious zing of need, along with a disturbing disappointment at his words.

Apparently, her face conveyed that disappointment without authorisation, because he smiled—oh, she wished he wouldn't smile—and murmured, "You disagree?"

"I don't," she said. "I think you're right."

Nate sighed. "This was a lot easier before I knew you. Now I can tell when you're lying."

She decided to ignore the more concerning part of that statement; nobody knew when Hannah was lying. "This?"

"This. Pretending I didn't want to touch you. Not cornering you in the kitchen like some kind of pervert. Resisting the urge to kiss you."

"You haven't kissed me."

"Yet." But then he closed his eyes and shook his head. "No. No. I'm not going to kiss you. I'm not going to touch you."

"Because you don't... like me." That was what she'd *thought*, but it was getting harder and harder to believe it.

Especially when Nate opened his eyes with a frown and asked, "What the hell are you talking about? Of course I like you."

"Right." She nodded calmly, as if she'd been aware of this all along. Which, really, she had—but it just seemed so impossible. When did anyone ever like her and want her all at the same time? Never, that's when.

Now, actually. Someone likes you and wants you now.

"The problem," Nate said slowly, as if making sure she understood, "is that you work for me."

"Oh," she said. "Well, yes. I knew that." *I just somehow didn't consider it at all, because I was far too preoccupied with pre-teen anxiety about who does and does not like me. Wonderful.*

Nate sighed, his expression suddenly, achingly sad. "This has ruined everything, hasn't it?"

To Hannah's surprise, something close to panic flared inside her. "What? No. I mean—I'm sorry—I shouldn't have said anything at all, I just—"

"Not you. It's not you." He laughed, the tension in his shoulders fading slightly. "You can't help yourself. You're ovulating."

"Oh, for God's sake. Are you ever going to forget I said that?"

"Not in a thousand years." His gaze dropped, for one heavy moment, to her lips, and Hannah's chest tightened. He lowered his head, but their mouths didn't meet. Instead, she felt his breath against her jaw, her ear, her throat. It felt like he was dragging his lips or his tongue, or even his hands, over that sensitive skin—but he wasn't. He didn't touch her. Not once.

Hannah felt slightly faint. If he ever *did* touch her she might just die. A thick, thrumming heat formed in her belly and moved lower, lower, lower, settling between her thighs. She felt like an ocean struck by lightning. She felt like a woman who'd never worried. She felt like he'd better hurry up and kiss her before she expired in anticipation.

"You weren't supposed to know," he said, and for a moment she imagined she felt the brush of his lips against her throat. But that was just a fantasy. "I didn't want to put you in this position. I'm sorry."

"Know what?" Why did she sound so breathless? If she'd had room for an emotion other than need, she might've been embarrassed.

"How much I want you."

"Oh. Well. I mean, I already thought…"

He pulled back with a slow smile. "You thought what?"

"Um… I thought you might, perhaps, *possibly*, be slightly attracted to me—"

"You *knew*?"

She rolled her eyes. "Well, Nate, I am thirty years old, and sometimes people are interested in me—"

"Only sometimes?"

She gave him a warning glare. "And when they are, they tend to display certain signs, and I have become adept at recognising these signs—"

"You knew." He laughed. "Oh, Hannah. I don't know why I thought I could hide anything from you. No-one could hide anything from you."

You'd be surprised. "I assumed you'd get over it," she said. "Which you will, once you get to know me."

Nate gave her an odd look. It was the kind of look she imagined he'd give the Queen, if the Queen suddenly ripped off her clothes and started pole dancing. "Hannah. I do know you. Knowing you is one of the reasons why I fantasise about kissing you senseless."

"You... fantasise..." She shook her head and decided not to focus on the kissing part. "What are the other reasons?"

"There's only one other reason."

"Which is?"

He stared. "You know, there's this thing called a mirror. And if you looked into one, all sorts of things might become clear to you."

"Shut up," she snorted. "Okay. I think we have enough information to proceed."

He raised a brow. "Proceed?"

"Let's review."

He raised the other brow. "Review?"

She was getting very good at ignoring him. "You have developed some sort of attachment to me. Likely because I made that fried plantain last week—"

"Hannah."

"And because your artistic temperament makes you susceptible to physical attraction—"

"This is amazing. I can't even tell if you're insulting me."

She tried not to smile. Smiling would ruin the academic approach she was determined to take. "Meanwhile, I have fallen victim to a dormant crush that should have died many years ago—"

"Wait, what?"

"But didn't, because you left town before anything could happen to kill it off."

"Is this your incredibly roundabout way of admitting you have a crush on me?"

"*Had*," she corrected. "I *had* a crush on you. It's sort of reappeared, like a virus, but once it's dealt with, my immunity will be complete, and it will never return. At least, that's my theory."

He watched her for a moment. He looked even more handsome since his haircut—which should be impossible, since he'd already been the most handsome man on earth. Yet there he stood, more gorgeous than before. And maybe a little bit… sad?

When had that happened? Why was that happening? He shouldn't look sad. She did not want him to look sad.

"Your crush on me," he said, "is a virus."

"That's… how I've been thinking of it," she admitted.

It was a perfectly sensible metaphor. So why did she feel slightly guilty? Hannah pushed that niggling doubt aside and ploughed on.

"I also have a theory that whatever you feel toward me is due to the novelty of having someone to cook and look after your kids—"

"Don't," he said, his voice oddly tight. "Don't say that. I

wish you *didn't* look after the kids. I wish I didn't need you to. If I didn't need you, I could just... want you."

She bit her lip, studying his face. She didn't understand him. She'd been *trying* to understand him—she was usually so good at that—but she still couldn't quite grasp... *this*. The way he looked at her. The way he watched her now, with something dark and heavy in his gaze.

"Listen," he sighed. "This—today—it's all been a bit of a fuck-up. And I'm sorry, because I shouldn't have done any of this, and because I thought I was hiding things well, but obviously I wasn't. You're wrong about... about me. About this. But it doesn't matter, because I'm your employer, and you live here, and I can't have you."

He sounded so depressingly hopeless, her heart squeezed in her chest. "Don't worry," she said. "It'll be fine. Give it a few weeks and you'll forget this ever happened."

He pulled away, freeing her from the cage of his arms, stepping back with a frown. "Forget *what* ever happened? Today? Or the fact that I want you at all?"

Without Nate surrounding her, Hannah felt suddenly unmoored. She shook her head against the sensation, and against his words. "You don't want *me*. I'm just around. It happens to the best of us."

He did not look pleased. He didn't even look reassured, or relieved, which was what she'd been hoping for.

In fact, all of a sudden, he looked thunderous. "You're just *around*? That's what you think this is? Are you fucking serious?"

Oh, she wished he wasn't shirtless right now. "There's really no need to get upset—"

"I'm not upset, Hannah. I'm pissed."

She blinked. "Why?"

"Why? *Why?* Because I am not this kind of guy! I don't lust after women who work for me! I don't spend hours thinking about women I can't have and shouldn't want. I don't take advantage of people—I don't even *think* about it. But I can't stop thinking of you. And dreaming of you, and wishing I could touch you, and trying to make you smile— and you want to tell me it'll *blow over?* Do you know how many times in the last few years I've wished I could want someone like this? I didn't think I could! And now it's you, and I shouldn't, and I— fuck!" He broke off with a low growl, dragging his hands through his hair as he turned away.

Hannah watched him, her brain so full of wild and reckless thoughts, it suddenly felt too big for her skull. As if she might burst. There was too much to take in, to consider, to analyse—and over the top of everything she *should* be thinking, Nate's voice played like some kind of recording. Not for the first time, she wished her own ridiculous memory to hell. Because now she'd have to go the rest of her life recalling those words, and the way he looked at her as if it were all true, as if he wanted her like nothing else.

This couldn't be happening. Even the most passionate moments of Hannah's life, from filthy one night stands to so-called-love, hadn't made her feel like this. These things didn't happen in real life—or maybe they did, for some people, but not for her. For her, everything was numb and distant and swaddled in cotton wool, and she appreciated the protection, the *safety*, enough to forgo that raw emotion…

So why did she feel everything like a blade scraping over bare skin right now? Why did she believe him?

"Nate," she said, her voice a ragged whisper. "Look at me." She hadn't known what she was going to say before the words came out of her mouth, but they felt oddly right.

Then he turned, and she *knew* they were right. She'd needed to see him, just like this, looking as confused as she felt. There were no tricks here. He was just as lost as she was.

"Come here," she said.

He shook his head. "I can't. I can't."

"Why not?"

"If you let me, I'll—" He broke off. "No. No. I can't touch you."

She moved toward him, as slowly and steadily as he'd done to her ten minutes before. This time, she stalked *him* into a corner—against the cool expanse of the kitchen island. He reached back and gripped the counter until his knuckles were paper-white.

Nate dragged in a breath, his eyes pinned to hers, a sort of desperation gleaming from their depths. "What are you doing?"

She had no idea. She knew, logically, that she was standing in front of him, barely a breath between their bodies—and now she was raising a hand, and she would put that hand on him, and it would feel fucking good, and it would change everything.

But she didn't understand where all this torrential need had come from, or how it was overpowering her common sense and forcing her to do this. All she knew was that when he looked at her, she saw something worth chasing.

Something that turned her into a wilder version of herself, something that felt like a drug without adverse effects. She'd heard people talk about losing their minds with lust, and she'd thought they were childish—too cowardly to admit that they'd acted with complete consciousness, using something as bland and ordinary as desire to be their shield.

She was starting to think she'd never really known desire. It certainly wasn't bland and ordinary now. It wasn't as anxiety-inducing as a crush, either, or as easily contained as thoughtless lust.

Desire, apparently, had a life of its own.

Hannah let her fingertips trace the words tattooed over his chest, words that stemmed from the dark branches of a barren tree. "No gods, no kings," she murmured, smiling slightly. "You don't love my God, Nate?"

He let his head fall back, his eyes closed. "I'll love whatever you tell me to. Take me to church. I don't give a fuck."

She laughed. "I won't hold you to that." But her laugh was shaky, almost as shaky as she felt. Adrenaline must have been tearing through her veins, because her hand was far from steady when she brushed over the tiny silver bar through his nipple.

He sucked in a breath, his hips jerking forward. They were already standing so close, and the action brought them firmly into contact. Hannah felt the rigid outline of his dick press against her belly, and the fact that he was even hard at all dragged a moan from her throat.

His eyes snapped open, burning into her. "Fuck, I want to kiss you."

She ran her hands over his chest, his shoulders, drinking in the hard muscle and soft skin, pushing her body against his, the pressure just enough to tease—him or her, she wasn't sure. Either. Both. "What else do you want to do?"

"Hannah…" His voice cracked, her name a plea.

"Just once," she said. "We'll do this just once, and then we'll go back to the way it was before."

There was a pause, too long and far too weighty. She thought he'd say no. She knew he'd say no.

Until, finally, he said, "Once."

Something in his voice struck her as odd, but the hunger in his eyes wiped her mind clean.

"And then we'll be okay," she said.

He didn't reply, exactly. Instead, he kissed her.

CHAPTER FOURTEEN

NATE HAD BEEN a lot of things, but he'd never been a liar before.

Usually, when he did wrong, he admitted it. When he was at school, if he'd punched a guy or smoked some weed he'd say, "Yeah, Ma, I punched that guy. I smoked some weed." Even when he'd been in court after an anti-fash protest that turned into a brawl, he'd happily pled guilty to affray because... well, because he'd done it.

But here he was, after thirty years of honesty, letting Hannah believe that one time would be enough. He supposed, technically, that the lie didn't matter. Because one time wouldn't be enough, but it *would* be the end. She clearly wasn't interested in more, and Nate... Nate would only allow himself this, anyway. Only this. And only because she'd asked for it.

Funny how none of that made him feel any better. Funny how none of that stopped his mind from whispering, *You are absolute scum.*

Funny how he knew, almost instinctively, that kissing her would silence the voices in his head.

Hannah's cheeks felt so sweet and delicate in his hands. The way her eyes fluttered closed, as if she'd been waiting for this, sent a warmth through him that had nothing to do with the need in his blood or the ache in his cock. How she'd ever thought he didn't *like* her, Nate had no idea. But after this, he had a feeling she'd never forget it.

His mouth found hers and something in him clicked into place. He'd thought she'd taste of lipstick and lust and burning flames, but instead, she was... she was cool mint and a hint of sugar, and something he couldn't identify. That mysterious something, earthy and intimate, drew him in the most. It made him deepen the gentle touch of their lips, made him pour out his passion until she finally opened for him. He swept his thumb over the velvety skin of her cheek as his tongue explored the heat of her mouth.

She moaned, a sweet, whimpering sound, and Nate lost what little restraint he'd had, wrapping an arm around her waist to haul her closer. Only, the closer they got, the more he noticed the height difference between them. So he took the only sensible option and picked her up.

Only to be rewarded with a shriek and a smack to the back of the head. "Put me down!"

"Don't be difficult."

"*Nate!*"

He rolled his eyes, put her back on her feet, and sank to his knees.

"What the hell are you doing *now?*" she demanded.

He didn't answer. He couldn't, because this new position put his face on a level with her cleavage, swelling gently beneath her loose, white shirt. To Nate, Hannah's tits were sort of like his nose: obviously, he knew they were there, but his eyes generally refused to show him. Anytime he'd come close to looking at her chest, guilt forced his gaze to slide away without registering any of the details.

But apparently, his eyes were feeling more cooperative today. Because he could see, quite clearly, the hint of deep brown flesh displayed by her loosened top buttons. He could even see the tiny mole that kissed the curve of her left breast. He wanted to lick that mole.

He could also see the rise and fall of her chest as she panted softly, its rhythm almost hypnotic. He heard every sharp inhale, every shaking exhale, because this was Hannah and he felt everything about her, even when he shouldn't. He had no idea how, but he did. He'd hear her calling his name from miles away and he'd see her reaching for him in the dark. He knew that she was reaching for him now even though she hadn't moved a muscle.

So he undid the button that strained over her breasts, his hands seeming bigger and clumsier than usual. Still, he managed to open her shirt and push down the cups of her bra. He managed not to come on the spot when she released a high, tight whimper. He managed not to moan out loud when her tits fell into his palms. Nate caressed the ripe mounds, savoured her silky skin, and watched her face.

She was beautiful. She rolled her lips inward, frowning ferociously, her expression pained. She wrapped a hand around his wrist and nodded, breathless, while he tried not to smile. Apparently, Hannah wouldn't say anything so human as *More*. That was just fine. That was just perfect, since it was her.

He wanted to taste her. Badly. And since it had been decided that, for just this one time, they'd both get what they wanted...

He released her, leaving her shirt slightly dishevelled. Her nipples, hard and dark, were visible through the white fabric now that her bra had been made useless. He left that single button loose, so that if she bent or turned or made any sudden movement, he'd see exactly what he wanted to see.

"Hold up your skirt." Firm words, so she wouldn't hesitate, because if she did, he might die. When she gathered up the fabric with eager, efficient hands, he closed his eyes for a moment, just to thank his lucky stars. When he opened them again, he found heaven.

Hannah's tongue darted over her lower lip before she said, "Can I kiss you?"

Nate's blood pounded through his ears. He ran his hands over her thighs, tracing whisper-fine ridges that might be stretch-marks, then sharp, raised lines that were definitely scars. "You can do whatever the fuck you want. Always. Please."

A slight smile tilted her lips before she leaned forward and cupped his jaw. He hadn't expected that. If he looked down, he'd probably see her tits spilling out of her shirt, but he couldn't tear his gaze from her face—from those electric eyes, sending a shot of pure power through him with every glance. He was hypnotised by the soft pressure of her hand and the way she frowned when she was turned on. Then she kissed him, and all he could think about was touching and tasting and drowning in her.

While her lips branded him, while she ruined him with

nothing but the heat of her tongue and the feel of her palm on his face, Nate's hands roamed from her thighs to the curve of her arse. It was covered in ordinary, sensible cotton, completely expected and impossibly arousing. He could feel his cock leaking pre-come even though she'd barely touched him. It was just that hand, the hand she was using right now to stroke his cheek, and… fuck.

He pulled her underwear down, and she let him—or maybe she didn't notice, because this was the kind of kiss that distracted people thoroughly. But, no, she knew, because she lifted each of her feet in turn to help him ease off the fabric. He put them in his pocket. Once might be enough for her, but he knew that he wouldn't stop needing her. He'd still lie awake at night thinking of her. And when that happened, he wanted her fucking underwear.

She pulled away, breathless, and said, "Kissing you is unbelievable. Why is that? Why have I never kissed anyone like that?"

"Maybe you've never kissed the right person."

She blinked slowly. "Maybe I haven't."

He wanted to kiss her again, but he wanted something else more. The sharp, sweet-edged scent of her arousal was sending him out of his mind. He pressed the heel of his hand against his dick, as hard as he could, but it didn't help. Slinging her legs over his shoulders and spreading her open and licking her clit until she screamed, *that* would help.

So he pushed her toward one of the stools at the kitchen island, and she sat. His hands shaking, Nate grasped her thighs. They were so soft, so different to his own lean muscle; he wanted hours to drown in her, but this would have to be enough. He'd make it enough.

She resisted a little when he tried to push her thighs apart, so he kissed the side of one knee and murmured, "Spread your legs for me, beautiful. I want to see."

"Is that all?" she asked, her voice shaky, her smile somewhere between sweet and nervous. He didn't want her to be nervous. He didn't know she *could* be nervous. His heart clenched like a fist.

"I won't do anything you don't want me to. Just tell me."

"I know," she said. "I know. You… you can do whatever you want." It was almost the same thing he'd said to her. Nate wondered if she'd experienced this sharp zing of satisfaction at the words. Did she feel even half of the things he felt?

Doubtful. She was too perfect for emotions this messy. She was too sensible to let need and adoration spill all over an impossible situation like theirs.

That depressing thought was easy to ignore when Hannah spread her legs, though. Mostly because he nearly died at the sight. The only reason Nate's soul didn't leave his body was that, if it had, he'd miss this: the sight of those plump, pouting lips, the way they parted to reveal that hint of pink, deep inside. He spread her wider with his thumbs, his touch gentle—he made sure—but so obviously eager, he was surprised she didn't laugh at his desperation.

Instead, she slid a hand through his hair and arched her hips towards him, murmuring something that might have been his name. He decided to pretend it was, because the idea felt pure and perfect as a cloudless summer sky. She was so wet and swollen and open, her clit begging for his tongue, but he wanted to tease her first. He would have, too, if she hadn't tightened her fingers in his hair and said, "Please. Please. I can't breathe."

Nate knew exactly what she meant. So he bowed his head and dragged his tongue over her sweet cunt.

"Oh my *God*," she breathed, her voice low.

He did it again, so fucking slowly, lapping up her juices as if he'd been dying of thirst. She was intoxicating. He couldn't imagine a future that didn't involve his head between her thighs. He'd live and die here and consider himself blessed.

Nate slid his tongue into her fluttering entrance, caressing the hidden flesh, tasting her. Then he moved on to her clit, swollen and stiff and demanding attention. She clenched her thighs around his head so fucking tight, it felt like she was trying to suffocate him. Was it bad that he wanted her to? He felt his cock leaking against his belly, felt his balls ache, and thought that if he didn't come soon, he might die. He might actually fucking die.

But, despite the desperation heating his blood, Nate kept his pace slow. He stiffened the tip of his tongue and flicked delicately at her swollen nub—and when she ground against him, seeking more pressure, he wrapped an arm around her hips to pin her in place.

"Fuck, Nate," she gasped. "Oh my God oh my God please don't stop."

There. That was what he wanted; for her to fall apart the way he was. For her to come undone. He didn't speed up, but he did ease a finger inside of her, nice and slow. She was so fucking wet, so ready, her cunt gripping the single digit. So he gave her another, and another, and fucked her hard, even as his tongue worshipped her softly.

God, she'd take his cock so beautifully. He could almost feel it.

And he could feel her getting close, too, closer to the edge. He didn't falter, because he wanted, *needed* her to come. And she was going to. She *was*. Until, all of a sudden, the hand in his hair began to push him away, and her moans turned into a hoarse, "Wait, wait, wait—"

He stopped, his heart racing. "What? Are you okay?" She didn't sound okay.

But she said, "I'm fine."

He studied her face. She was biting her lip, white teeth sinking into smudged red lipstick, her frown too deep, too serious.

"Hannah," he said, "you're not fine. If I did something wrong, tell me. Please tell me." His hand found hers, their fingers twining together. Just touching her like this made his heart beat twice as fast, which was... concerning, to say the least. But he couldn't think on it too hard, because he was more worried by the look on her face.

"You didn't do anything wrong." At least she seemed to mean that. "It's me."

"What's you?"

"I don't—I can't..." She released a heavy sigh and sat up straighter, her skirt falling down over her thighs. "I'm sorry. Oh, God. I don't know why I can't just lie to you."

"Lie to me?" Nate stood, his near-painful erection softening with alarming speed. He'd been wondering what it would take to make his dick relax around Hannah. Apparently, the possibility that he'd just committed some unforgivable act worked just fine. "Sweetheart... could you explain this like I'm five?"

She laughed, which made him feel a bit better—even if she clamped her lips together immediately after, like she regretted releasing the sound. He sat down on the stool beside hers, and held her hand, and waited.

Eventually, she said, "I get kind of self-conscious sometimes. During... you know, stuff. Things."

He arched a brow. "Stuff and things."

"Sex," she whispered with a glare.

"Did you just whisper *sex*?"

"Piss off. I'm trying to explain, here."

"Okay, okay." He held back his smile. "Sorry."

With a haughty sniff, she continued. "I'm just going to be blunt. Blunt! It's nothing to be ashamed of. It's perfectly normal. I'm just going to come right out and..." She eyed him warily. "You're not going to be weird about this, are you?"

He had absolutely no idea what she was talking about, but he said, "Nope."

"Okay. Fine. Okay, so, I can't... orgasm."

He was so astonished by that statement, he didn't even make a joke about the fact that she'd whispered *orgasm*. "Um... Hannah... not to be a dick, but I'm pretty sure you can."

"Well, yes, I can," she agreed. "Just not in front of anyone."

"What?"

"I can do it *myself*." Aaaaand now he was imagining Hannah doing it herself. Wonderful. "Although I don't often bother. But usually—not always! Just, *usually*, when I'm with someone else, I get so anxious, and it just..." She shrugged. "Doesn't work."

"But you were going to. Just then, you were going to come."

She stared at him. "I—well, maybe. Maybe. Maybe I would have."

"So why did you want to stop?"

"Because I…" She broke off, her gaze flitting away from him, her lips pursing as if she were embarrassed. "I don't know. I just get nervous. I don't know. I mean, usually, when I'm with someone—well, mostly when I'm with a man —I fake it. Because people take it so bloody personally, and… oh, God, you're not going to take it personally, are you?"

"What? No, of course not. Don't worry."

"Good. Some people are absolutely awful when they think their abilities in the bedroom are being questioned." She rolled her eyes. "And they don't seem to realise that sex can be perfectly enjoyable without all that fanfare at the end."

It was both alarming and not entirely surprising to hear Hannah refer to an orgasm as *fanfare*. In such disdainful tones, too. Nate knew he should keep his mouth shut, but he really couldn't stop himself from asking: "Are you sure you know what an orgasm is?"

She scowled. "Of course I do."

"So you've had one. You have had an orgasm."

"*Yes.*"

"When? How? Tell me."

"Oh, for God's sake. I promise you, Nate, I have had an orgasm. I have had multiple orgasms. They are absolutely lovely, under the correct circumstances. I just think sex is so much less pressure when you take orgasms out of the equation. I hate it when people want to make me come. They get all insistent and militant, like there's a goal to reach—and you know, usually I like goals, but sex is supposed to be…"

"Easy?" he suggested. But no, that didn't sound right. "Fun. It's not supposed to feel like work."

"Exactly! Exactly. So, that's that. No orgasms. For me, I mean. I'm assuming you'd like one, though."

"Ah…" This was really not going as Nate had planned. Actually, this whole day was like some kind of trip. He'd somehow gone from a hangover, to a haircut, to Hannah calmly ask him if he'd like an orgasm. "Well, no. I mean, if you're done," he began, but she gave him a pitying look and shook her head.

"We're only doing this once," she said. "I'm certainly not going to stop before I get you naked. You don't mind stripping off for me, do you?"

And just like that, Nate was hard again. Fascinating.

CHAPTER FIFTEEN

HANNAH HADN'T INTENDED to make a fuss. She'd *intended* to take the edge off of this awful, intense arousal Nate sparked in her, fake an orgasm when she'd had enough, and be on her merry way.

But she'd gotten carried away. And things had felt so impossibly, breathtakingly blissful that she'd thought, for a moment she might actually do it. Or rather, that *he* might actually do it—make her come. Which is when the icy fist of her inhibitions gripped her. *Sigh.* But at least he'd been so very reasonable about it all. And at least he was now ripping off the rest of his clothes, just for her. That more than made up for her annoyance at herself.

When Nate shoved off his jeans to reveal thickly muscled thighs covered in sparse, black hair, Hannah was seized by the strangest urge to lick or suck or bite... *something*. She just needed something in her mouth. Preferably something that tasted like Nate. And then he dragged down his briefs, releasing the solid, ruddy length of his cock. It hit his stomach with a soft, rude sort of slap, and Hannah decided that the thing she needed in her mouth was right there, thank you very much.

But she couldn't do it in the kitchen. God, no. Because then she'd know exactly how it felt to kneel on the cold tiles and suck him, and she'd never get the memory out of her head. In fact, she decided, she couldn't do it anywhere in the house. The desecration of this particular stool was bad enough. She'd have to bleach the damned thing to high heaven just to soothe her guilt.

"Let's go outside," she said.

Nate squinted at her, as if he suspected he'd misheard. "Outside?"

He was so gloriously *naked*, with all that taut skin and those lean muscles, Hannah felt like saying, *Or here. Or the moon. Wherever you want, actually.*

But somehow, she stood firm in the face of disgraceful sexiness. "Yes. Outside."

"It's going to rain, you know."

It was true that the air beyond the patio doors vibrated under the weight of an impending summer storm, and heavy clouds had covered the bright sun. But she didn't really care. "Do you mind? You used to love the rain."

"How did you know that?"

She shrugged awkwardly. "I don't know. When we were at school, you always wandered around in the rain. And you always looked calmer. I thought you liked it."

"So you just… noticed," he said slowly, with a look on his face she couldn't quite decipher. One of his soft looks, the kind that made her uncomfortably melty in the middle, like a brownie. Hannah did not want to be a brownie.

"Whatever. Just get outside before I change my mind." She stood with a huff, marching off towards the garden. Bold move, considering she was worried about him changing *his* mind. But she had to leave first anyway, because if he led the way, she'd end up staring at his arse. That arse befuddled her enough fully clothed; Hannah didn't think she'd survive seeing it naked.

Nate followed her out, thank God, and didn't even falter when she said, "Shall we sit down?" He just sat, right on the grass, as if it hadn't been an absolutely ridiculous suggestion. Overhead, the sky darkened. Thunder rumbled. It kind of suited her suddenly dour mood.

The problem, Hannah realised, was that she'd never... well, she'd never wanted anyone this much. And now she was overthinking things quite awfully, and she'd never snap out of it, would never get back to that lovely state of mindless lust—

"Come here," he said. He leaned back on one hand, and the other grasped his cock, stroking lazily. "You're miles away."

"I..." She licked her lips, her eyes on the hypnotic pull of his cock. "I was planning on staying over here, actually." *Over here* being three feet in front of him, where she had an excellent view. And he seemed to know that, because he spread his legs further, until she could see his heavy sac, moving with each stroke. The underside of his dick looked like velvet, but she knew, if she touched him, it would be iron-hard. Would it be so bad, to touch him?

No. No, it wouldn't. This was an indulgence, after all. She was supposed to make the most of it. She *would* make the most of it.

So, despite her words, Hannah moved towards him. Crawled, actually. Because she was teetering on the edge of that magical arousal, the kind strong enough to take away her constant gnawing worries. And then his gaze fell to her chest, and she realised her breasts had spilled out of her shirt and were swaying as she moved. Maybe it was the sensation that gave her a last little push, or maybe it was the way he groaned and stroked himself harder, his hips lifting, his teeth sinking into his lower lip.

She crawled between his spread thighs, her eyes focusing on the flushed head of his dick, the way it leaked tiny beads of pre-come like slick jewels. He rasped, "You want me in your mouth."

It wasn't a question, but she answered anyway. "No."

"I know when you're lying, Hannah." Lightning flashed overhead like some kind of divine judgement, like punctuation to his gently teasing words.

"You don't know. You can't know." She pushed his hand away from his length and bent her head, running her tongue over the underside of his cock. Nate tasted of raw heat and skin and salt and desire.

His head fell back as he groaned. "I do. I do. I think about you so much and I watch you so closely—"

She slid her tongue over the tip of his cock, suckling the swollen head.

"Fuck," he spat. "*Fuck.* Oh, you look so fucking good. Jesus. Suck me. Touch me. Hannah, please, I need you—"

She couldn't let him finish that sentence, just in case that *was* the sentence. "*Hannah, please, I need you.*" So she sucked hard, taking his cock as deep as she could, cutting off his words and drinking in his ragged moans. He felt so thick, so hard and impossibly long, filling her mouth. When he grabbed her hair, she whimpered, the sound muffled. When he hit the back of her throat, she held him there, even though she couldn't swallow. After a few seconds she had to release him, gasping for air. His cock gleamed, all wet from her mouth, and the sight was hotter than it should've been.

So she did it again. And again. And again.

"Oh, fuck, like that," he growled, his face twisted with something that might have been agony or ecstasy or both. "Perfect. So perfect."

Without warning, the heavens opened. She'd forgotten about the storm altogether, but she couldn't forget it now. Cool rain drenched her dishevelled clothes and dripped over Nate's naked body, the scent of his skin mixing with the scent of fresh, wet grass.

Still, she sucked him hard. Hard enough that he hissed out a breath and wound his fingers through her hair and moaned, "Your *mouth*, Jesus, baby—you're gonna make me come."

And, since that was the whole idea, she kept going. Kept going as the rain poured down her hollowed cheeks. Kept going until his hips, which he tried to keep still, jerked as if he couldn't control them. Kept going until he choked out her name and thrust into her mouth and spilled hot come down her throat.

He sat there, panting and apparently dazed, while she caught her breath. Her lipstick was smudged all over his cock. And, she finally noticed, his face. She should probably be worried about the state of her own face, but she couldn't bring herself to care when the taste of him was still sharp on her tongue and her clit was throbbing between her thighs.

Nate let out a heavy breath. "Get over here." Before she could move, though, he caught her wrist and pulled her into his lap. And then, one arm around her waist, the other gently cupping her face, he kissed her. Naked, under icy rain and hot sun, his hardness beginning to soften against her thigh, he kissed her. She should probably be horrified by this entire situation. She'd never felt better in her life.

Except for the heavy weight of her own arousal, which really ought to have calmed down by now. She'd had him, hadn't she? Quite thoroughly. Far more thoroughly than she'd ever dared to imagine.

He broke the kiss and groaned. "Fuck. Why do I feel like I could do that again?" He studied her, his eyes going from her face to her heaving chest and tight nipples. "You want to do that again."

"I thought we—"

"Now. If we do it now, it's still just once."

"Is it?"

"Yes." He smiled slightly as he pulled up her skirt, shoving fistfuls of damp fabric out his way. "And you want to. Don't you?"

What she *wanted* was to lie—but she couldn't. The only thing escaping Hannah's lips were these embarrassing, gasping little whimpers. They got even worse when he pushed her skirt up around her waist and touched her. His hand delved between her thighs, and then his fingers nudged her aching clit, and she moaned.

But maybe he hadn't noticed. Maybe he didn't hear.

He touched her again, firmer now, massaging the stiff

nub. He had definitely heard. He watched her with that infuriating smile—how could a smile, just a *smile*, be sexy? But it was. Even sexier when he said, his voice low, "Fuck, you're wet. You like my come in your mouth?"

Well, no point denying it. "Yes."

He shifted so that the heel of his hand rubbed her clit, the pressure just as perfect, while his fingers eased into her pussy. Hannah writhed in his lap, even as she gasped out, "You don't—you don't have to—"

"I want to," he insisted, his voice fierce. "Let's clear that up right now. I want to touch you. I want to put that look in your eyes. I want every single one of your moans. I could do this forever and still enjoy it. I'm not expecting you to come —I'm not expecting anything from you, so don't even think about that. I just want you to take it, and tell me you want it, and beg me for more."

She couldn't help but kiss his sweet, filthy mouth, when it produced words like those. She kissed him and kissed him and kissed him, and he kept stroking her in a way that made her thoughts swirl. Her body felt languid and electric all at once. Maybe minutes passed, or maybe it was an hour; she had no idea, because for once, she wasn't counting. She wasn't hyperconscious of exactly how long it was taking her to come, because… well, she wasn't going to come. She didn't have to. She didn't need to. And apparently, that was okay.

Their kisses went from slow and slick and teasing to unapologetically deep, his tongue thrusting into her mouth as his fingers thrust into her pussy. At some point, he laid back on the wet grass and pulled her on top of him, his free hand running over every inch of her body as if he couldn't get enough. She didn't think about the gentling of the downpour around them, the way rain slid over her bared skin like a caress. She didn't think about the soft earth they lay on, and she certainly didn't think about the passage of time.

Because he kissed her so hungrily, and breathed her in, and touched her like he needed her. And then, all of a sudden, she felt an impossible tightening between her thighs, as if something sweet and ripe were about to burst.

"Nate," she murmured into his mouth. "I—"

"Relax. Just relax. Kiss me."

So she did. And he kept touching her, everywhere, and then the tightening happened again, and again, until...

Until she released this long, low, rolling moan that echoed the rich, deep pleasure rushing through her, taking over her body in the best way possible. As if her arousal was a river that had just burst its banks, overflowing into every nerve ending until she was limp and tingling and absolutely astonished.

Hannah forced her heavy eyes open to find Nate watching her with obvious satisfaction. He pressed a quick kiss to her lips. "You okay?"

"I... you made me come."

"Eh. I think it was a team effort." He kissed her again. "God, you're beautiful. You know that, don't you? You must know that." His lips found her cheek, her jaw, her temple. His hands cupped her arse, kneading absently while his mouth moved on to her ears. He was *kissing* her *ears*. Even worse, she was thoroughly enjoying it. She felt wonderful. Fantastic. She could do this a thousand times over.

Which was the problem, really. Because she couldn't.

"Well," Hannah said, once she was sure her voice would work properly. "Thank you very much."

He laughed. "You're thanking me? Really?"

"Yes. That was extremely well done. We should be fine now."

He froze, as she'd worried he might. And then, after a pause, he pulled back slightly to look at her. "Oh, yeah. That's right. Because this was supposed to... cure us."

"*Inoculate* us," she corrected. "Or me. And fulfil your—" Then she remembered how angry he'd been, when she'd suggested he had some kind of nanny fetish. "Well, it's done now, is what I mean."

"Yep," he said. "It's definitely done now." He wasn't holding on to her anymore. He certainly wasn't kissing her anymore.

But he looked pleasant enough, reasonable enough. He was always reasonable, really—unlike most people. It was one of the reasons she liked him so much.

Platonically.

And now she'd be free to feel that platonic liking without having the waters muddied by her rampant libido or her half-dead crush. And he'd be free to platonically like her back, and eventually get over his unfortunate attraction.

She scrambled off of his lap, because sitting there suddenly felt strange—which was probably an indication that her plan was already working. The grass beneath her felt colder than it had before, more like mud than some romantic earthy cushion. Which made sense, since there was nothing romantic about grass. Or rain. Or Nate.

He stood, woefully naked, and she tried very hard not to look. "So," he said. "We're just, ah... back to normal."

"That's correct."

"Employer and employee." He winced slightly as he said those words.

"Yes indeed."

He studied her for a moment, and she felt her cheeks heat. If he questioned her, even slightly, she'd crumble. She knew it. She'd lose her head and start waffling on about feelings and connections and a load of other nonsense that she didn't want to examine too closely.

But in the end, that didn't happen. Because Nate nodded slowly, and murmured, "Well, I better go. I wanted to pick up the kids today." He marched off into the house before she could point out that school wouldn't end for hours, yet.

Ah, well. It was probably for the best.

CHAPTER SIXTEEN

Hi Nate,

I know you said the sequence by the lake was fine during our call, but I was considering increasing the exposure a little bit. I don't know what you think?

Best,

Lisha.

Lisha,

DO NOT TOUCH THE EXPOSURE. Unless you want your model to look like the ghost of a croissant, in which case, go for it.

Nate.

So, *that* had been a terrible idea.

Nate stood in the playground, waiting for his kids with even more impatience than usual. He felt like he hadn't hugged them in a century—even though he'd actually hugged them yesterday morning. Whatever. It didn't help that he'd been wandering the streets of Ravenswood for hours, waiting for school to end.

Because he'd needed to get out of the house. Because he needed to avoid Hannah.

When he looked at her, this twisted combination of guilt and desire choked him. It felt like acid, burning away inside, leaving him raw and vulnerable. He had realised two things on his tragically meandering walk. Firstly, that he'd just become exactly the kind of man he despised: the kind who bent rules and principles, instead of just rules. And, secondly, that he felt far too strongly about Hannah. *Far* too strongly. As in, the intensity of his affection for her was starting to seriously concern him. After all, their shared childhood aside, he hadn't even known her that long. So why did it hurt so fucking badly when she pushed him away?

Time doesn't matter. You fell in love with Ellie at first sight.

True.

But he hadn't *realised* he was in love with Ellie until at least three months later. Nate reminded himself of this fact triumphantly, before his hazy brain grasped that it wasn't actually helpful to his situation. In fact, all things considered, it was rather damning information.

You are not in love with Hannah. Just because you want to spend all your free time with her and you'd like to fall asleep holding her and you think she looks perfect when she comes, doesn't mean you're in love with her. You're just confused because she sucked the soul out of your dick.

Which made way more sense, right? The sex had overwhelmed him because it was so impossibly *good.* That was all.

Nate wasn't what you'd call a ladies' man. About a year after Ellie died, he'd picked up some girl at a bar and had his first one night stand. He didn't come, but he did throw up. It had been a delightful experience all round, clearly, like ripping off a plaster. These days, when he had the time and inclination, he found an agreeable woman and did what needed to be done.

Which, now he thought about it, sounded more grim than erotic.

He wasn't used to good sex anymore. But he'd known it would be good with Hannah; better than good. He almost wished he'd been wrong, except not really, because he'd enjoyed himself way too fucking much for that. Aaaand now he was back to the guilt. Which, aside from anything else, was an inconvenient emotion to grapple with while surrounded by a gaggle of mums.

Oh, God, the mums.

"Nate, my darling, are you alright? You look like you've swallowed something awful."

I have. It's the reality of my own weak moral fibre. "No, no. I'm fine, thanks, Caroline."

"You sure, babe? Won't judge you if you've managed to catch a fly." Caroline cackled, slapping him on the back, and her friends all laughed merrily along.

It wasn't that *every* woman on Hollygate Primary's playground made a beeline for Nate, or anything like that. 99% of them were more concerned with keeping an eye on their toddlers, or catching up with friends, or trying not to fall asleep at a picnic bench. But that last 1%... that last 1% were a pain in the fucking arse. Because for reasons he couldn't quite grasp, that small group of yummy mummies had developed quite the attachment to him.

Caroline was still cackling, and, against all odds, Nate could feel his hangover returning. Or maybe the migraine threatening his tender skull had nothing to do with last night's drunkenness. Maybe it was a brand-new ache brought on by Caroline's reckless good cheer.

Beside Caroline stood Kieran, her razor-sharp bob gleaming in the early morning sun. Kieran was a doctor. A private consultant, actually. Nate knew this because she never bloody shut up about it.

"I'm surprised to see you here," she said. "In the afternoon, I mean. It's usually your nanny who comes after school, isn't it?" She said *nanny* the way most people would say *dog shit*.

"Yep," Nate grunted. They waited, as if he should say more, but he couldn't. He was too busy dealing with the fact that he'd wanted to correct Kieran—not just her superior tone, but her words. He'd wanted to say, *"Hannah's not the nanny. She's..."*

What? She's what? The nanny whose mouth you came in? I bet they'd love *to hear that.*

God, he wanted to punch himself in the face. Was that a thing? Could that be done? Well, he'd find out when he tried it later.

There was an awkward pause as the women around him shared an indecipherable, edgy sort of look. Then Caroline said, in what she probably thought was a delicate tone, "Having trouble?"

"With what?" he asked, his voice a little rougher than he'd intended.

Kieran tutted. "*Her*, of course. Don't worry. We don't gossip, do we girls?"

"No, no," the women all agreed. Kind of like how his kids said *"Noooo,"* in tandem when he asked, *"Did you guys pour that juice all over the carpet?"*

"I did think," Caroline was saying. "I mean, when I realised you'd hired Hannah Kabbah, I went home and I said to my Mitchell, *I should pull Nate aside—*"

Nate looked up sharply. "Why?"

"Oh, sweetie. Don't you know? Gosh, I definitely should've said something."

He gave Caroline a steady look. "I know everything I need to know about Hannah. What I'm asking is why the hell you'd think you could talk shit about her."

There was a sharp little intake of breath all around them at the word *shit*. Oh fucking well. He really was not in the mood. Caroline set her shoulders and forged ahead—which was pretty brave, since Nate was well aware that his face looked like thunder right now.

Thunder. Lightning. Hannah's mouth, wet with rain, and her slick hands all over him, and her—

"Clearly," Caroline sniffed, "you don't know as much as you think. If you did, you wouldn't let her *near* your children."

"I wouldn't let *you* near my children," he said calmly, "because when you drive yours to school every morning, you're still drunk from the night before. Which we can all smell on you, by the way. And while we're talking about who would and would not get near my kids…" He speared

Kieran with a glare. "You can wipe that smug look off your face, because I saw your shitty fucking Facebook post about vaccines and autism. What the hell kind of doctor are you, anyway?"

Kieran stepped back, a hand fluttering to her chest. "I—"

"Shut up. That was a rhetorical question." He turned to glare at every other member of the now deathly-silent circle. "Hannah Kabbah watches my kids because she's smart, she's honest, she's compassionate, and she knows what the fuck she's doing. That's it. That's what I need, that's what she's got. If you want to talk shit about her, I can't stop you. But you better not do it where I can hear. You won't like the result."

For a moment, silence reigned in their little bubble despite the chatter of the playground around them. Then, after a sharp jerk of the head from Caroline, all of the women began drifting away with narrowed eyes and resentful mutterings.

If he'd known it was that easy to get rid of them, Nate would've sung Hannah's praises weeks ago. She was all he ever thought about, anyway.

"I really think you're making a mistake," Caroline said. "But if you won't be told…"

"I think you made a mistake when you named your kid Majorca," he replied flatly. "But I keep that to myself. Because I know how to mind my business."

She stared at him for a moment, her mouth working soundlessly. Then, finally, she spat, "Fuck you!" before striding off toward her friends.

Which left Nate alone to deal with the fact that he was angry. Really fucking angry, furious in a way he hadn't been for ages. His head began to pound, and his jaw ached from grinding his teeth, and his knuckles cracked from clenching his fists.

He wasn't worried, though. It would pass. It was natural for his temper to rear its ugly head when a bunch of snide, self-important fucks disrespected the woman he'd fallen in love with. He thought he'd stayed pretty cool, all things considered. He *could've* mentioned the fact that Caroline's husband, Mitch, visited the house across the street from Nate's every Tuesday and Thursday at 2 a.m., but...

Wait.

Through the red-hot, shimmering haze of anger, and the fog of guilt and shame that still clouded his head, one word smacked Nate in the face.

Love? He was in love with Hannah? He was. In love. With Hannah. He felt his lips move slightly as he mouthed the words to himself. *In love with Hannah. I am in love with Hannah. Am I—?*

"Nate?"

He looked up to find Cheryl Brown, a woman whose son was friends with Josh, eyeing him warily.

"Are you okay?" she asked. "You look like you're going to be sick."

"I'm fine," he managed. "Just... a bit hot."

"Oh, yeah." She gave him a sympathetic nod. "This sort of weather makes my boys queasy. Sunshine, then rain, then sun again. Well, if you're sure you're alright..."

Which he was, technically. His brain was just struggling to absorb the fact that he was *in love* with *Hannah.*

"Fine," he choked out. "Really."

Cheryl didn't look convinced, but she nodded politely and pushed her buggy away.

So. Hannah. Love. In. Right. Because that made total sense. Why the hell not? Why wouldn't he fall in love with the most inappropriate, off-limits, sweetest, funniest, sharpest woman he knew? The woman who seemed both all-powerful and made for him to protect, the woman who —well. This list was supposed to be sarcastic, but it was starting to sound completely understandable.

Oh, fuck. He was in love with Hannah.

The school bell rang. The kids would be out soon, and here he was sweating over the fact that he'd accidentally fallen in love with the nanny. This was even worse than accidentally fucking the nanny in the garden. Because what was he supposed to *do* about it? He couldn't tell her. He couldn't even ask her out, for Christ's sake. As long as the power between them was so skewed, he couldn't do *shit*. There was a word for guys who started relationships with women whose livelihoods they controlled, and that word was not pleasant.

It wasn't as if she loved him. Fuck, if he'd thought she even *wanted* him he might've tried... something. But she didn't. She didn't. She'd compared wanting him to a fucking *virus*, for Christ's sake.

A few classroom doors opened, and a handful of teachers led out their students. Just the sight made Nate relax slightly, because soon he'd see the kids—*finally*—and even if his brain was scrambled eggs right now, he always felt better when he was with them. Calmer. More sensible.

Josh's class came out first, and Nate practically ran over at the sight of his son's little face.

"Daddy!" Josh cried. He attached himself to Nate's leg with an enthusiasm that made Nate both happy and guilty. More guilt! Perfect. It would fit in so nicely with all the... other... guilt.

He bent down to ruffle his son's hair. "Hey, kiddo. Sorry I missed you this morning."

Josh giggled. "You were *snoring*. Hannah showed us!"

He tried not to wince. "I heard."

"Where is she, Daddy? I thought she took us home, now."

He'd been hoping that the kids would *distract* him from Hannah. Which, now he thought about it, was pretty ridiculous, since they talked about her all the goddamn time. Because *she was their nanny.*

"I think your sister's class is out," he said, clearing his throat. "Let's go and get her."

"But where is Hannah?"

"At home. She's at home. We swapped today. She took you in the morning, and I'm getting you now."

Josh gave a cheerful, chubby-cheeked smile. "Okay." He put his hand in Nate's, as usual. Because Josh loved him. Josh trusted him. Josh had no idea that his dad was actually an official predator who did terrible things to inappropriate and vulnerable women.

Stop that. She asked for it. She literally *asked for it. She wanted to.*

Just like she wanted to be miles away from you immediately after.

It didn't make any sense. Or maybe it did, and he just didn't understand. Maybe loving Hannah was slowly draining his brain cells. But that didn't sound right either, because being around her made Nate feel smarter. And stronger. And kinder. And just… generally better than he was capable of being on his own.

Which was when it came to him. He was thinking about this all wrong. He was panicking about all the variables when he should be asking himself: What would Hannah do? If she found herself in this situation, what would she do?

Wait, his mind supplied. *Stay calm and wait. If she wants anything else from you, anything at all, she'll say so. But you can't ask her. You can't pressure her.*

Hmm. He didn't like that thought. He didn't like it at all. Because it sounded a lot like, *Chill the fuck out and see if she makes the next move. Which she might never, ever do.* That was all well and good, but the last time Nate had noticed he was in love, he'd proposed on the spot. He did not have high hopes for his ability to chill the fuck out.

Ahead of him, he saw the door to Beth's classroom open. Her teacher led out a gaggle of chattering seven-year-olds, and within seconds, Beth was running over to him with a big grin on her face, pushing her tongue through the rapidly-closing gap in her front teeth.

She slammed into him like a rocket, and when she looked up, he saw himself in her big, blue eyes. Not the real him, the him who thought too much or too little, who made mistakes and had to leash his temper like an attack dog. He saw the version of himself she believed in. The version who was more patient, more principled, more perfect than he could ever be.

He'd really like to be that Nate. For Beth, and for Josh, and for everyone he loved.

Which, he supposed, meant leaving Hannah alone.

Great.

CHAPTER SEVENTEEN

Hannah: How come there's only one of these huge cookies on the table? Who's it for?
Nate: You.

∼

HANNAH WAS USED to tangled thoughts, but not like this. Her worries had never wound her up like bondage porn.

And she'd never thought about things like bondage porn during her daily life, either—but, apparently, that was her style now. Her mind had become some sort of hyper-sexualised filth machine that put everything in lustful terms, and it was all because three weeks ago she'd gone absolutely bonkers and let Nate... kiss her.

Etcetera.

Well, to be honest, she hadn't *let* him do anything. *She'd* kissed *him*.

Etcetera.

Hannah wandered toward Ravenswood's play park with Josh clinging to one hand and Beth clinging to the other, letting their discordant chatter wash over her. These days, only the kids had the power to tear her mind away from their dad. When they were around, she could concentrate on watching them, and making them laugh, and feeding them at regular intervals. When they were at school, all she could think about was whether Nate had said her name strangely at breakfast, and whether Nate was still up late every night researching his mother's condition, and whether Nate had gotten over his attraction—and why the hell *she* hadn't.

Because Hannah had been forced to admit that her grand plan was a fucking failure, at least on her part. Being with Nate had *not* fully inoculated her against the deadly crush virus. Instead, her weird, flushed feelings had mutated into something disturbingly intense. Something so strong, she'd been on edge for the past three weeks, trying not to let her maelstrom of emotions escape.

What if she slipped up and kissed him? What if she told him the truth?

I have never wanted anyone the way I want you. And I can't stop.

It would be a fucking disaster, of that she was sure. She'd been grappling with this issue for some time now, and no matter how she looked at things, the important facts hadn't changed.

1. Sensible women did not sleep with their employers.
2. Or develop feelings for their employers.

3. If sensible women accidentally slept with and/or developed feelings for their employers—it happened—they remedied the issue by never doing it again.

4. Even if she lost all sense and tried to do it again, Nate's recent sweet-but-distant politeness clearly showed that *he* wouldn't do it again. Possibly because

5. She may have scarred him for life by seducing him in the first place.

It was all looking very grim, to be honest. But at least things between them were proper and professional, now. *Extra* proper and professional. Which was exactly how Hannah liked it. Just imagine if Nate *hadn't* started acting like a fond nineteenth century butler around her. Imagine if he'd decided that, actually, he couldn't stop thinking about her, and they needed to kiss—and so on—every day for the foreseeable future.

Then she'd be involved in some sort of sordid sex-pact that involved sneaking around behind the backs of innocent children and throwing all her dignity to the wind, and what have you.

She looked down at the kids, and thought of their chubby-cheeked smiles and wild imaginations and exhausting energy, and decided once and for all that things were better like this. Much better. Because she'd rather work through this awful, yearning hunger and still feel decent, than have the thing she wanted and feel guilty.

"Hannah!" Beth shrieked, suddenly yanking on Hannah's hand with far too much force for a seven-year-old. "Ohhh my *Goddd*"—this was Beth's latest Cool Girl Phrase— "look at that DOGGY!"

Hannah would love to look at the doggy who'd inspired such excitement, but she was too busy trying not to fall on her arse. Josh had started yanking her hand too—actually, he was practically swinging off of her arm, and he was surprisingly heavy. Of course, he did that to Nate all the time, without any effect on his dad's general uprightness. He seemed to think of Hannah as similarly solid, which was both flattering and likely to result in her embarrassment.

"Josh," she said, sounding a little more desperate than she'd intended. "Please stop jumping!"

It was only 4 p.m., so the park was filled to the brim with excitable kids and their stuck-up, glowering parents. Glowering parents who would absolutely *love* to see Hannah Kabbah land on her arse.

Why did she still live here, again?

Since Josh was an angelic child—once you got past his obsession with frogspawn and his hatred of underpants—he stopped yanking Hannah immediately. So did Beth. But their screeching only increased, because all that diverted energy had to go somewhere.

"*Look!*" Beth bellowed. Then she pointed boldly across the park, just in case her words hadn't been clear enough. When Hannah followed Beth's tiny, jabbing finger, she understood all the excitement.

"Goodness me," she murmured. "That is… quite a dog."

Dog didn't seem entirely accurate. Was it a bear? Or a fluffy, cheerful-looking wolf? Perhaps some sort of bear-dog-wolf hybrid? Maybe. It stood by the nearest park bench —*taller* than the bench, mind—looking enormous and beastly with its thick, chestnut fur, floppy ears, and lolling tongue. Its tiny eyes and shiny nose reminded Hannah of a teddy bear. She'd never seen a teddy bear that huge, though.

A woman sat on the bench beside the dog, scratching its head in an absent sort of way. She was older than Hannah, maybe in her forties, with golden-brown skin and long, dark hair. She had the kind of sparkling eyes and deep laugh lines that made her look friendly; even now, when she was staring blankly into space. Hannah was surprised to see that none of the children at the park were harassing the woman and her fantastic dog already. Beth and Josh were absolutely dying to.

"Can we go and say hello?" Beth was asking, practically breathless with excitement. "Please?"

"Please please please please please?" Josh added. They were like a coordinated attack team of cuteness. Who would stand a chance?

"We can say hello," she allowed.

A little cheer went up.

"*But* we must remember our manners. The dog might not want attention. The lady might not want attention for her dog. So we'll go over, and *politely* say hello, and *ask* if the dog likes to make friends. And you mustn't touch it."

The cheer was replaced by groans. "Han-*nah!*"

"But it's so *fluffy!*"

"No touching unless I say so. If I bring either of you home with a dog bite your dad will murder me on the spot."

"Daddy would *never* murder you," Beth said solemnly. "Daddy *loves* you."

The words jolted Hannah for a moment. But then she remembered that Nate told the kids he loved them at least twenty times a day. They were probably so used to the word that they threw it out to describe any sort of affection.

"Well, he loves *you* much, much more. And either way, I would prefer to keep both of you unbitten." Hannah crouched down and poked Josh's belly, startling a giggle out of him. Then she ruffled Beth's unruly hair. "So, what are we going to do?"

"Remember our manners," the pair said in unison. Sort of. Josh seemed to forget what he was saying halfway through, probably because one of his friends was waving from the see-saw. But she trusted that he understood the key message.

"Alright." Hannah stood and took their hands again. "Let's go."

It really was odd, she thought as they drew closer, how alone the woman seemed. She was sitting so close to the gated-off play-area where the children congregated, and the dog was practically a kid-magnet, but no-one even looked over…

In fact, the parents huddling together by the swings were *not-looking* rather pointedly. She recognised that forced, hyperaware ignorance from her own years as a social pariah. The obvious exclusion was enough to remind Hannah of the gossip she'd somehow managed to forget; gossip about someone new in town.

The woman, sensing their approach, looked over. Hannah saw the right side of her face for the first time. And the scars.

Ah.

Well, that explained it. What self-respecting Ravenswood motherfucker—sorry, *mother*—would let their darling child within five feet of a woman who dared to look out of the ordinary?

"Hello," Hannah smiled as they came to stand by the bench. She squeezed the kids' hands and they managed two semi-shy *hellos* of their own. "Sorry to bother you. We were just admiring your dog."

The woman smiled back, her dancing eyes lighting up. One of the three dark scars on her face came perilously close to her eye, and another almost nudged her lips. Maybe that was why her smile only seemed to work on one side. "Well, hi," she said, sinking a hand into the dog's mass of fur. "Duke loves being admired." The creature twisted its head to lick her wrist, its tongue almost as wide as her bloody forearm. Good Lord. Turning her attention to the kids, the woman asked, "Would you like to pet him? Are you allowed?"

Hannah hummed at the woman's questioning glance. She should probably say no.

But then the woman added, "He's *very* good with kids."

Well. It would be a lot easier to cautiously refuse if both dog and owner didn't seem so thoroughly *nice*. Niceness was rather disarming.

"Go on then," Hannah said.

Beth flew forward like a missile, cooing over the dog as if it weren't twice her size. Hannah had a minor moment of panic—*Is this adorable? Is this highly dangerous? Oh dear*—before noticing that Josh hadn't followed his sister's example. He was still clinging to her hand.

"Are you scared?" the woman asked him. "You don't need to be. Duke is really friendly."

Josh plastered himself against Hannah's thigh and remained silent.

The woman's lips quirked. "Or are you scared of *me*? I'm friendly, too, you know. For a pirate."

Josh un-plastered himself, just a little bit, and eyed the woman skeptically. "A *pirate*?"

"That's right." She cocked her head, winked, and said, "That's how I got these scars."

"Oohhh." Apparently, Josh was now completely convinced. "Are you a good pirate?"

"I don't eat children, if that's what you're asking."

He considered this claim for a moment before deciding that this particular pirate seemed a trustworthy sort. "Okay." Just like that, he let go of Hannah and joined his sister in the dog-stroking extravaganza.

The woman watched him with a smile before looking up. "Hi. I'm Rae."

"Hannah." It seemed awkward to stand there like a lemming, so she took a seat on the bench, putting the kids' book bags down with relief. Who knew half-eaten snacks and sheets of homework could be so heavy?

"Are they yours?" Rae asked, nodding at the kids. Which was funny. Typically, Hannah had to deal with people thinking she'd abducted Beth and Josh, even when they pulled her skirt and played with her braids and called her 'Banana'.

"I'm their nanny." Which reminded her, actually. "Guys, come here a sec." They did, with sighs and eye rolls, abandoning their new furry friend to stand in front of Hannah and allow themselves to be kissed. When their pale foreheads were marked by her purple lipstick, she released them. And then, in answer to Rae's arched brow, explained: "Makes it easier for me to find them in a crowd and harder for people to claim I'm kidnapping them."

"Ah." Rae paused. Then, wrinkling her snub little nose, she said, "This town's fucking weird." Her gaze flicked over to the kids. "Sorry."

"They're not paying attention anyway. And yeah, it is. If by *weird* you mean full of stuck-up, Stepford pod-people."

Rae laughed. "Yeah. That. How long have you lived here?"

"My whole life," Hannah admitted, hoping she didn't sound as pathetic as she felt.

Rae winced, her shoulders rising awkwardly. She seemed to do everything with her full body, like her feelings were too intense to convey through facial expressions alone. "Really? Damn. Why?"

"Well, there are actually some great people here. Just a few. Plus, I don't trust my mother to survive unsupervised, and I don't trust my sister to supervise." *And if I left, knowing the way these people look down on me, it would feel like letting them win. Maybe I'm petty. I like taking up their space.* "How long since you arrived?"

"Am I so obviously new?"

"It's a small town. I know everyone."

Rae shrugged. "I think it's been a month? I'm losing track of time since I stopped working. I moved here from the city to waste my ex's money and try being a lady who lunches."

"Oh? How's that going?"

"Slowly. Might be less boring if I had someone to lunch with. Do you, by any chance, eat?"

"I do," Hannah nodded. "Often at lunchtime, in fact. Perhaps we could eat together."

"Perhaps we could!" Rae slid a mischievous glance towards the parents huddled in the park, most of whom were now openly staring. "Do you think they want an invitation, too?"

"Knowing that crowd as I do," Hannah murmured, "they're probably terrified by the sight of us together. Because I am known around town as a lunatic, and you, being from the city, must *also* be a lunatic."

"Wonderful," Rae said happily. "We'll have to make sure people see us together often. Don't you think?"

Hannah smiled, and meant it, for the first time in a while. "I do."

NATE HADN'T BEEN in the best mood recently, but today he was positively cheerful. Shirley's latest appointment had yielded semi-good news; she was eligible for surgery to remove most of her tumours. And if it went well, she could stop taking methotrexate. And if she stopped taking methotrexate, she would, in her own words. *"Stop feeling half-dead all the bloody time."*

So he was feeling pretty fucking good.

Even sitting at the dinner table opposite Hannah wasn't enough to dampen his happiness—not that Hannah typically made him *un*happy. It was more her complete indifference to him, combined with his pathetic longing for her, that usually ruined his day. But right now, as Nate enjoyed the excellent pasta made by his excellent nanny, he could almost convince himself that her indifference was a good thing. Kind of. Somewhat. One of them had to be sensible, after all.

Josh was chattering on about his day at school and how he'd learned his twenty-rows. Nate had no idea what twenty-rows were, but clearly Josh was an expert on the topic. In fact, his son just might be a genius.

"And after maths we went outside and played rounders," Josh was saying, "and Ava laughed at me because I couldn't catch, so I put a cone on her head."

Yes, Nate decided. His son was indeed a genius.

"Joshua," Hannah murmured in a tone that suggested she disagreed. "What did we say about expressing anger?"

Josh sighed heavily. "Use your words."

Oh. Right. Yeah. Nate cleared his throat and added, "You mustn't put cones on people's heads, Josh."

Josh sighed again, even more heavily. It was a wonder his tiny lungs could handle that much air. "O-*kay*."

"Good boy." Nate turned to Beth, trying very hard not to look at Hannah in the process. Which was difficult, when Hannah was sitting right there, wearing a bright white shirt (who wore *white* to eat pasta? The woman was both brilliant and terrifying) and purple lipstick. He'd taken a picture of her in that same lipstick just last week.

Not that she'd noticed. His photograph-Hannah-by-stealth campaign was going extremely well. In fact, it might be the only thing that was going well between them. That, and treating each other appropriately. They were doing *great* there.

Not that he absolutely fucking hated it, or anything.

"Beth," he said brightly. "How was your day?"

"It was good!" Beth said. "We found a monster doggy."

His brows shot up. He looked over at Hannah—which was okay, because he was looking as a baffled parent rather than a lovesick pervert. She met his gaze with a wry smile, which was also okay, because she was just being a capable and caring nanny. "It was a very safe and friendly monster doggy," she assured him, her tone dry.

Then the moment passed. Now they were just Hannah and Nate smiling at each other, and everything became unbearably intimate and potentially inappropriate again. He looked away.

"It was *this big*, Daddy," Beth said, raising her hand to improbable heights.

"*This* big," Josh corrected, kneeling on his chair and thrusting his arm into the air.

"THIS big—"

"Alright! Sit down, both of you. We don't stand on chairs at the dinner table." He could practically see Hannah having heart palpitations. "It was a very big dog, is the message I'm receiving."

"Yes." Beth nodded. "And the lady who owns it *says* she's a pirate—"

"She *is* a pirate," Josh insisted. "I know she is. She told me."

"I don't believe it."

"*I* do!"

"If she was a pirate," Beth said, "she'd be on the ocean. *Obviously*, she's not a pirate. Is she, Hannah?"

Hannah hesitated, spearing pasta onto her fork. "I'm not sure. Perhaps she's a retired pirate."

"Will you ask her?" Josh prodded.

"Send her a message!" Beth suggested. "And tell us what she says."

Something about those words pricked Nate's attention even more than a monster-dog-owning pirate. "A message?"

Hannah focused her attention on her food and said demurely, "We swapped numbers."

His eyebrows flew so far up his head, they might have disappeared into his hairline. "You did?"

"We did."

"*Why?*"

She pursed her lips and blatantly avoided meeting his eyes. "The usual reasons. Long-distance communication, etcetera."

"They are going to be ladies who eat Lunchables," Beth said seriously. "I also eat Lunchables, but I am not a lady yet."

Hannah finally looked up, but not at him. She gave Beth a fond smile and said, "Lunch, poppet. We're having lunch."

At which point Nate realised that the sharp, suspicious feeling tightening his chest was jealousy.

He stuffed a forkful of pasta in his mouth and decided not to think about it.

Only he couldn't stop.

CHAPTER EIGHTEEN

Ruth: Can you put silk in the washing machine?
Hannah: Depends. Why?
Ruth: Evan got me new pyjamas.

NATE KNEW he was being ridiculous. Not because he suspected that Hannah had a date, but because he was not happy about it.

He'd been 99.9% sure that she liked women, because she had a habit of checking them out rather obviously in public. She seemed to think no-one would notice. It was quite high up on the list of adorable things about her.

He was also 99.9% sure that Hannah hated making friends. She only seemed to have a few, and one of those was her sister—so she probably hadn't randomly picked up a new one at the park. Of course, that logic also suggested that she wouldn't randomly pick up a date at the park. But

238

he knew from experience that she could be very direct when she wanted to sleep with someone.

Which brought him right back to his completely unreasonable jealousy. Dinner was over, the kids were in bed, and Nate was loitering in the living room because he knew that once Hannah took off her makeup and put on her 'inside clothes'—he'd given up trying to understand what that meant—she'd come down to tidy up.

What are you going to do, ask *her about it?*

Yes.

Well, you can't, because it's none of your business.

Wrong.

Nate didn't have much experience with jealousy, but apparently it wiped out half of his IQ points and all of his common fucking sense.

He sat on the sofa and glared at the Hot Wheels cars littering the carpet. Then he glared at the blank TV screen. Then he glared at the fort, which was still standing. He'd lain in that fort with Hannah. The woman who may or may not be a pirate had never lain in a fort with Hannah. She certainly wasn't in love with Hannah, whereas he was, so if this mysterious dog owner had any sense of fair play whatsoever she'd fuck off.

On the heels of that unbelievable nonsense, Hannah arrived. He looked up as she faltered in the doorway, peering at him with what appeared to be concern.

"Nate? Are you okay?"

He grunted in response, because if he actually opened his mouth, something ill-advised might come out. Like, *Don't have lunch with a dog-owning pirate.* Or, *I'd really like to kiss you again, but only if you swear on the Bible that you want it too and you're not afraid of losing your job if you say no.*

He thought it was best to avoid those sorts of statements. He was trying to keep things light.

But Hannah was making it difficult. She came over to the sofa with a swish of her swirly, knee-length skirt and said, "Nate. Seriously. You're worrying me."

He'd rather *not* worry her—since he loved her, and since she already worried too much—but he couldn't exactly explain what his problem was, could he?

"Sorry," he said. "I was thinking."

She squinted at him as if he were a page of 8pt font. "About what?"

Well… "Do you have a date?" he blurted out, a burning coal of jealousy wreaking havoc in his chest. Really, he needed to know. If she *did* have a date, that might complicate his make-Hannah-fall-in-love-with-me mission. It was best to be forewarned.

"A date? Why on earth—wait. Do you mean with Rae?"

He shrugged, because that was what casual, unconcerned people did, right? They shrugged. "The woman with the dog."

"Rae. No, I don't have a date." She narrowed her eyes. "Why would you care if I had a date, anyway?"

For about half a second, Nate considered lying. Then his brain finally woke up, and he realised that a question like that from a woman like Hannah could potentially be translated as, *Please tell me why you'd care if I had a date.*

That was probably wishful thinking. It had to be. Only now she was doing that shifty-eyed thing she did whenever she was embarrassed, and she'd crossed her arms over her chest, and... oh, fuck it.

"Because I'm jealous." Nate set the words free with a sigh that was half relief, and half annoyance with his own big mouth.

She huffed out a laugh, but there wasn't much humour in it. "*Jealous*? Seriously? What does that even mean?"

"In my case, it means that the thought of you with anyone else makes me want to set something on fire."

Those words hovered in the air between them for an uncomfortable few seconds before her calm facade evaporated.

"Ohhh, you are such a fucking *guy*," she snapped. "I cannot *believe* you!"

Well, Nate reflected. It turned out honesty was not always the best policy. He should've stuck with the plan, shouldn't he? Why hadn't he stuck with the plan?

Because she had a date with a pirate. Sometimes plans get rearranged.

"Three weeks," Hannah whisper-shouted. Whisper-shouting was never a good sign, with her. "Three weeks, Nate! And you haven't said a word!"

"A word about what?"

"About *us*!" she hissed, fury flaring in her eyes. "Which was fine. It's fine. It's *fine*. But now you think I'm seeing someone else, all of a sudden you're *jealous*?"

"It's not *all of a sudden—*"

"Yes it fucking is!"

"Hannah, I..." He broke off just in time, the word *love* ready to roll off his tongue. "I like you! Okay? Of course, I'm jealous."

"Oh, you like me? You *like* me? But ever since we... ever since we had sex—"

Jesus Christ, she was still whispering *sex*.

"You've been acting like I'm just some... some..." she scowled, frustration all over her face. "Some *acquaintance*! A friendly acquaintance! I am not an acquaintance, Nate! I put your *thing* in my mouth!"

He blinked. "Did you just call it—"

"Oh, for fuck's sake, will you focus?"

Good point. "Hannah, I swear to you, you've got this all wrong."

"Don't tell me I've got it wrong! I never get it wrong!"

Shit. She was actually upset. *Really* upset, if she was reverting to know-it-all Queen of the World mode. Nate paused for a moment and took in the stern set of her shoulders, the harsh line of her jaw. He knew when Hannah was angry, and this wasn't it. Not exactly. Right now, she was too tough, too brittle—as if she might break.

Hannah was hurt.

A frantic sort of panic rose up in his chest, because *he'd* hurt her. And that was just... no. No.

Nate was on his knees in front of her before she could blink. He caught her face in his hands, just to make sure she looked him in the eyes as he spoke. "Give me thirty seconds. I know you're thinking a lot right now, but just stop for thirty seconds. Stop and let me explain. Because I *can* explain."

After a tense, silent moment, she whispered, "How?"

He'd take that as permission and talk fast. "I have feelings for you, and I've known that for a while. But I also know that as long as I pay your salary it'll never be right for me to pursue you. I've already crossed a lot of lines—"

She snorted. He grinned. If she was giving him attitude, she was already better than she'd been a second ago.

"All the lines," he corrected. "But, sweetheart... after that day in the garden, I think you made it pretty clear you didn't want things to continue. I thought I was being ridiculous, just hoping you'd change your mind. But I did hope. Thing is, I knew that even a word from me could feel like pressure, in this situation, so I kept my mouth shut. I was trying not to push. Maybe I tried a little too hard," he admitted ruefully. "Because I never meant to make you feel like... like an acquaintance."

She sighed. "I can see you trying not to smile, you know."

"Sorry. It's just... an acquaintance? Really?"

"It seemed accurate."

"Okay," he said solemnly. "Fair enough. But I swear, I was just trying to be good. That's all. I didn't want to make you uncomfortable. I didn't know how you felt about me."

"You still don't know how I feel about you," she said archly.

He smiled. "Well, are you gonna tell me?"

"No."

His smile grew. "Okay. Are you gonna kiss me?"

Hannah eyed him thoughtfully. "That's quite a good idea." Then she grabbed his T-shirt with both hands, dragged him closer, and pressed her mouth to his.

And time stopped.

It stopped. That was the only explanation. How else could his lungs hesitate, his heart stutter, and his mind freeze all at once? How else could every worry that buzzed steadily through his head suddenly fall silent?

There was nothing, now—no work to complete or meetings to schedule or doctors' appointments to dread. Nothing but Hannah's hands fisted in his T-shirt and Hannah's tongue slipping tentatively into his mouth. Nothing but the softness of her lips, nothing but the way her thighs cradled his hips as she pulled him closer. Nothing but the scent of her, fresh and real and so familiar, and the hoarse little sound she made in the back of her throat as his hands settled at her waist…

Nothing but her. Nothing but heaven. Nothing but bliss.

She let go of his shirt and smoothed her palms over his chest, trailing sparks of desire with her touch. Her fingers nudged the little bar at his nipple and lust shot through his body. Nate's hips thrust forward of their own accord and found the edge of the sofa—not what he wanted, not Hannah, but enough to alleviate his sudden, desperate need for pressure.

She wouldn't tell him how she felt, but Nate let himself pretend. Let himself imagine. When she moaned softly into his mouth again, he decided that meant, *I need you.* And when she raised a hand to glide over his jaw, her thumb stroking his cheekbone, Nate interpreted that as, *I care for you.*

And when she pulled back, panting, her eyes wide and her pupils dilated, he almost heard, *I love you.*

Almost. But not quite. Even his imagination wasn't that powerful.

Still, what she actually said was pretty fucking great. "The inoculation was a failure." The humour faded from her voice, until she sounded achingly serious. "I can't stay away from you."

He was holding her too tight. But she didn't seem to mind, and he didn't want to stop. "So don't. Ever. I don't want you to."

"But you were right," she murmured. "What you said about power, I mean."

He closed his eyes. Took a deep breath. Tried to ignore the jagged pain in his chest.

She kissed him again. Gently, carefully, pressing her lips to the corner of his mouth. "I'm not worried. You can't hurt me. But I don't want you to feel guilty. You already feel so guilty all the time."

He didn't even know where to start with that. Was it bad that he cared most about her second sentence? *"You can't hurt me."* Not *won't. Can't.* Nate might have power over her job, he realised dully, but he clearly had none whatsoever over her emotions.

Well. That was okay. It was enough that she wanted him. It would have to be enough.

"I wouldn't feel guilty," he said, "as long as you swear to me that... that you'll never put my feelings before yours. That you'll never be afraid to tell me the truth. No matter what." He opened his eyes to find her smiling gently.

"I'll never be afraid to tell you the truth," she said. "And to prove it, I will tell you right now that I want to kiss you again. And stuff."

He arched a brow, but it was hard to look sardonic when a pathetically happy grin was spreading across his face. "And stuff?"

She rolled her eyes. "You know what I mean."

"We really need to work on your dirty talk."

Hannah looked down at the erection straining his jeans. "I think I get along just fine without it."

HANNAH WATCHED as Nate opened the door to his office with a baffled expression on his face.

"You don't mind, do you?" she asked teasingly. "It's not, like, top secret in here?"

He rolled his eyes, stepping back to let her in first. What a gentleman. "No, it's not top secret. But I don't see why we're here."

"Because we're doing *things*," she murmured, looking around the spartan little room. "Remember?"

"Yeah," he said dryly. "I remember."

Hannah was too distracted to laugh at his tone. She was busy studying the mysterious office where Nate spent most of his daytime hours. Honestly, it was a bit of a disappointment. She'd expected some dark and sophisticated den of creativity, but it was just a plain, clean and tidy space with a desk, a chair, a huge Mac, and a shit ton of cupboards.

Still, at least the desk was big. That suited her purposes.

"You know," Nate said as he shut the door behind them, "*I* was thinking we could have sex on a bed."

She wandered over to the desk. "What if the kids come into your room?"

"You've been here for months, Hannah. When have you ever known the kids to wake up at night?"

"Better safe than sorry."

"Plus, we could use *your* bed."

She turned to face him, wondering if she should explain her reluctance. She was supposed to be telling the truth, right? About everything. That seemed like the only way to make this work—although, truthfully, she still didn't believe that this *could* work. Situations like these didn't end happily for Hannah. They ended up with her eating Chunky Monkey alone in her bedroom while reminding herself that no-one could make a fool out of her unless she let them.

She wouldn't expect anything of Nate, and she wouldn't trust his sweet words or his soft lips or his honest eyes. Because people, she knew, could care about you—could love you, even—and still fuck you over if they thought it was necessary. If—*when*—Nate fucked her over, she'd be okay. Because she was expecting it.

In the meantime, she'd hopefully get more orgasms. At the very least, she'd enjoy sex without panicking about her *lack* of orgasms. So really, what could possibly go wrong?

"If we go to your room," she explained, "or my room, I'll be nervous the whole time. Even if I *know* the kids won't wake up—"

"You'll still worry," he finished gently. "Okay. I get it. Is this why you dragged me outside last time?"

"I didn't drag you," she said demurely. "You came quite willingly."

Nate smiled. "I did, didn't I?" There was a sharp *snick* as he turned the door's lock. Then he crossed the room far too quickly for her liking, and suddenly she was trapped between the desk and his broad body. "I think I'd follow you anywhere. You won't take advantage, will you?"

"Um… no," she squeaked.

One of his big hands wrapped around her wrist. He held

her there for a moment, his thumb resting against her pulse, before his palm slid down to meet hers, their fingers twining together. "I think you're lying. I think you'd happily take advantage of me." He raised her hand to his lips and kissed her knuckles. "It's one of the many, many reasons why I like you so much."

"Really?" she croaked. "Ah." Funny how a racing pulse and a growing wetness between her thighs could erase most of Hannah's mental faculties. She'd had no idea, before now.

"Yep." He stepped forward, urging her back until her arse bumped into the desk. Then he leaned down and brought his lips to her ear. "So. There are four ways I could fuck you in here, Hannah. I know because I've thought about it a lot."

Oh, Jesus. She was overheating like an old laptop. What if she fainted? She'd never live it down.

"I could bend you over this desk," he said. "I think about that one the most." He shoved her skirt up abruptly with one hand, and then his fingers were digging into her arse while his mouth brushed gently against her ear. "I'd spread you open and watch my dick slide into you. Watch you get me nice and slippery."

A whimper escaped her lips. Almost instantly, his mouth was on hers, as if he wanted to swallow the sound. He kissed her hard, caught her lower lip between his teeth, then released her so fast she felt dizzy.

And then, as if nothing had happened, he went right back to whispering in her ear.

"Option two," he said, "is the chair. You in my lap. I'd get to suck your pretty tits while you bounced on my cock. But I think that would make me come fastest, you screwing me. And I'm trying to impress you." He bent his head and kissed her throat. She felt his lips smiling against her skin for a moment before his tongue slid out to trace her pounding pulse.

"Which brings us to option three," he said. "It's quite simple. I take you up against the wall."

She tried, and failed, to breathe normally. Arousal couldn't actually choke someone, could it? In an effort to bring herself back down to earth, she reminded him: "I'm too heavy for that."

He laughed. It didn't sound like his ordinary laugh. It was lower, darker, edged with something white-hot. "You have no faith in me, do you sweetheart?"

"I'm just saying—" She choked down a gasp and grabbed Nate's shoulders as he picked her up and kissed her.

She'd never had a kiss like this before. Not even with him. Because this time, when his lips eased hers open, when his tongue traced every sensitive part of her mouth, it felt... urgent. As if he were a starving man devouring a meal. Like he was pouring himself into her with every giddy press of his lips. He took her mouth slowly, deliberately, holding her so tight, she swore his fingerprints would be burned into her skin.

She barely registered that they were moving until her back came into contact with the wall. Just like that, she was pinned: cool, smooth plaster behind her, Nate's hard chest and harder cock in front. He pressed his thick length against her belly and Hannah rocked her hips, desperate for something to ease the heavy pressure between her thighs.

His kisses moved from her mouth to her jaw, her throat, her ear. And in between the hot press of his lips and the glide of his tongue, he growled, "Tell me what you want."

As if she had any idea right now, with this pulsing need taking over every inch of her body.

"Hannah. Tell me now."

"Wh-what's option four?"

He smiled against her skin. "I was hoping we wouldn't get to option four."

"Why?"

"Option number four is me fucking you on the floor like an animal. Like I wanted to three weeks ago."

A cresting wave of desire rolled through her and she shuddered against him. "Why didn't you?" she whispered.

"Because I can't take something I don't think you want to give."

Hannah swallowed. "That's what you need? Just… to know what I want? And you'll give it to me?"

"Yes." His gaze met hers, so raw and honest, she almost wanted to look away. "I'll give you anything you want. Always. So, tell me. What do you want, Hannah?"

"The—the chair," she blurted.

He smiled. "Why am I not surprised? You want control, love?" His hooded gaze met hers, and for a moment she thought she saw… affection?

Stop it. Stop trying to turn this into a fairytale.

"I always want control," she said.

"Sounds exhausting."

"You should know."

"Touché." He carried her over to the desk, set her down on its smooth surface, and sat in the huge, leather chair in front of her. Her legs dangled on either side of his bent knees. She bit her lip as he reached forward and opened the drawer just to the right of her shin. And then bit it harder as he produced a stack of condoms.

"In your office?" she asked, trying to sound teasing. Her voice came out a little too raw for that. "Seriously?"

He shrugged, a smirk tilting his lips. "Only place in this house with drawers that lock." And then, his tone barely changing, he ordered calmly, "Take your clothes off."

CHAPTER NINETEEN

HE SAID it so casually that, for a moment, she didn't even register the words. But then his meaning sank in, and her cheeks flushed in a way that had nothing to do with the need dancing through her veins. "Just like that?" she asked. "Just… take them off?"

"Yes, love." He stood up and pulled his T-shirt over his head in one move. "Like that," he said, while she tried not to drool over his chest. He bent forward and pressed a kiss to her temple, and then his hands came to the hem of her T-shirt. Slowly, Nate raised the fabric, exposing inch after inch of her flesh to the cool air and the rasp of his calloused palms. "Like this," he whispered. "Okay?"

She nodded, wetting her lips as he drew the clothing higher. "Okay."

Once she said that, he moved slightly faster, speeding up, then easing back—as if he were trying not to rush, but failing. She liked that. She liked that a lot. She liked it even more when he finally pulled her T-shirt off completely, groaning as his hungry gaze landed on her bare skin. Nate closed his eyes and sank his teeth into his lower lip. Hard.

Hannah looked down at herself and found everything in its usual place. Not-particularly-pert breasts in their boring, nude bra. Belly as soft and wobbly as ever. Rolls present and correct. She still had those raised, circular little scars from a childhood bout of chicken pox, and she still had…

"A tattoo?" he croaked. "Seriously?"

"What? You have a thousand."

"I'm me," he said, sinking to his knees in front of her. "You're you." His thumb traced the lines on the right side of her lower belly, the pentagon and the hexagon and the diagonal strokes.

"It's—"

"Serotonin," he finished.

She nodded jerkily. She'd never explained it to anyone. And no-one had ever known. "In case I ever need a boost."

A slight smile teased his lips. "Press here for happiness?"

"In an ideal world," she smiled back.

He kissed her. Right over the tattoo. And then he kissed her again, and again, his lips straying from the ink until every inch of her belly was tingling from the warmth of his mouth. Until her heart was pounding and her muscles melting.

Then he stood, hooked his thumbs under the waistband of her skirt, and said, "Up."

She lifted her hips without hesitation, because somehow, it didn't feel weird to be naked with Nate. Sometimes nakedness felt odd to Hannah—even when she was alone. But right now, it was fine. Right now, it was good.

He let her skirt fall to the floor, and then he ran his

hands over her bare legs, his gaze reverent. "You," he rasped out, "are unbelievable."

"What does that mean?" she asked lightly, as if she didn't care. As if he wasn't sweeping his thumbs over the old self-harm scars on her thighs right now.

He looked up. "It means that if you weren't sitting in front of me, I wouldn't believe anyone could be this fucking sexy." There was a fire in his eyes so fierce, she couldn't doubt him for a second. But even if she had, the way he kissed her would have made things clear.

And the way he stroked his hands over every inch of her skin, every soft curve and dip, as if he couldn't get enough.

And the way he yanked off her knickers in between shoving down his jeans, like he didn't know which to do first, like he couldn't think straight beyond *You, me, naked.*

No, she couldn't doubt him. Even if she'd wanted to.

He ended up naked first, because Hannah dragged off his underwear with an urgency she didn't bother to hide. If he could look at her so hungrily, and touch her so desperately, she could let him see how badly she wanted him. That was safe, wasn't it? That was even. So she stripped him off until he stood before her completely bare, his cock rising up from between those muscled thighs.

Then he unhooked her bra, the last piece of fabric between them, and stared at it. "Hannah... does your bra have pockets?"

"Um, yes."

He gave her a look brimming with amusement. "I didn't think bras came with pockets. Do they come with pockets?"

"No," she admitted.

"Did you... did you sew pockets into your bra?"

"Yes. Don't laugh! Don't laugh! We're having sex!"

For some reason, that just made him laugh harder. "Hannah," he wheezed between chuckles. "Why do you keep whispering *sex*?"

"I don't know!"

He cupped her cheeks and kissed her, even though he was still laughing. And that made *her* laugh, until they were just two naked weirdos giggling into each other's mouths.

"Holy shit," he snorted, "I—I adore you. I really do." He kissed her cheek. "You're perfect. You're perfect."

The tender words squeezed ruthlessly at her heart. Her poor, foolish heart, which was falling in love with him right this second, totally and tragically. It would not end well. But she'd never felt like this, and she'd certainly never been *adored*. It felt good, and it probably wouldn't happen again. So Hannah decided to go with it. For now.

She wrapped her arms around his neck, running her tongue along the soft, inner seam of his mouth. Nate's laughter faded into a groan, and his hips rocked forwards. When his cock nestled against the swollen folds of her pussy, they each dragged in a ragged breath. And then Nate reached between their bodies and nudged the blunt head of his dick against her aching clit.

"Oh, fuck," she sighed, her head falling back. "What—? Ohhh, yes."

He rocked against her, running his lips along the line of her throat. "More?"

"*Yes.*"

"Tell me."

"I can't—"

"Tell me." He pulled her closer, his forehead bumping

against hers, his gaze gentle as ever despite the need burning there. "Trust me. Tell me what you want."

Hannah bit her lip as she studied him. Maybe it was because his face had become so dear to her, or maybe it was the heat suffusing her body and the lust racing through her veins, but she wanted to.

So she fumbled around until she found the condoms he'd dropped on the desk. Then she slapped them against his chest and got as close to dirty talk as she was ever going to get. Wrapping her free hand around his cock, her fingers covering his, she murmured, "I want you. Inside me. Please."

By his low, agonised moan, anyone would think she'd just given a porn-worthy speech. He took a condom, ripped it open, and rolled the slick latex over his length. Then he sat down, but he didn't pull her into his lap as she'd expected.

Instead, he hooked his hands under her thighs and eased her forwards until she was almost hanging off the desk. "Spread your legs," he said softly.

Slowly, Hannah let her knees fall apart. He drew in a sharp breath, and then she felt his thumb glide over her entrance in a teasing circle. Her heart rate spiked.

"I have to make sure you're ready," he murmured, easing the tip—just the very tip—of his thumb inside her.

"I am," she gasped, her hips jerking forward, her arousal demanding more. More pressure, more heat, more of that blunt intrusion. She wanted his thickness between her thighs, but anything would do. As long as it came from him.

"I don't know," Nate said. "You *are* wet." He withdrew his thumb and she whimpered as he licked the digit clean. "But you're so tight," he went on. She sighed in sweet, agonised, semi-satisfaction when he touched her again.

"I'm fine. I swear I'm fine. Please, Nate, please."

"Be patient," he said. But he dragged in a breath, his lush mouth tightening, and she knew he wasn't totally in control. She could push him.

She spread her legs wider and ran a hand up her body. The way his eyes followed the path of that hand, the hunger all over his face as he watched her, sharpened Hannah's arousal even further. This was a power she hadn't often felt, and the heady edge of control ramped up her own desire.

She slid the same hand back down her body until she found the aching bead of her clit. When she circled that swollen flesh, Nate moaned as if she'd touched *him*. When she did it again, he finally pushed his fingers inside her, long and thick and perfect.

Pleasure spiralled through her, from the sweet friction of his touch to the feel of his body against hers. Nate wrapped an arm around her waist and dragged her closer, thrusting his fingers deep, filling her up.

"Ah, Hannah," he breathed. "How am I supposed to go slow when you look at me like this?"

"You're not supposed to go slow." Her hips jerked in time with his thrusting hand, sensation fizzing through her nerve endings. "I don't want it slow."

He groaned and bent his head towards her swaying breasts, catching one dark tip in his mouth. When his tongue flicked over her nipple, she almost forgot how to breathe. He sucked hard, and fucked her with his fingers, and she rubbed frantically between her thighs because something good was within reach and if she didn't get there soon it might never happen at all.

Nate released her breast with a lick and whispered, "God, you feel so good. So good. Look at you, playing with yourself." He kissed her neglected nipple, sucked it into his mouth for a second, then let go, his stare focused between her legs.

"Nate!"

"What, sweetheart? You want more?" He licked her again. "I'm surprised you're not being bossier, all things considered. But you don't need to be, do you? I'm yours anyway." He caught her nipple again, sucked harder—and she broke. Snapped. Even though she'd felt it coming, the orgasm shocked her witless. It felt as if everything that held her body together had dissolved, as if she were just a ball of sobbing pleasure, as if her spasming pussy was the only part of her that still *felt* at all.

She was distantly aware of him whispering into her skin, murmuring words she couldn't be hearing right. *"Hannah, my love, you own me. Forever. You own me."*

Delirious. She was delirious because she'd never come that fast or that hard. But she returned to herself when she felt him grip her hips, lift her off the desk, and pull her into his lap. Her knees landed on cool leather, straddling his thighs. She opened her eyes to find him watching her, his black pupils swallowing the blue of his iris, his mouth red and swollen, his cheeks flushed. Because of her. He looked like this, lost to desire, because of her.

Nate caught her hand and guided it to the place where his cock jutted up between them. "Use me," he rasped, his tone commanding even as he gave himself to her.

So, she did.

~

EVERYTHING WITH HANNAH was more intense than it should be—more intense than seemed humanly possible. So Nate should've been prepared for the pleasure that stole his breath when she sank down onto his aching cock.

And yet, the sensation destroyed him. The feel of her hot, wet cunt gripping his length; the soft flesh of her thighs brushing his as she rode him; the sight of her eyes fluttering shut and her lips parting on a sigh... It all wrecked him. Fucked him up completely. Fucked him up *perfectly*.

God, he loved her.

Nate's hands gripped her arse, her hips, her thick waist and soft belly, claiming every lush curve in the only way she'd allow. Never, in a thousand years, would he have enough of this. She fucked herself so hard and so deep on his cock, he was ready to come within seconds—but he couldn't, because she wasn't done with him. She clutched his shoulders and moaned and rocked against him, and he wondered if she'd *ever* be done with him.

He hoped not.

Nate pulled her closer and kissed his way up her throat. She tasted so good, so fucking good, everywhere. When she moaned and arched into him, pleasure arced from the base of his spine to the root of his cock like an arrow, so intense his breath caught. His control was unravelling way too fucking fast. Then she took his face in her hands and kissed him, and he was fucked. He was absolutely fucked.

"I'm going to come," he panted against her lips. "But if you stop—"

"Do you want me to stop?"

"Fuck, no, Hannah. Never."

"So come." She rose up until only the tip of his cock kissed her slick heat. Then she sank down again, rolling her hips, and it was as if he'd been waiting for permission. Sensation ripped through him as he cried out her name, his vision blurring slightly—but not enough to hide the look on her face, the way she watched with lustful eyes as he came for her.

The disorientating grip of pleasure eased, and his head fell against her shoulder. He was gratified to notice that she was sweating as much as he was, panting as much as he was.

And clinging to him the way he clung to her.

This time, she didn't push him away. She didn't force distance between them. She kissed a spot just below his right ear, which meant she'd noticed the little, old-fashioned camera tattooed there. No hot licks, no wicked bites, just a single, sweet kiss.

Nate raised his head to smile at her. "You okay?"

Clearly, this was a day full of blessings, because she smiled back. "I'm great."

"You haven't changed your mind?"

She ran a finger over his eyebrow, his cheekbone, up the bridge of his nose. "Me? No. I don't change my mind."

Well, that was good fucking news for him. "Neither do I."

She arched a brow. "We'll see."

"*We'll see.*" As if she… expected him to? That stung. But, he reminded himself, she was so cautious. And their situation was complicated. And she didn't know that he loved her.

Maybe he should tell her.

Yeah, that'll go down well. You make up after three weeks of weirdness, have sex, and immediately confess your undying love. She'll react wonderfully.

Okay, never mind.

Instead, he kissed her gently, his thumb stroking over that unexpected tattoo on her belly. "We will see." Because he'd show her. "In the meantime, I think we should both refrain from dating pirates. And dog owners. And any combination of the above."

She snorted. "I was never dating Rae. Relax."

"I'll relax if you agree that this is exclusive." That seemed like the only thing he could push for right now. The only thing that wouldn't make his wary Hannah nervous. But slow and steady won the race, didn't it? That's what he always told the kids, anyway.

She stared at him for a moment, biting her lip. He kept his expression calm and his muscles loose, even as his heart pounded like a drum. Then, finally, she spoke. "Exclusive and secret. Right?"

He should've expected that, he supposed. It made sense, after all. And from Hannah, he'd take what he could get. So Nate nodded, and smiled, and said, "Exclusive and secret. Obviously."

But the words were bitter on his tongue.

CHAPTER TWENTY

"The mental *is* physical."

— HANNAH KABBAH, *THE KABBAH CODE*

T<small>HERE WAS</small> a clock in Hannah's head. It was ticking.

She didn't know when her time would run out, when the bomb would detonate or whatever the fuck, but she knew it would happen eventually. Every time Nate wrapped his arms around her and buried his face in her hair, the ticking got louder. Every time he played absently with her braids, or made her breakfast, or held her hand, it sped up.

It only stopped when he bent her over his desk and kissed his way up her spine and fucked her hard.

She was trying her best to ignore that damned clock, and sometimes she even succeeded. Because being with Nate, even if it was illicit and undefined and everything else that would usually make Hannah's skin crawl… well, being with Nate made her happy.

The only real problem was keeping the source of that happiness a secret. Even Beth had started asking her why she was always singing—badly—and why she wasn't quite as strict anymore. On Sundays, Hannah went to church and thanked God that her little family consisted of one unbelievably oblivious mother and one adorably unobservant sister.

Until the fourth Sunday, when she went to her mother's for dinner and found Evan sitting in the living room, his arm around Ruth's shoulder.

Hannah froze in the doorway. Her sister's boyfriend turned his head to look at her. "Hey Hannah. How are you?"

Terrible. Because you—*you are not my mother or my sister. You don't live in the clouds, and you read facial expressions without trying. So I'm fucked, Evan. That's how I am. I'm absolutely fucked.*

She allowed herself that small, self-indulgent moment of panic before pushing it away, pasting a smile on her face, and chirping, "Great, thanks! You?"

The words sounded plastic even to her own ears, but she didn't let her smile falter. No-one ever got anywhere without a can-do attitude, now, did they?

Evan paused before answering. "I'm good. How's the party planning?"

"In full swing!" she laughed nervously. Zach's birthday was coming up, and Nate was throwing him a surprise party. For the past few weeks, they'd been making the arrangements together—and taking occasional breaks for certain extracurricular activities. Aaaand now Evan was staring at her as if he knew all about those extracurricular activities, and he was going to burst out with the truth and shame her completely.

Actually, she might be imagining that. Her ever-present anxiety expected him to leap up and shout, *"Aha! I can tell just by the look on your face that you've been sucking Nate's dick when you should've been setting up a Facebook event!"*

But all that came out of his mouth was, "Cool. Blog going okay?"

Hannah's cheeks heated. She looked past him to glare at Ruth. "You *told*?"

Ruth blinked like a cornered rabbit. "Was I not supposed to? I thought it was Mum I couldn't tell."

And then, like a cherry on top of that clusterfuck cake, Patience Kabbah floated into the room and asked, "What is a blog, Hannah?"

Great. The one time Hannah needed her mother to be oblivious, the woman started paying attention to conversations.

"Nothing, Mummy. It's a… a computer thing."

Patience wrinkled her nose. "Ah. Come and help me with dinner, now. You want me to take your hair out later?"

"Oh, yes. Yes, please."

"Good." Patience floated away again like a cloud of absent-minded, cinnamon-scented perfume. Hannah followed, flashing Ruth a death stare over her shoulder.

What? Ruth mouthed.

Later, Hannah mouthed back, pouring every inch of sisterly menace she could into a half-second glare. Which was rather a lot.

But Ruth, the cow, seemed unconcerned.

~

ALL THROUGH DINNER, Hannah was cool, calm and generally Hannah-like. Not giddy, not overly cheerful or excessively relaxed; just her normal, ordinary, stick-up-the-arse self. She thought she did quite a good job of it, too. It wasn't hard, with nerves stiffening her spine and sharpening her tongue.

But when she and Ruth stood to clear the table after dinner, Evan pulled the plates from Ruth's hands. "Sit down," he said. "I'll do it."

Then he looked at Hannah and she knew that she was busted.

By the time they reached the kitchen, she was so nervous that the *click* of the door shutting behind them almost made her drop a crystal glass. She had a minor heart attack when it wobbled in her grip. If she smashed the crystal, Mum might be upset enough to *glare* at her. Or speak sternly, even. Hannah didn't think her nerves could take that.

While she was staring, frozen, at the glass in her hand, Evan put down his plates. Then he took the crockery she was holding and put that down, too. *Then* he put his hands on her shoulders and said solemnly, "Something's wrong with you."

She scowled. "Nothing's wrong with me. Get off."

He gave her a suspicious look. "You're distracted. And... weird. You keep doing this thing with your face."

"What *thing?*"

"Kind of like a smile. A *weird* smile—"

"You can stop saying 'weird' now."

"—but then you cut the smile off really fast. Like it's not

supposed to be there." He narrowed his eyes. "Yeah. Something's up with you. I don't like it."

She huffed out a breath. "Oh, piss off. You're not my dad, you know." But really, Evan behaved like *everyone's* dad.

"I'm kind of your brother." He folded his arms and leant against the kitchen counter.

"You are *not* my brother."

"I'm your brother-in-law."

"Oh, did I miss the wedding? Congrats." She rolled her eyes and shoved him out of the way. Or tried to. He didn't move, the giant fucker. "I need to get in that cupboard," she gritted out, glaring hard enough to kill.

Oh, if only.

Evan studied her for a moment, his eyes searching. "If you were ever in trouble," he said gently, "you'd tell me. Or Ruth. Or someone. Right?"

"Yes," she lied. "Of course."

He didn't seem convinced—but he did step away from the cupboard. As she crouched down to find the Fairy Liquid, he murmured, "I've got my eye on you, Hannah Kabbah."

Great. Just what she fucking needed.

Respect thy mother and thy father.

It wasn't Hannah's favourite commandment. She didn't typically need motivation to respect her mother, and she absolutely refused to respect her so-called father—but then, God probably understood why.

Truthfully, Hannah only ever thought of those words when she found herself in a situation like this one: sitting on the floor with her back against the sofa, arsecheeks slowly going numb, Mum dragging at her freshly washed hair with a comb

Respect thy mother and thy father. Respect thy mother and thy father. Respect thy mother and—

Patience hit a button on her decades-old hair straighteners and a cloud of steam poured out, singeing Hannah's ears.

"Oww!" she howled. "Mother! Please!"

"Stop moving your head," Patience tutted. "Is not hot."

"Why am I even letting you *do* this?"

"I want to see how much your hair has grown," Patience reminded her.

"That won't matter if you burn it all off!"

"Cha. Duya. What's wrong with you? You're arguing so much today."

Oh, fuck. She was supposed to be Ordinary Hannah right now, and Ordinary Hannah let her mother do whatever she wished. Ordinary Hannah was quiet and obedient at home. But Hannah hadn't been ordinary for a while now. She was swooping to the top of a rollercoaster with Nate, the pleasure exhilarating, the threat of an inevitable drop looming large. Oh, how she dreaded that drop.

It might break a fundamental part of her.

"Now, no fidgeting," Patience ordered, as she made another sharp parting. The edge of the comb felt like a knife. Patience's usual airy-fairy delicacy vanished like smoke in the wind when it came to styling her children's hair.

Not that Ruth would let their mother near her head like this. No; clearly, Hannah was the fool of the family.

I am thirty fucking years old, sitting on the bloody floor while my mother straightens my damn hair and puts a bump in the front like it's 2001. God has forsaken me. And if I find Him, I will be having stern words.

In the midst of that internal rant, Patience spoke again. Her voice was absent, soothing as always, but her words hit Hannah like a fist to the gut. "I know something is bothering you, angel."

Fuck. Now her *mother* was noticing? Hannah gritted her teeth into a tight smile and stared at the TV screen in front of them. "It's nothing." Her eyes latched onto the familiar sight of Noel Edmonds's silver bouffant.

Take my word for it. Don't ask me any questions. Focus on Noel and his shiny hair. Tut at the contestants for taking pointless risks.

"You mustn't lie, Hannah. It's a sin. What is wrong?"

Clearly, psychic suggestion wasn't working. "Nothing's wrong."

"Is it the job? With the children?"

Hannah almost choked at the question, slapping a hand to her throat. *Nice. Subtle. You really played it cool there, Kabbah.*

"The father," Patience pushed, her concern clear now. "He treats you well?"

Arguably too well. *Definitely* too well. "He's nice," Hannah managed to croak. "You know he's Zach's older brother, right? Evan's friend Zach, I mean." Any association with Evan, no matter how tenuous, was a positive mark in Patience Kabbah's book.

But she didn't sound mollified. "I know who Nate Davis is, Hannah. I am in a book club with his mother."

"Ah."

"He comes to see her often. He drives her to places. He seems like a very sweet boy."

"Mmhm."

"You went to school with him, didn't you?"

I went to school with a lot of people, Mum. "Yes. He was in my class."

"He ran off to worship the devil in London, didn't he?"

Hannah tried not to smile. "I couldn't say. But I will remind you that he's here to help his mother, and he has two kids, and his wife passed away—"

"God rest her soul."

"God rest her soul. So, we should be good Christians and speak nicely about him." Honestly, this conversation was odd. Patience Kabbah was not the sort of woman to gossip about people, or disapprove of people, or even *think* of people. She typically existed on another plane. Hannah sometimes wondered if she even knew what day it was.

And yet, somehow, she'd noticed that her daughter was acting strangely. She'd even managed to pin down the cause, whether she realised it or not.

Hannah's heart ricocheted around her chest. *Fuck.* Her mother had been playing them all along. She was secretly a hyper-aware Sherlock Holmes in sheep's clothing, and now she was on the cusp of ferreting out Hannah's biggest secret. This could not stand.

She searched frantically for a topic important enough to serve as a distraction. The murky waters of her mind had never been more fucked up—but out of nowhere, a suitable subject bubbled to the surface. It was one she'd been avoiding for a while, one she'd desperately wanted to drown. Now she clung to it like a life-raft, blurting the words out abruptly. "Do you ever hear from Dad?"

Silence fell, heavy as January snow. Hannah tried not to wince as another puff of steam passed over her sensitive scalp. A full minute passed, filled only with the tinny applause of the *Deal or No Deal* audience.

Then, finally, Patience said, "You have never asked me about your father. Not for years. Not once since he left."

Well, no, Hannah supposed she hadn't. She didn't like talking about him. The word 'Dad' tasted like rust on her tongue. Of course, once upon a time, she'd *loved* talking about him. She'd told all the kids at pre-school: "My dad's rich and he comes to see us *every month,* all the way from Sierra Leone because he *loves* us, and he buys us whatever we want because he *loves* us…"

Yeah. Kids were easily confused. And rich men, it turned out, were easily bored. Even with their second families.

"I didn't need to ask," she said finally. "You told us what happened." They'd been given an unfulfilling, childish sort of explanation at the time, and then a more complete story when they were slightly older. By which point, the most important thing had already become clear: their father was not coming back.

Really, what more was there to ask about?

"True," Patience allowed. "But you have never asked why I fell in love with a married man in the first place."

Hannah's jaw dropped. "I… you…" *I would rather die than ask anyone about something like that, but especially not my mother.*

Patience gave a little laugh and patted Hannah's shoulder, as if she'd heard that thought. "We are very different, angel. But I do love you so." She sighed and ran the straighteners over another section of Hannah's poor hair. "You know, I don't like to speak badly of your father in front of you girls."

Did that mean Patience spoke badly of their father at all? If so, she certainly hid it well.

"But," the older woman went on, "Now that time has passed, I have decided that he did not behave correctly. I think, perhaps, he used our positions to his advantage. I worked for him, you see. Did you know that?"

"No," Hannah whispered. She certainly had not known that. The words settled greasily in her stomach, heavy and sickening.

"I cleaned his office," Patience said. "And he was there so much—he was a lawyer, you see—it was as if I lived with him. Things were not fair between us, I don't think. Of course, it all worked out for me, in the end." She pressed a quick kiss to the top of Hannah's head. "But I understand now, why my mother was so angry at the time. It is not something I would want for my daughter. Especially not you. You are not like me. You are very sensitive."

Hannah should snort at that, should mock the idea that she could ever be considered more 'sensitive' than her wispy mother. But for some reason, she couldn't bring herself to make a sound.

Instead she sat rigid, locked into place by her own screaming thoughts. It was as if the volume had been turned up on all the snide whispers she'd spent the past month ignoring. *Relationships aren't for you. No-one's going to catch you if you fall. Happiness is always temporary.*

The clock ticking in the back of her skull had never been so loud.

Finally, she croaked out, "You don't need to worry about me, Mummy. You really, *really* don't."

"I'm sure." Patience patted her shoulder absently. "You are a very sensible girl. So much more sensible than me."

That was Hannah, alright. Sensible.

NATE WASN'T WORRIED about Hannah, exactly, but he *was* wondering where she'd got to. She returned from her mother's around the same time every Sunday, but today the kids' bedtime came and went, and she didn't appear.

It was only when the summer sky began to darken that he heard her key in the front door. And even though she'd left just that morning, he couldn't stay put in the kitchen, planning food for Zach's surprise party, when he knew she was in the house. He went to her so fast, he might've been embarrassed if he weren't past the point of caring about that shit.

He loved her. And he couldn't tell her yet—not until his top-secret plans came to fruition—but he also couldn't hide it.

She was in the hall, hanging up her keys by the door. He circled his arms around her waist from behind, bending down to murmur in her ear, "Hey."

"Hey," she said.

It was just one word, but it sent a skitter of unease down

his spine. She sounded… off. Flat. Like she was lying. But you couldn't lie about *"Hey"*. That didn't make any fucking sense. Nate turned her in his arms. She moved to face him stiffly, slowly, as if the air was thicker than it should be.

He looked down at her smooth, blank face and felt something like panic shake him. "Are you okay?"

"I'm fine," she said, pulling away from him. Manoeuvring around him as if he were just an obstacle in her path.

He followed her into the living room, trapped between the urge to reach for her and the fact that she obviously didn't want him to. Forcing his frozen tongue to work, he said, "You changed your hair."

She shot him a dour look over her shoulder, pushing the thick, dark mass out of her eyes. "I don't want to talk about it."

"You don't like it?"

"Does it matter?" She sat down with a sigh. "I'll probably get braids again in a couple of weeks."

"Okay." He sat beside her. "Well, I think you look nice."

Her lips pressed into a hard line. She glared at him as if he'd just insulted her stationery collection. Then, out of nowhere, she said, "I don't want to have sex tonight."

Oh. He was so relieved, he didn't even laugh when she whispered 'sex'. "Is that why you're being weird?" he asked, reaching out to catch her hand.

Her eyes narrowed further. He wondered how she could even see, at this point. "I'm not being weird."

Sure you're not. "Honey, it's okay if you don't want to have sex. We don't have to have sex all the time."

"But we do," she said.

"We do?"

"Have sex all the time, I mean. Usually."

Nate shrugged. "Well, yeah. But we don't *have* to. If you're not in the mood, it's fine. We can sit in the garden. Or watch that baking thing on Netflix. Whatever you want."

She eyed him suspiciously. "What if I never really wanted to have sex again? Like… what if I just… didn't… you know."

He didn't know, exactly, but he kind of got what she was saying. With a sigh, Nate tugged gently at her hand. "Will you come over here?"

"Why?"

"Because I feel like you're pulling away from me and it's stressing me out."

He hadn't meant to say that, exactly. He'd meant to give her some sanitised version of the truth, but the words slipped out. And as soon as they did, some of the hardness in her expression faded. She frowned slightly, biting her lip. "I'm sorry. I didn't mean to—I'm not trying to stress you out. I just—"

"I know," he said. "Don't worry. It's okay." When he pulled at her hand again, she crawled over the cushions and into his lap. The minute she settled against his chest, the deafening rush of blood in his ears quieted. His rampaging heart slowed. He kissed her temple and held her in silence for a moment, waiting for the last of his panic to fade.

Finally, he trusted himself to speak. "Hannah, I don't care if you never want to have sex again."

She snorted. "Sure."

"I don't. I'd have to masturbate a hell of a lot more…" She huffed out a laugh, bringing a smile to his lips. "But I can handle that. Sex isn't as important as being close to you.

I just want to make you happy." He tilted her chin up with one finger, making sure she met his eyes. "If that means I never fuck anything but my hand, I'll deal."

She held his gaze for a moment before looking away. "Okay."

Did she believe him? For once, he had no idea. But if she didn't yet, she would. Eventually.

"Are you alright?" he asked. "Are you having a hard time?" He'd been through difficult patches himself; times when he felt disconnected from his body. When the idea of anyone touching him like that made him nauseous. It wasn't a bad sign for everyone, but it usually was for him. It might be for her, too.

But she shook her head. "No. I'm fine. Really."

"You sure?"

"It was just theoretical. I remembered that sometimes I have phases where I don't want to, and I wondered..." She trailed off, giving him an odd, tight smile that slowly softened into something real. After a beat, he felt her whole body relax. She ran a hand through his hair and said lightly, "You need another trim."

The casual touch felt like a blessing. "Whatever you say. You're in charge of my hair, after all."

"Oh, I'm in charge?"

"You didn't know?" He kissed her cheek. "It's your call."

Everything is your call. Trust me. I love you.

She studied him for a moment, her dark eyes fathomless. "Are you sure about that?"

"Well," he teased, "I don't like any of the barbers around here, so..."

There was only the slightest pause, a fraction of a breath,

before she laughed. And then she changed the subject. She asked him about his day, and the kids, and the party plans, and she seemed fine. Perfectly fine.

But he couldn't shake the feeling that he'd said the wrong thing.

CHAPTER TWENTY-ONE

Rae: I think I saw the kids with their dad on Sunday. Is he tall, kinda pale, heavily tattooed, extremely hot?
Hannah: I don't know about that last part.
Rae: ??? Is your vision okay?
Hannah: He has really bad breath.
Rae: Huh. That's a shame.

"Where's Zach?"

"Late," Hannah said, her voice rising over the chatter of guests. "He texted me. Work stuff."

Nate scowled. His little brother was a *blacksmith*. Blacksmiths shouldn't have regular nine-to-fives, never mind all this overtime. Blacksmiths should take time off whenever they wanted and pound iron in ye olde forge by the dark of night, or whatever. Right? But Zach seemed to work for some kind of tyrant, so here he was, late for his own surprise party.

About thirty people milled around the house and a soft rock playlist hummed along in the background. The patio doors were open to let in the summer night air, and Hannah had made a shit ton of food, and most people seemed to be having a good time. Ma had already fallen asleep, so he'd put her upstairs with the kids—but he was trying not to worry too much about that. Hannah kept telling him, *"Worry doesn't pay bills or raise children, and it certainly never healed anyone."*

He wasn't sure if the words themselves were helping, or if it was just the source. In the end, it didn't really matter. Last week he'd managed to sleep for five hours at a time, so he wouldn't question his newfound relaxation too closely.

Once Hannah answered his question, she floated casually away from him without another word. She'd been doing that ever since the party started. Maybe she was nervous around all these people, or maybe it had something to do with her little sister glowering at everyone from the corner of the room, but Hannah seemed... jumpy. Eager to jump away from *him*, at least.

She'd been acting weird for a few days, in fact, but he told himself not to overthink it. It was probably stress—plus paranoia about hiding their relationship tonight, since they'd never had to pretend in front of so many people. It definitely couldn't be a problem between the two of them, could it? No. No.

Recently she'd been trusting him more than ever, sharing her emotions and everything. Like last week, when she'd looked across the kitchen with narrowed eyes and said thoughtfully, "Kind of weird how you never get on my nerves."

Nate was choosing to take that, rightly or wrongly, as an admission of eternal devotion.

Of course, she had no idea that certain plans of his were coming together, plans that would free them from all these complications so they could just... be. Once he told her, and everything was wrapped up neatly, he could shout from the rooftops that Hannah Kabbah belonged to him. Until then, she could be as cautious as she wanted, even if it hurt. He was a patient man. So, so patient. Really fucking...

He watched as Hannah slipped through the crowd and wandered, alone, into the hallway.

Ah, screw it.

He followed.

She was hovering by the window beside the front door, peeking out between the curtains. Nate smiled as he watched her, then grinned wider when she turned around and jumped at the sight of him.

"Oh," she gasped, pressing a hand to her chest. "Jesus, Nate!"

"Sorry. Looking for your friend?"

"Who, Rae?" She bit her lip. "She keeps texting me reasons why she's late. But I don't think she's coming. I think she's shy. No, I was looking for Zach."

"Ah. Well, maybe she'll turn up eventually." He reached out and caught her hand. She let him, a reluctant smile teasing her lips—so he pushed his luck and twined their fingers together, pulling her closer.

"Bad idea," she whispered.

He raised her knuckles to his lips. "I know. But I have something to tell you."

"Now?"

"No, not now. I wish. Later. I'm just getting ahead of myself." He wrapped an arm around her waist and kissed her, letting her feel his adoration with every slow glide of their lips. *I hope I'm not alone in this. I hope I'm not wrong about the way you look at me.*

When he pulled back, the expression on her face was sweet enough to melt him completely. She smiled hazily, her gaze warm and soft, and Nate's heart bounded around his chest like an excitable puppy.

Then a knock came at the door and she practically leapt away from him.

There was no logical reason for that to sting. They were a secret. They *had* to be a secret, for now. But that reality didn't quite fit with his need to kiss the tension out of her whenever and wherever he damn well pleased.

Hannah opened the front door to reveal Zach standing with his hands in his pockets, his hair still damp. "Let me guess," he said dryly. "You threw me a party."

She gave a mock-gasp. "How did you know?"

"I'm psychic. Or I just saw thirty-odd people and a shit ton of balloons through the window."

"Well, that's what happens when you're late to your own surprise," Nate winked, stepping forward to pull his brother into a hug. "Happy birthday, man."

Nate didn't get a second with Hannah for the next two

hours. Not a single second. Every time he caught her eye, she looked away. Every time he manoeuvred past chattering guests to reach her, she disappeared like smoke. At one point he caught her in the kitchen eating a spring roll, which confirmed what he'd already suspected: she was freaking out about something. Because Hannah didn't even *like* spring rolls, but she'd probably eat a tree branch if she was stressed enough.

As soon as he asked her what was wrong, though, that bloody sister of hers appeared. Ruth Kabbah looked exactly like Hannah, except for her permanent glare—Hannah's was only *semi*-permanent—and the fact that she seemed to be wearing pyjamas. For some reason, whenever she was around, Hannah got as uptight about 'unnecessary familiarity' as she did in front of the kids. Like Ruth was still five, or something. So he had to let her go. And he didn't miss the way Ruth eyed him suspiciously as she and Hannah wandered off arm in arm.

Nate couldn't shake the oddest feeling that something was slipping through his fingers.

Maybe that was why, the next time he saw Hannah alone, he didn't give her a chance to get away.

HANNAH WAS SEARCHING through the fridge for a snack—the party food had depleted tragically over the course of the evening—when Nate appeared behind her. He put his hands on her waist, the brief contact lighting her up, and murmured, "Come outside."

She stiffened, and not just because anyone could walk

into the kitchen and see them. She'd been trying so desperately to cut back the uncontrollable, overgrown weed that her feelings towards him had become—but they still sprawled over the garden of her mind like some kind of dandelion infestation. All it took was a touch from him and she forgot to be sensible.

It was making her nervous.

"Why?" she asked, staring into the fridge as if it could save her from the inevitable.

"I want to talk to you." He'd said that earlier—that he had something to tell her. And ever since, anxiety had been bubbling up inside her like something in a witch's cauldron.

"About what?"

"Nothing bad." He kissed her neck. "It's a surprise."

The words made her relax, which just stressed Hannah out even more. She didn't want to trust him like this. She didn't want this urge to melt into his touch. She didn't want this feeling of calm and safety to fall over her like a warm blanket whenever he was around.

She didn't want to love him.

But it was becoming painfully clear that she did. She loved Nate. She was secretly fucking the man who paid her wages, and she'd managed to fall in love with him on top of it all. Her mother had been right, in the end. Hannah wasn't strong enough for this.

She wasn't strong at all. Because when he took her hand, she let him. When he pulled her out into the dark heat of the garden, she let him. When he pressed her against the house's rough cobblestones and ran a finger over her cheek, she let him.

"You look beautiful tonight," he murmured, a smile softening his features.

"Thanks," Hannah managed. It was hard to concentrate on a conversation when her brain was kind of collapsing. She'd decided that, whatever he had to say, it couldn't possibly be good. Yes, he'd claimed it was a 'surprise', but what did that even mean? Hannah hated surprises. What if it was something terrible, but he didn't want her to make a fuss? What if he was just letting her down gently?

The ticking in the back of her mind was louder than ever, every obnoxious little *click* reminding her that this was the real world and happy endings did not exist. Or, if they did, they simply weren't for her.

And yet... she didn't say anything. Not a damned thing. She should be demanding answers, but she just stared up at him like a love-sick cow. Hannah was considering putting up posters around town. Clearly, she had misplaced her backbone. Perhaps some kindly older person had come across it on a morning walk?

"Are you okay?" he asked. "You seem down."

"I'm fine," she lied. "Just panicking about... party stuff."

"Don't worry about all that, love. Everything's perfect." He tipped up her chin and pressed a soft kiss to her lips. "Just like you. Listen, I meant to save this until later, but—"

"Wait," she said, the word leaping out of her mouth without permission. Now, why had she said that? There must be a reason—a reason other than the unexplainable fear running icily through her veins, the fear that had stalked her like a predator ever since that talk with Mum on Sunday. Right?

Nope. There was no logical reason for her to cut him off. Just the fear.

She looked up and found Nate's brow furrowed, his eyes cautious. He was worried about her. Like he didn't have enough to worry about. She was fucking around, letting all her Ominous Despair overflow willy-nilly, and *he* was paying the price. Which was reason number 763 why Romance Was Not for Hannah.

Not that she'd been counting.

"Kiss me," she said finally. She didn't even know why. Maybe because her mind was sinking into a mire of stormy, indescribable feelings and kissing Nate felt like the only way out.

"Are you sure?" he whispered. For heaven's sake. Why couldn't he be like other men and slobber all over her without a moment's consideration?

Before either of them could think too hard about it, Hannah grabbed his face with both hands and dragged him down to her level.

He held her tight. Their lips met. It felt like drinking down devotion.

Flames ripped through her body, trying their best to burn away the thick, rubbery dread that squatted heavy in her chest. And still, it wasn't enough. It should be—she *wanted* it to be—but it wasn't enough. Because no matter how good this felt, how much she needed him, how much she *loved* him, that edgy, formless, almost-terror refused to fade.

And then a familiar voice cut into the moment, sharp and horrified. "What the fuck is going on here?"

Hannah jerked away from Nate so hard, she hit her head

against the wall. It was more of a glancing blow than anything else, but a second later she felt Nate's hands in her hair, pulling her close, running over scalp. "Are you okay?" he asked, his voice low. "Look at me."

"I'm fine."

"Just look at me, would you?"

She ignored him and looked at Evan instead. It was Evan who'd spoken, he and Zach standing a few feet away with bottles of beer and twin expressions of astonishment.

Muttering a curse, Nate yanked his phone out of his pocket and switched on the torch, shining it in her eyes.

"Would you stop that?" she snapped. "You're not a fucking doctor."

"I know how to check for a concussion," he gritted back, "and I'm checking whether you like it or not. So keep still."

"Hate to interrupt," Zach said slowly, "but, Nate, I have to ask. Did you just have your tongue down Hannah's throat? Because it kind of looked like you did."

Barely sparing his brother a glance, Nate said calmly, "Fuck off."

How the hell was his voice so steady? How were his hands so sure as they ran through her hair? Because Hannah felt as if her body and her soul were shaking at different frequencies, like she could fall out of her own flesh at any moment. Her heart pounded so hard, she was worried it might actually come loose. That didn't sound medically possible, but anxiety could be a real bitch sometimes.

"Hannah," Evan murmured, "you should come over here."

She wanted to ask why, but she already knew her voice would be humiliatingly shaky. In the end, it didn't matter, because Nate carried the conversation for her. "Why? She's fine here."

"With *you?*" She'd never seen Evan angry before. It had never really occurred to her that he *could* be angry. He was so eternally cheerful, so self-assured and utterly implacable. But right now he seemed absolutely furious, his voice hard. "Forgive me if I don't trust the guy who runs around grabbing his employees."

Nate flinched as if the words were a blow. She wanted to take his hand. She wanted to say something. But she couldn't. She couldn't move. She felt cold sweat dripping down her spine, followed by the icy finger of self-doubt and a white-hot blade that felt a lot like pain.

And then, through it all, resignation. Cold, heavy, unavoidable.

"Not that it's any of your business," Nate said, "but this is not whatever the hell you're thinking."

"Well what the fuck is it?" Zach snapped. "Because it *looks* pretty fucking bad, Nate."

"Hannah and I—"

For some reason, those were the words that unlocked Hannah's stiff jaw and watered her dry throat. Those were the words that allowed her lungs to function again. Those were the words that inspired her to step in front of Nate and voice her deepest fear as if it were the truth.

"It's nothing, Zach. This is nothing." Her laugh sounded so real, so genuine—a touch of embarrassment, a dash of self-deprecation. "An experiment, I suppose. Nate was just humouring me. Honestly, I'd rather not explain." She rolled her eyes at her own strange ways. "It's complicated. But nothing to worry about." Her gaze focused on Evan. "Really. I swear. It's nothing."

There was a heavy pause. And then Nate said, his voice hollow, "Right. Nothing."

She whipped her head around to look at him. He was watching her with the very worst emotion on earth written all over his face.

Disappointment.

Hannah couldn't bear the sight of it. It triggered a tight iron mesh in her mind, one that covered her thoughts like an unnavigable blanket. If she'd battled through the barrier, she'd have found reasonable notions like, *This isn't that big of a deal,* or, *You should stop and let yourself breathe through this panic,* or even, *Nate would never hurt you. Ever. And you know it.* Those truths were all lurking, somewhere, in her head. But Hannah couldn't see them, couldn't hear them, couldn't find them. So they might as well have not been there at all.

"I'm... I'm going to find Ruth now," she managed. For some reason, those magic words made Zach and Evan step aside as she hurried back into the house. Which was lucky, because they obviously hadn't believed anything else she'd just said.

She found Ruth in a dark and quiet corner of the living room, clearly having a grand old time staring into space and muttering to herself. Hannah was almost sorry to interrupt, but desperate times called for desperate measures—and her brain melting in the flames of burning panic before sliding out of her ears like goo definitely qualified as *desperate times.* She grabbed her sister's hand, ignoring the curious stares around them, and tugged her towards the door.

Ruth blinked once, cocked her head, and followed without question.

It was the silence between them, reassuring and familiar as the feel of Ruth's hand in hers, that let Hannah maintain her composure. Until they finally reached the front door and opened it to find Rae on the doorstep, her hand raised as if to knock.

"Oh!" she said. "Hannah! I'm so sorry I'm late. I was being—hey, are you okay?"

Hannah had lost count of the times she'd been asked that question tonight. But she'd never, not once, answered like this:

"No."

CHAPTER TWENTY-TWO

"WELL," Evan said pleasantly. "You have about thirty seconds before I lose my temper and punch you in the face. I recommend you use those seconds to explain."

"Hey," Zach frowned. "He's my brother. I'll punch him in the face."

"No-one's punching me in the face," Nate gritted out.

Evan snorted. "That's what you think."

"Oh, for fuck's sake. You know what? Go for it. Hit me. Maybe that'll feel better than watching her run off like I'm a fucking leper." Nate tunnelled his fingers through his hair and turned around, staring into the garden's moonlit shadows. He sucked in a breath and forced his galloping thoughts to calm.

"It's nothing," she'd said, her voice light and even. Hannah was a terrible liar. He always knew when she was talking shit.

But when she'd said those words, it sounded as if she

meant them. And all of a sudden, Nate wasn't sure if he knew her as well as he thought.

You're in love. People in love have bad judgement. People in love lie to themselves. People in love create fantasy worlds where everything is wonderful and the object of their affections feels the same, but you know Hannah's been weird this week, and you've felt her drifting away from you, and...

"Hey," Evan snapped. "I'm not fucking around. I don't appreciate people taking advantage of my family."

It didn't make the slightest bit of sense, but the accusation in Evan's tone made all of Nate's worries disappear. Every last gnawing hesitation in his mind faded, replaced by the only truth that made sense.

Hannah kissed him when he couldn't sleep. Hannah made fun of the shitty stick-and-poke tattoo on his knee. Hannah was his. They weren't *nothing*. And if she'd managed to convince herself they were, that was okay. It was easy to lose sight of something when you kept it in the dark. He'd find her and hold her hand and tell her that he loved her until she remembered that they were everything.

He turned to face the two suspicious men, spreading his hands helplessly. "I love her. I am in love with Hannah. We are together. Our situation right now is not ideal, but life usually isn't. I'm working on it. Okay?"

The silence that fell was punctuated only by the music floating out through the patio doors and an owl's occasional hoot. For long, tense moments, Nate studied Evan's glare and Zach's scowl.

Then he lost his patience.

"If you have something to say, say it. If not, get the fuck out of my way. I need to find her."

Finally, Zach shrugged. "Alright. I mean, I do technically trust you not to be a creepy, manipulative predator. I just really like Hannah."

"So do I," Nate ground out, turning to look at a stony-faced Evan. "Which is why I need to go and find her."

Evan nodded, his eyes still narrowed. Then he stepped aside. Which was good, because Nate *would* knock the guy out if absolutely necessary, but it would probably take some work. Plus, Hannah wouldn't like it.

"If you hurt her," Evan said, "I will make a trophy out of your balls."

Nate shrugged as he strode past the other men towards the house. "Pretty sure she'd do that herself."

He heard Evan's snort of laughter just before he stepped into the kitchen.

HANNAH HAD NEVER SAT on a curb before, but she was sitting on a curb right now. Which was one of multiple signs that her mind had become an absolute shambles.

"There we go, honey," Rae soothed, her hand circling Hannah's back. "Let it out."

Oh, yes. That was another sign of Hannah's deteriorating mental state. She was *crying*. In *public*. Well, on a darkened street in the middle of the night, but still. Beside her, Ruth sat in awkward silence, radiating sympathetic mortification.

After a disturbingly long and snotty period of time, Hannah managed to stem the flow of rogue tears—they did *not* have a permit or a licence, damn them—and wipe her nose. If rubbing her wrist over her damp face could qualify as wiping her nose. Good God, she was acting like Josh.

Oh, Josh. And Beth. It had started to hit her over the last few days—when she'd realised that this arrangement between she and Nate couldn't last—that she might actually lose her job. She might not be the kids' nanny anymore. She might never stir marmalade into their porridge, or solve their arguments with empirical evidence, or move their toys in the night to convince them that fairies were watching them sleep.

Aaaand now she was crying again. Shit.

"Oh dear," Rae said. "Well, better out than in!"

Ruth seemed to disagree. She caught Hannah's wet face in both hands, locked their gazes together like magnets, and said sternly, "Han. Stop that."

The sobs shaking Hannah's body slowed down. The jagged feeling in her gut, was, for a moment, numbed. She managed to frown and tut, "Bugger off."

Ruth patted her on the head like a dog. "Good. Very good."

There was a pause as Hannah waited for more tears to come. They did not. Perhaps because she was scowling so ferociously. "You're just trying to irritate me," she accused, swiping at her wet cheeks.

"I don't have to try," Ruth said, very seriously. Then she looked over Hannah's shoulder at Rae and asked, "Who is this?"

Rae smiled slightly. "Charmed, I'm sure."

"Rae, this is my sister, Ruth Kabbah. Ruth, this is Rae…" She trailed off.

"McRae," Rae supplied.

Hannah stared. "Your name is... Rae... McRae?"

"God, no. Can you imagine?" Apparently, Rae didn't feel the need to explain further, because she moved swiftly on. "Now, why don't you tell us what's got you so upset?"

Ah. See, this was one of the many reasons why Hannah preferred to keep all emotions to herself. People couldn't just let you have a minor breakdown, then move on with their day. They were always demanding *explanations*. Hannah didn't like explaining herself. To anyone. Ever. It was just so exhausting.

But for some reason, right now she felt an almost physical urge to spill her guts. The whole sorry story was on the tip of her tongue. She looked from Rae's sympathetic face to Ruth's worried little frown, and decided—well. There was no reason *not* to tell them, now was there?

"Nate and I..." Oh dear. Telling was harder than she'd thought.

But, to her surprise, Rae cut her off with a triumphant, "Aha! I knew it!"

"Knew what?" Ruth demanded.

"Your sister is sleeping with Nate!" Then, after a moment, she added, "You *are* sleeping with him, right? Please tell me you are."

Hannah winced. "Yep. And... And Evan and Zach just caught us kissing in the garden, and they wanted to know what was happening so I tried to pretend it was... I don't even know what! Nothing, I suppose. But Nate looked so upset. And I've been upsetting him all week, I know I have, but I just can't stop thinking about my parents and I don't even know if we're really together and everything is *shit*." She dragged in a shaky breath, then looked hesitantly over at Ruth. What would she see on her little sister's face? Horror? Shame? Disappointment?

…A small, satisfied smile? Wait, that wasn't right.

Except, apparently, it was. Because Ruth's tiny smile swelled into a full-on grin before Hannah's eyes. And then, just to erase any doubt, she said, "You're dating Nate? That's lovely, Han. He has very big hands."

"That's what I thought," Hannah said. "The hands! Hands are so—wait, hang on. First of all, we aren't *dating*. And second, aren't you… I don't know, disgusted by my lack of principles?"

Ruth blinked. And blinked again. And then, finally, said, "Oh. You mean because you work for him?"

"Yes. That is exactly what I mean."

"Well. Do you actually like him, or are you doing it for other reasons?"

"I love him," Hannah said. *Oh, wait. Fuck.* She clapped a hand over her mouth as if to drag the words back in. "*Like* him!" she corrected, voice muffled. "I meant I like him! That's all."

Ruth and Rae shared a rather meaningful look before murmuring nonsense like *"Ah,"* and, *"Of course"*. Apparently, they were glossing over the whole *love* thing, for now. But that didn't help, because Hannah knew the truth, and it was beyond depressing. Her lower lip trembled like something out of a fucking *Oliver Twist* adaptation as she blurted, "But it's doomed!"

Oh, the drama. How very embarrassing.

Rae's hand resumed its soothing, circular passage over her back. "Why's that, poppet?"

"I—I—I don't *know*." Hannah admitted. "It just *feels* like it is. He says all these lovely things, but the more he says them, the more I feel like it just can't be real. Because nothing is *official*, and… and who gets lovely things, really? Who gets lovely, romantic things? In real life? No-one!"

"Evan's pretty romantic," Ruth said.

Hannah turned to stare at her sister in astonishment. "…Is he?"

"Yeah." Ruth leant back against the pavement and squinted up at the moon. "He's always doing romantic shit."

Actually, now Hannah thought about it, that wasn't really surprising. "Oh. I always thought you'd hate that kind of thing."

Ruth shrugged.

Huh. "Well, to be honest, I do understand that people have… that," Hannah admitted. "I *do*. I know they do. It's just—"

"You don't think you can," Rae said quietly.

Hannah looked up to find the older woman staring at the moon, like Ruth. Apparently, they were all moon-starers now. She might as well join in. Gazing up at the luminous slice of pearl, Hannah sighed. "No," she agreed. "I don't think I can."

"Because you're insecure," Rae said.

"What? No. I'm not insecure. I'm Hannah fucking Kabbah."

"You are quite insecure," Ruth agreed mildly.

Hannah turned to glare at her sister. "What on *earth* are you talking about?"

"Well, you pin all your self-worth on external validation, you have to be the best at everything to consider yourself even slightly accomplished, and you apparently don't think someone can like you enough to put up with a week of weird behaviour and an awkward moment in a garden."

Hannah stared at her sister. Or rather, the thing that *looked* like her sister, but was undoubtedly an observant and talkative alien who had been lurking among them, wearing Ruth's skin and learning their ways.

Then Alien Ruth asked, "By the way, how does Nate feel about sleeping with his nanny?"

"Not great." Somehow, Hannah managed to answer while grappling with the astonishing suggestion that she might… actually… be… insecure?

"Well, have you considered mentioning the fact that you don't *need* the job because you have £500,000 sitting in a trust fund that you refuse to use?"

"No, because I'm *still refusing to use it,*" Hannah snapped. "That trust fund is the physical embodiment of our father's guilt. I'm not taking money from someone who doesn't give a shit about me."

"Why not?" Rae piped up. "Speaking from experience, it feels really fucking good. Spending my ex's cash is basically a mini-orgasm every time."

Ruth snorted out a laugh. "I like her. She has a sensible attitude."

"*I* have a sensible attitude," Hannah insisted.

"Do you? Seriously, Han, isn't there anything you want to do with that money?"

"Can I focus on one problem at a time? I'm trying to figure out what my rampant insecurities mean for the state of my weird non-relationship."

"Well, I think you're about to find out," Rae murmured.

Hannah followed Rae's gaze until she saw a tall, broad

figure moving towards them, wreathed in shadow but still unmistakable. As he came closer, she made out the tense set of Nate's shoulders, the hands shoved into his pockets, the gleam of moonlight on his pitch-black hair.

They watched him approach in silence, as if all three of them had frozen.

"Hey," he said. His voice was low, rougher than usual.

The women had wandered for a street or two before they'd finally settled on this particular curb, so Nate must have been wandering around, too, searching for them. And yet, his voice held all of its usual patience, despite its hoarse edge.

But Hannah couldn't bring herself to meet his eyes. Not while her mind was helpfully informing her—*way* too late— that the ominous feeling in her chest could have been resolved days ago. All she'd ever had to do, she realised, was ask Nate where he saw this whole thing going. *Oh*, her brain said sweetly. *Didn't I suggest that course of action before? No? Was I too busy throwing you into random panics and making you disbelieve every reassurance he gave? Sorry.*

Wow. Hannah's brain was a fucking traitor.

And so were her sister and her friend, because both women rose like pop-up tents and scrambled for excuses to leave Hannah and Nate alone. Well; Rae scrambled. Ruth just said, "I'm gonna go," and went.

But not before giving Hannah one last, questioning look. A look that said, *Is this okay?*

Hannah nodded slowly in response. And it wasn't a lie.

When Rae and Ruth trotted off down the street, Nate sat. Usually, when he sat beside her, he'd touch her. Throw an arm over her shoulders, or take her hand, or fiddle with her hair. Now, though, he left space between them, his hands on the tarmac instead of on her.

Maybe yesterday, or even an hour ago, that distance would've made her think the worst. Today, it made her think that she'd pushed him away like an absolute donkey and now she needed to make him feel better.

Hannah wasn't the only one who deserved reassurance, after all.

But before she could speak, he beat her to the punch. "I'm sorry."

"*You're* sorry?" she echoed, finally allowing herself to study his face. That full lower lip was snagged between his teeth, a frown furrowing his dark brows. His jaw was tight, his gaze shadowed—and, yeah, apologetic. She just had no idea why. "What do you have to be sorry for?"

He ran a hand through his hair and the familiar motion squeezed at something tender in her chest. "A lot," he said. "Like… fucking around, dragging you outside when we have a house full of people. I know I shouldn't have put you in that position."

Hannah shook her head. "Nate, I *asked* you to kiss me."

"And I should've said no. Because I knew you weren't okay." He sighed. "I shouldn't have done any of the shit I did tonight. I've been chasing you hard, the last few days, because I thought I was losing you. And in case I haven't made it obvious, I don't want to lose you." His eyes, darker in the low light, pinned hers. "Ever."

His voice had been so steady, but it cracked on that last word. Her heart cracked a little bit, too. She couldn't sit here like they were strangers when it was starting to sink in that she'd… hurt him. She'd actually hurt him.

This, she decided, was the worst feeling in the world. Not disappointment, not losing, not weakness, or any of the shit she'd always cared about so much. Hurting Nate. That was rock-bottom.

Ignoring the tiny pieces of gravel that dug through the fabric of her skirt, Hannah shuffled over the pavement and climbed awkwardly into his lap. The minute his arms settled around her, the slow, ominous tick of that clock in her head finally stopped. And nothing happened. No bomb was detonated, nobody died or changed their mind or threw her away. She pressed a hand to his cheek and watched his eyes slide shut, as if her touch soothed him the way his presence soothed her. Then she began.

"I haven't been honest with you." The way he stiffened at those words, as if expecting a blow, filled her with shame. He was wary. She'd made him wary. "You were right. I wasn't okay. I've been so anxious lately—*way* more than usual. I should probably see my doctor again; I haven't been in a while. But..." she shook her head. "It's not just that. I mean, that didn't come out of nowhere. I've been so scared, Nate, because I realised that I love you. And I've never seen any evidence that loving someone can work out for me. I think the circumstances and... and keeping it a secret, that just made it worse, because it feels so fragile between us. Like smoke."

The words came out so easily, now, when they'd seemed impossible to reach just yesterday. Maybe it was because she felt more like herself after talking to someone. After crying with someone. After confessing. Hannah had never been good with secrets—not big secrets, not suffocating, *emotional* secrets. Setting all those words free felt like setting herself free too. When she looked up to check Nate's expression, she was slightly hesitant, but she wasn't choked by some nameless, fearsome dread.

And even her hesitation disappeared when she saw the huge, dopey grin on his face. "What?" she asked, an answering smile spreading her lips without permission.

He shook his head. "Nothing, nothing. Keep going."

Hannah tapped a finger against his dimple. "I think I'm done, actually. So what's this about?"

"You…" He laughed, the sound a little flash of joy. "Did you just say you love me?"

Something warm and sweet started to glow in her chest. "Yeah. I did. Because, you know, I do."

His arms tightened around her. He kissed her cheek, and then her eyebrow, of all places. Then the side of her nose, her chin… Actually, he was just kissing her face indiscriminately. Hannah supposed she should stop him—it was undignified—but she was quite enjoying it.

He kissed her ear next, then whispered, "I love you, too."

The warmth in her chest gained the strength of a sunrise. "You do?"

"Of course I do." He ran his hands over her as if he just wanted to feel that she was there. Her sides, her arms, her thigh—whatever he could reach, he touched, smoothing his palms over her skin. And then he pulled her tight against his chest, buried his face against her hair, and breathed her in. "God, I love you. I love you so much, Hannah. I should've told you weeks ago."

"Weeks?" she squeaked.

"Weeks," he repeated firmly. "I didn't know you felt like this, love. I didn't know you were so worried. I'm sorry."

"It's not your fault," she said. Her words were kind of muffled, since her face was smushed against the massive slab of his chest, but the message seemed clear enough.

And then Nate released her—kind of. She wasn't smushed against his chest anymore, but she was still quite firmly in his lap. He cupped her cheeks in his hands with the sort of certainty that suggested he didn't plan on letting her go. "I'm telling you right now," he said softly, "that this is real. It doesn't get any more real than this. I am in love with you, and I'm not going anywhere."

She laughed shakily. "Even if I'm really insecure and may or may not have daddy issues?"

He leant in until their noses touched. "You could have all the issues in the world, sweetheart. I don't give a shit. Just tell me when they're drowning you, okay?"

She dragged in a breath. It sounded disturbingly like a teary sort of sniff, but that couldn't be right. Surely, she'd cried enough for the next year, at least? "I think you have enough to worry about without handling my random neuroses."

"Hannah. When I can't sleep because my mind's moving too fast, you hold my hand and remind me to breathe. When my head hurts and my vision blurs too much to read, you do it for me. Even when you think I shouldn't be reading at all."

"Well," she muttered, "spending all your free time researching sarcoidosis can't be healthy."

"But you let me. And you help me. And you pour coffee down my throat the next morning, and you find ways to keep the kids quiet when my head pounds, and you make me smile when I want to cry. You keep me afloat. You keep everything and everyone afloat. Do you know how much I want to do that for you?"

She was starting to get that, yeah. Hence the sneaky little tears sliding down her face. "Um… okay. Okay."

"I know you can't magically start sharing your feelings," he said, "but I would probably die of happiness if you tried."

She huffed out a laugh. "Cool. Right. Good. Fabulous. Um… Nate, I'm so sorry if I hurt you. I never want to hurt you. Not even a little bit. Not even by accident. I just, I really fucking love you."

"Good," he said. "Because I really fucking love you, too." His hands slid into her hair. "So kiss me."

She did. And there was no creeping panic, no ticking clock, no tightly contained fear. Just Nate's soft, smiling mouth, and happiness.

CHAPTER TWENTY-THREE

Hannah: If you send me any more dog pics I'm blocking your number.
Rae: How are you not loving this? Where is your HEART, woman?!

"IF YOU THINK you're sleeping without me tonight," he said, "you've had too much champagne."

"I haven't had any champagne, genius." Hannah was standing in her bedroom doorway, hands on her hips, glare at full capacity. But he could see a slight twitch at the corner of her mouth, the only sign that she was fighting a smile.

Nate loved that smile.

It had barely left her face, in one way or another, since they'd returned to the party a couple of hours ago. Since then, they'd said goodbye to guests, checked on the kids and his mother, completely given up on the cleaning—which meant Hannah really *must* be tired—and gotten ready for bed.

Apparently, she hadn't realised that 'bed', to Nate, officially meant *A soft, horizontal place that includes Hannah.*

"Let me in," he murmured, reaching out to trace the slight curve of her lips.

"Nathaniel," she whispered back, "your *mother* is in the house."

He sighed. "This is going to be so much easier when everyone knows about us."

"And when would that be?"

"Soon. Come to bed and I'll tell you."

She hesitated, her eyes widening slightly. What with everything that had happened tonight, Nate still hadn't told her about his plan.

"I won't fall asleep," he reminded her. "You know I won't. I just want to talk."

She gave him a look that was somehow skeptical and flirtatious all at once. "Right," she drawled. "*Talk.*" But that hint of a smile became the real thing, even as she rolled her eyes. "Well, fine, as long as you don't fall asleep. You have to leave before anyone wakes up."

"Whatever you want."

Hannah shook her head as she turned away. He followed her into the room, shutting the door behind them, and watched for a moment as she climbed into bed. It was like watching a dream come to life. Her room was quiet and cool and painfully tidy, as always. The window overlooking the garden was pushed wide, letting the fragrant night air in, and her bedside lamp cast a warm glow over her brown skin and white sheets. She settled back against the cushions in her cute little PJs, her face free of makeup, her hair all wrapped up in that scarf.

This was what he wanted out of life. His kids snoring like jackhammers down the hall, his mother safe and sound, his brother sending him such loving texts as *I only thought you were a creep for 0.05 seconds at most*, and Hannah Kabbah waiting for him in bed.

Nate took his time sliding in beside her, wondering if it was possible to memorise an experience perfectly—from the feel of the sheets against his skin, to the sound of the mattress shifting as she rolled over to face him. He didn't want to forget this moment, ever.

He'd been in love with this woman for a fucking century, but he'd never lain in bed with her. She'd always avoided that, no matter what time it was or who was in the house. It had been one of the many ways, he realised, that she'd held herself quietly apart. But now she reached out to trace her fingers over his chest, and her feet tangled with his under the sheets, and everything was absolutely fucking perfect.

"As part of my new sharing attitude," she murmured, "I should tell you that it's mildly alarming when you do the whole 'mysterious' thing."

He kissed the top of her head. "Sorry. Okay, let me spit it out. I was thinking of ways that we could fix the boss/employee thing, and I kept hitting the same issues. No matter what happens, you still need a job, and I still need a nanny."

"You don't need a nanny," she said. "I'd watch the kids for free."

"Jesus, Hannah. That would be even more ethically questionable than what I'm doing now."

She laughed, and the sound made him smile. "Fair point. So… what, then?"

"Well, as you know, I have your agreed-upon salary sitting around the house already. And, as of last week, I also have several au pairs flooding my email with references. So I was thinking, maybe… you take the money, I get a new nanny, and everyone's good. For the time-being, at least." He studied Hannah's face, which was, at best, blank. "What do you think?"

She rolled her lips inward, her frown more considering than anything else. "I… don't know."

"Okay. Talk to me."

"Well, first of all, I don't want just anyone watching the kids."

He bit back a smile. "It's all arranged through this specialist company with a mile-long vetting process. But I was thinking maybe you could help me choose someone?"

"How do the interviews work? Like, Skype?"

"Yeah."

She wrinkled her nose. "I want to see this company. Maybe call them and talk to someone…" she trailed off, shaking her head. "We can work on that part. I like the idea, though."

"So, you don't feel like I'm getting rid of you?"

She gave him a gentle smile. "No, honey. I mean, you are getting rid of me. Except not really, because I'm still going to stick my nose in your business all the time."

He kissed the aforementioned nose, and said, "Good."

"I'm not sure about the money thing, though."

Nate was prepared for this argument. In fact, he was prepared for all arguments, because he'd planned this discussion very carefully. Of course, in the end, it had still gone awry—but things were running much more smoothly now.

"It's only fair," he said. "We signed a contract, right? You're past the probation period, and you haven't been dismissed. You're not choosing to leave, you haven't broken any terms—"

"Haven't I?" she asked innocently. "Because I don't think snuggling was in the contract."

"We're not snuggling."

She gave his arm, which was wrapped rather tightly around her waist, a pointed look. And then she shifted her knee, which appeared to be trapped between his thighs. And then she kissed his chin, and Nate realised that they were practically on top of each other.

"Okay," he admitted. "We may be snuggling."

"It's more like *you're* snuggling *me*, really."

"Snuggling is a group activity. We're snuggling."

"Weeeelllll…"

"If you keep arguing, I'm going to kiss you."

"Oh no," she deadpanned. "Please. Stop. Don't."

He snorted. "Shut up. You can't distract me, Hannah. We have a plan to discuss."

"Ah, yes. The money issue. Well, I get what you're saying about the contract, and I would love to take some of this random house cash off your hands, because knowing it's in here makes me beyond nervous—"

"Why?"

She stared at him as if he'd asked the silliest question in the world. "Um. What if the house burns down? What if we're burgled? And so on, and so forth? Banks exist for a reason, Nate."

"If it bothers you so much, just take it."

"All of it? I don't think *that's* in my contract."

"Well, you have to take something." He sighed. "Come on, sweetheart. Work with me here."

"I don't know. I might not need it, anyway."

Nate frowned. "What do you mean?"

"Well, I don't think I mentioned this before, but I have a trust fund. It's not huge, as trust funds go, but I could definitely live off it for a while."

"Why the hell do you have a trust fund?" On the heels of that question, common sense arrived to smack him with the answer. "Oh. Ah... is it something to do with your dad?"

"Mmhm." Her tone was casual, but their bodies were too closely intertwined for him to miss the tension running through her.

"Okay," he said slowly. "So you're not sure if you want to use it?"

"Exactly. I've never used it. Ever. I suppose that makes me prideful."

"Not necessarily," he said gently. "But even if it did... is pride a sin?"

"Yes," she said promptly. "Literally, yes."

"Oh. Well, so is pre-marital sex, right?"

She glared. "You're really not helping."

"Sorry, love." He kissed the little arrow that appeared between her brows, until the frown was smoothed out. "Honestly, I understand. I wouldn't want to take anything from my dad, either. Yours is a twat, mine's a twat, they're all twats and you're entitled to deal with that twatness however you like."

"You think?"

"I do. You can spend the money he gave you, or you can give it away, or you can burn it. Symbolically, I mean. Please don't actually burn it. People are starving." When she bit back a laugh, her hesitance melting away, he felt a surge of happiness. Funny how making Hannah smile felt like a lifetime achievement every time. "Seriously, though, it's up to you. I want to pay you, and I think it's right to pay you, but that's your choice too. Think about it. Okay?"

She nodded slowly. "Okay. I will."

"Good. And in the meantime, I was thinking *maybe* we could tell our families, at least, about our plans."

"That sounds good," she agreed. "Although after tonight, the only family members who don't know are our parents and the kids."

"Actually, Josh and Beth have both asked me if you're my girlfriend. Multiple times. And I did say no, but I don't think they believed me."

"Girlfriend? Oh, Jesus."

"Kids are smart." He shrugged. And then bit back a groan as her fingers, which were gently circling his chest, grazed his nipple. Fuck.

"So, it's just our parents," she said. "I'm not sure how my mother will take it."

"Oh?" he croaked.

"You never really know with her. She's absolutely baffling, and this thing between us is... odd. Hard to explain." Hannah shrugged. "What about yours?"

"Not sure," he managed. Then he cleared his throat as a

sudden realisation struck him. "By the way, Hannah, you do know that we're a couple, right?"

"Well," she said slowly, "I know that we're exclusively sleeping together…"

"No. We're exclusively *dating*." Which, he was beginning to realise, may not have been explicitly clear. "You didn't think we were dating?"

She pursed her lips, her gaze sliding away from his. Then she frowned and squinted down at their bodies as if she could see straight through the sheets. "Do you have an erection right now?"

"Stop staring at my dick when I'm trying to romance you."

"That's you romancing me? *By the way, we're together?*"

"Well," he said reasonably, "if I'd gone with, *Dearest Hannah, light of my life, would you do me the great honour of becoming my girlfriend?* you might freak out."

"Girlfriend?" she squeaked.

"You are a girl, right?"

"I'm thirty, Nate. *You're* thirty. You're a widower, for God's sake!"

"My very mature girlfriend, then. My very *adult* girl-friend. My womanfriend, if you will."

She laughed so hard, he had to cover her mouth. They were trying to be quiet, after all. And if he just so happened to cover her mouth with *his*…

Well, that was called creative problem solving.

WHEN NATE WOKE up the next morning, the first thing he

felt was pure joy. It shone through him as if his heart had become a little sun, pumping golden light through his veins instead of blood. Because he woke up in Hannah's bed, with her arm slung over his chest and the soft sound of her snores in his ears. Hannah *snored*. He was ridiculously pleased about this fact.

And then he was suddenly, instantly horrified. Because he'd just woken up, which meant he'd been *asleep*. Long enough to feel better than half-dead, even. Which was too fucking long, judging by the soft glow filtering through Hannah's open window—and the distant sound of his early bird children, nattering away somewhere in the house.

Nate barely resisted the urge to bolt upright. Instead, he slid Hannah's arm gently off him, eased out of bed, and padded quietly out of the room.

A quick check proved that the kids were indeed up, their beds rumpled and abandoned. So, apparently, was his mother. Fan-fucking-tastic. Nate threw on some clothes that may or may not have matched and hurried downstairs. He found them all in the kitchen, the kids eating porridge and his mother standing by the kettle.

"Daddy!" Josh grinned. "Grandma made a love heart with my jam!"

"She didn't make a love heart with *my* jam," Beth sniffed, "because that's for *babies*."

"I don't know where she's getting these strange ideas," Shirley said mildly.

"She has this friend at school," Nate murmured. "Lily." Lily had very strong opinions about what was and was not babyish, and Beth seemed to take those opinions quite seriously. But Hannah said the whole thing would blow over.

He kissed his daughter's head, and then his son's, before meeting his mother's eye. "Morning, Ma. How are you?"

"Very well, thank you, darling. Coffee?"

"No thanks."

She arched a brow. "Cutting down?"

"Trying. Thanks for feeding the kids. I overslept."

"Where?" she asked.

"Sorry?"

Her voice softened even as her eyes narrowed. "*Where* did you oversleep, Nathaniel? Because it wasn't in your room."

Ah. He ran a hand through his hair. "Right. Well, this doesn't usually happen. Ever, actually. It never happens." He cast a wary look over at the kids, who appeared to be discussing the merits of raspberry jam versus marmalade, before continuing. "But I fell asleep with Hannah. Because we are together. Which I was going to tell you, at some point." He cleared his throat. "And she's not going to work for me anymore. As soon as we find someone else. You know, because we're together." Did he already say that? He'd already said that.

There was a slight pause, before, much to Nate's relief, his mother smiled. "Well," she said, patting his cheek. "I did think you liked her a little too much. But as long as you're not taking advantage of the poor girl."

He sighed. "It's kind of disturbing, how everyone seems to think I would."

"Life is full of surprises, darling, and most of them are unpleasant. But I'm glad you aren't one of those." She looked thoughtful. "And I do rather *like* that girl, you know.

Both of those Kabbah girls. They're a credit to their mother. Oh, does Patience know? She's in my bookclub."

"Not yet, no."

Shirley laughed. "I see. Well, I suppose I'll just have to keep my mouth shut." Then the humour in her eyes faded and she raised a hand to touch the cord around his neck. Beneath his T-shirt, Nate's wedding ring hung warm against his chest. "I am pleased," she said gently, "that you feel so strongly about someone. Strongly enough to take risks."

"So am I," he murmured. He didn't explain that he was in love, or warn his mother that he'd be proposing to Hannah as soon as he was convinced she'd say yes. He didn't need to. Shirley would see for herself, soon enough.

Everyone would.

WHEN HANNAH TOLD her mother that she was, in fact, dating the man she'd been working for over the last few months, Patience's response was short. Resplendent on the cushioned throne that was her favourite armchair, her attention torn quite fully from *Deal or No Deal*, she stared at her eldest daughter for three long seconds.

And then she said, "You will bring him to dinner."

So, a week later, Hannah brought him to dinner.

Not so long ago, the Kabbah dining table had been half-empty every Sunday. On the day Hannah dragged Nate to her mother's house, leaving the kids under Zach's question-able care, the table was almost filled to capacity. Evan and

Ruth sat on one side, Hannah and Nate on the other, and Patience settled at its head.

Where she proceeded to display a side of her personality that even her daughters had never seen before.

It began shortly after grace, when everyone else took their first mouthful of food while Patience stared darkly at Nate and asked, "How many nannies have you had, Nathaniel?"

He choked down a mouthful of rice. "Uh… Just Hannah, Ms. Kabbah."

"Most of the youngsters around here call me Aunty," Patience said.

Hannah started to relax.

"But you may indeed call me Ms. Kabbah."

Hannah stopped relaxing.

Across the table, Ruth gave her a wide-eyed stare that might have been comical if it hadn't reflected Hannah's own alarm. She then performed a series of utterly obvious head bobs that Hannah interpreted to mean something like, *"Is Mum on crack?"*

Hannah responded with a minute brow lift that meant, *"Possibly. Prepare to seek medical attention."* Under the table, she gave Nate's rigid thigh a reassuring pat.

"Hannah," Patience said in severe and unfamiliar tones. "I see no reason for your hands to be anything other than visible during this meal."

Was it possible to die of embarrassment? Yes. Clearly it was. Because Hannah was literally dying, right this second.

Turning her stare away from her eldest daughter and back to Nate, Patience spoke again. "What do you do, Nathaniel?"

"I'm a photographer," Nate said. "Though I work more in creative consultancy, these days."

"Hmm." Patience arched a brow. Hannah didn't even know her mother *could* arch a brow. "That doesn't sound like a real job."

"Mother!"

"Yes, Hannah?"

"Will you just let him eat?"

"Of course, darling. I am only making conversation." Patience gave her usual placid smile and looked down at her food, finally picking up her cutlery. Hannah's heart rate slowed. Then Patience added casually, "Of course, *he* could have simply let you work, but—"

The whole table spoke at once. Hannah threw down her fork and snapped, "Stop, or we're leaving."

Evan, bless him, said gently, "Patience, I don't think—"

And Ruth bellowed over them all, "For God's sake, Mum. Get over it."

Patience shrugged her narrow shoulders, her expression unapologetic. "This is my house. I will say whatever I wish."

Hannah had been prepared for some minor discomfort, but she was not even slightly ready for this. At all. She jerked back her chair and stood, grabbing some part of Nate —maybe his hand, possibly his arm, potentially a fistful of his shirt—as she made her escape. She dragged him out of the room without looking back, and didn't stop until they were both safely trapped in the downstairs toilet. She locked the door.

And then she looked at him. Blinked. Looked again. Blinked harder. Looked a third time, sure that her vision must be faulty.

But no. She was not mistaken. Nate was definitely doubled over in silent laughter.

Relief and disbelief flooded her buzzing mind. *"What* is so funny?" she demanded, her voice hushed. She was trying to be outraged—how dare he laugh while she was having a minor internal crisis? — but, as always, the sight of his smile brought hers out in response.

"She's you," he whispered back in between chuckles. "She is literally you."

Hannah gaped. "My mother is nothing like me."

"She's exactly like you."

"She lives on another planet! She doesn't notice anything or anyone! She is physically incapable of concern, stress, anxiety, or any emotion stronger than mild amusement and general contentment!"

"Unless," Nate said, his laughter finally calming, "she thinks her children are in trouble."

Hannah paused, those words sinking in. "Oh. Oh. I suppose you're right. Hmm." She cocked her head. "That's actually rather sweet."

"I agree." Nate slung an arm around her shoulders and pulled her closer, kissing her cheek. "Are you okay?"

She thought about it for a moment. "Yes."

"Not stressing out?"

"Not really."

"Not worried I'm going to disappear because your mother said photography isn't a real job?"

She snorted. "Should I be?"

"No." His gaze caught hers, searing as blue flame. "You don't need to worry about me. Ever." He ran a finger over Hannah's collarbone, up her throat, along the line of her jaw. Her eyes fluttered shut as a trail of electricity followed his touch, skating over her skin and setting her alight.

Until he added, "And I'm going to tell your mother the same thing."

Hannah's eyes popped open. "Tell my *mother?*"

"Yep." He winked, kissed her forehead, and unlocked the door. Leaving Hannah to stand alone in the loo and wonder if everyone in Ravenswood had lost their minds today, or if the phenomenon was confined to her mother's house.

NATE MIGHT UNDERSTAND the source of Patience Kabbah's animosity, but that didn't make it any easier to sit at her table again and meet her eye. See, he kind of needed Hannah's mother to like him. Because Hannah, whether she realised it or not, adored her mother. And Nate couldn't be the thing that caused problems between them.

So he held Patience's gaze and said, "I'd just like to make a few things clear."

She gave him a glare that reminded him of Hannah's, if Hannah's were powerful enough to blow up the fucking sun. Across the table, Ruth and Evan practically leapt to their feet. "We'll be in the kitchen," Evan said, before giving Nate a sympathetic look. Which was reassuring, since not so long ago he'd wanted to punch Nate in the face.

"Bye," Ruth muttered. She picked up her plate and kept eating, even as she hurried out of the room.

Which left Nate, Patience, and the monumental weight of a mother's disapproval. Hannah, apparently, was still hovering in the toilet. Possibly hyperventilating, so he'd made this quick.

"Ms. Kabbah," he said, "I completely understand why you don't like me. I have kids. I get it."

"It is not that I dislike you," she said sharply. "I am friends with your mother, you know. I think—I *thought* that you were a lovely boy. But I will not have you hurting my Hannah."

"I know," he said. "But I'm not going to hurt her. I love her."

She cocked her head. "How convenient."

"Actually, it was extremely *inconvenient*, all things considered. Things would've been a lot simpler if I could just stop loving Hannah. But I can't, and I don't want to. I'd rather walk over glass every day for the rest of my life than give her up." He sat back, watching a series of unreadable emotions pass over the suspicious woman's face. "If you want to—if you *need* to—you can spend all year needling me. And the year after that. And the decade after that. Because I'll still be here."

She studied him with narrowed eyes, her mouth a razor-sharp line. Then, finally, she said, "If you will be here so very long, I suppose you may call me Patience."

He tried not to grin even as relief blossomed in his heart. "Thank you. Patience."

She flicked him an arch look. "Go to find my children. I cannot believe they are running all over the house during dinner. These girls." She shook her head despairingly and picked up her fork as if nothing had happened.

At which point, Nate gave up on holding back his smile.

~

A COUPLE OF HOURS LATER, Hannah and Nate wound their way through Ravenswood's meandering streets. The afternoon sun had become the low, ripe disc of evening. Its glow warmed Hannah almost as much as the feel of Nate's fingers laced through hers.

"I don't know how," she said, "but you really saved that nightmare."

His lips quirked. "Your mother and I had a talk."

"About what?"

"My undying devotion."

"Ah." She chuckled. "Well, it worked."

"I should hope so. I meant every word of it."

She faltered for a moment, her steps slowing, her eyes wide as she looked sharply up at him. "You… did?"

"Yep." He pulled them to a complete stop and turned to face her. And then, to her absolute horror—and, disturbingly, her slight excitement—he sank down onto his knees. In the street. The quiet, abandoned street, but still.

"What on earth are you doing?" she hissed. "Get up!"

"I can't." He took her hands. "I'm being dramatic."

"Nathaniel! Are you *proposing*?"

"No," he laughed, "but thanks for the enthusiasm."

Her cheeks heated. "Sorry. I just—"

"Hannah." He squeezed her hands. "When I propose—" she almost choked at *when* "—you will be warned well in advance so you can organise the whole thing to your satisfaction. Okay?"

Her heart swelled. "Really?"

"Really."

319

She was getting dangerously emotional, and all because he was going to let her arrange her own proposal. Oh, dear. "You're the best."

"I know." He dodged as she tried to flick his head. "Settle down, woman. I'm declaring myself, here."

"Oh, I see. Sorry. Do go on." She cleared her throat and tried to look demure, but it was difficult to maintain with an enormous smile splitting her face.

Nate kissed her hands, one at a time, before he began. "Hannah. I wasted a lot of time and made this whole thing harder than it needed to be by holding back. I didn't want to scare you off, I didn't want to move too fast, I didn't want to throw my feelings all over the place like confetti. But I'm not going to hold back anymore. Because I'm pretty sure that even if you do get overwhelmed, you won't shut me out —and if you did, I'd find a way to open you up again regardless."

She laughed, but the sound was choked by something that sounded disturbingly like tears.

"You," he said softly, "are my sunshine. You're my moon when I can't sleep. You're every star in the sky when I'm lost. You're a galaxy, and I am constantly in awe of you. I'm yours—completely, utterly—for as long as you'll have me. And I pray that's a long damn time, because I don't ever want to be without you."

It wasn't that Hannah *wanted* to sink to her knees along with him; it was more that she had to. Her legs kind of buckled. Plus, she suddenly needed more contact than just their joined hands. So she ignored the bite of gravel on her shins and knelt, throwing her arms around him, quiet sobs shaking her body.

"I love you," she choked out, her face buried against his shoulder. "I love you. Even when I can't tell you and I can't touch you and I can't think straight—"

"I know. I know."

"*Always*, Nate."

"I know." He threaded his hands through her hair, raising her head. She glimpsed the adoration in his eyes for a second before his lips met hers.

And then she felt it. With everything in her, she felt it.

EPILOGUE

A YEAR LATER

HANNAH GAVE her trust fund to Ruth. Ruth leant some of it back to Hannah. They were calling it an advance, since Hannah was writing and planning to self-publish a book based on her blog.

Writing wasn't always easy, but mental blocks were a hell of a lot more bearable when she was breathtakingly happy with every other aspect of her life. And especially when she was—*finally*—happy with herself. Even on days when the world seemed slightly grey or completely terrifying, that undercurrent of contentment made it easier to stay afloat.

Today wasn't one of those grey or terrifying days, though. Hannah left the local café she liked to work in and took a slow walk home in the summer sun, watching pairs of cabbage butterflies dance. By the time she made it back, it was just after four. But when Hannah stepped into a house that should be filled with childish chatter, she found it silent.

It was a mark of the progress she'd made that her first thought wasn't, *Oh dear, everyone's been brutally murdered.* That was only her *third* thought. "Clarisse?" she called, wondering if the kids' au pair had taken them out into the garden.

But it wasn't Clarisse who responded. Nate appeared at the top of the stairs, looking all handsome and smiley and— ugh, just too fucking good. "You're back," he said.

"Looks like it." She grinned up at him, any concerns she'd had disappearing. "Where is everyone?"

"Out," he replied helpfully. "Come up here, would you?"

"Why?" She came before he answered, because she wasn't worried. Hannah still didn't like mysteries, but she'd come to realise over the last year or so that Nate was never really being mysterious. Right now, for example, he was watching her with barely hidden excitement and a slight hint of nerves, everything he felt written all over his face.

And he answered promptly, too. "I have a present for you. I think you'll like it."

"I do love presents." She reached the top of the stairs and his arms slid around her waist. He kissed her, soft and slow and gentle, as if he could spend hours doing nothing else. Which, she knew, he could. Sometimes he did. The memory of those times, along with the teasing caress of his tongue, combined to send tingles of heat running over Hannah's skin.

But before he could really spark something, Nate pulled back. She studied the creases at the corners of his smiling eyes, the faint scars on his pale face, and felt her heart squeeze. She loved him so much. And somehow, loving him felt just as good as being loved *by* him. To call this sweet, secure sort of happiness a blessing felt like an understatement.

"Come on," he whispered, leading her towards the bedroom they now shared. After Clarisse had been hired, Hannah had moved out of Nate's house for almost eight months. But eventually he'd persuaded her to come back. She didn't regret it. She didn't believe she ever would.

Hannah entered the room expecting some extravagant surprise, but the neat and tidy space looked the same as usual. Except, she noticed, for a little leather book sitting in the centre of the bed. Moving closer, she picked it up and realised…

"This is a photo album."

"Yep," Nate said.

She bit her lip on a smile. "What's in it?"

"Three-hundred and sixty-five days."

Hannah arched a brow.

"That's how long it's been," he said, "since you told me I could take pictures of you."

Oh, fuck. "I… I forgot about that."

"I know you did." He smiled, slow and sexy, leaning against the doorframe. "But I didn't."

Well, crap. Looking at 365 photos of herself was not Hannah's idea of fun, but she loved Nate's pictures. And she loved the fact that Nate was taking pictures at all. He'd been doing so more and more ever since Shirley's symptoms had begun to improve, and nothing made Hannah happier.

So she wasn't going to refuse to look. That would just be childish. But she did sit down first, just in case the sight of her own awkwardness was painful enough to bowl her over.

Then she took a deep breath, opened the album, and looked at the first picture.

She knew it was her—or rather, the palm of her outstretched hand and the inside of her wrist. The garden formed a verdant backdrop, blades of grass standing out bright and sharp against her skin. Yes, it was definitely a picture of her. But something about it seemed too perfect, too bright and alive, to be anything as mundane as a slice of reality.

The next image was just as ethereal. The tips of her braids hung against the small of her back, dark plaits striking against her white shirt and scarlet skirt. She could see a thin band of brown skin where the two items of clothing didn't quite meet, and even that—just plain skin— seemed somehow…

"Magical," she murmured. Then she looked up, the question suddenly urgent. "How do you make normal things look so magical?"

He gave her a one-shouldered shrug, but his eyes were serious. "Maybe that's just you."

"Don't flatter me. It's some fancy, technological photography thing."

His lips twitched. "No comment."

"Come here. Sit with me."

He came over slowly. When he sank on to the bed beside her, she finally realised why he seemed slightly edgy.

So she leaned over to kiss his cheek. "I like them. Thank you."

Something about him relaxed, even as he shook his head. "You only just started."

"I already know I love them all. But I suppose," she sighed dramatically, "I'll look through the rest. Just to make sure."

He laughed and tugged one of her braids. "Go on, then."

So she did. She flicked through 365 pictures of herself, from her lipsticked mouth to the shadow of her profile in the moonlight, to Josh's legs dangling between hers as he sat on her lap. She saw 365 versions of herself through the eyes of a man who loved her. And when she was done, Hannah set the album carefully aside and threw herself—literally *threw* herself—at Nathaniel Davis.

He caught her, obviously.

They fell back against the bed, him laughing, her covering his face in kisses. "Hold on," he managed to say between chuckles. "I'm not done."

"Oh?"

"No. I just wanted to let you know that I'd like you to start planning your proposal. If you're amenable."

Was it possible to break your own face by smiling too hard? Hannah really hoped not. "I'm definitely amenable. Enthusiastic. Eager, even."

His brows shot up. "You are? For real?"

"For real." She ran the tip of her nose over his throat, his jaw, his cheekbone. Just touching him, simply because she could. "You're mine, and that isn't changing. Might as well make it legal."

With a wicked grin, he rolled them over until his body covered hers, his hard chest pinning her against the mattress. "I'm yours?"

"That's right." She pressed a kiss to his throat. "And I'm yours."

His answering whisper rolled over her skin like a touch. "No matter what."

The End.

AUTHOR'S NOTE

One thing I love about being an author is that my platform allows me to raise awareness. Of what? Well, of anything, because the world is a vast and terrifying place and there are always 50,000 things going on that we *should* know about, but usually don't.

In this book I am shamelessly raising awareness of sarcoidosis, which is an issue close to my heart. A lot of chronic illness sufferers are ignored or misdiagnosed due to our society's ableist attitudes. Over twenty years ago, my mother nearly died for that very reason. Doctors ignored her complaints of throat pain until the tumour growing in her windpipe almost suffocated her to death. Even after her emergency surgery, no-one thought to investigate what had *caused* that tumour.

Decades later, her mysterious illness returned with a vengeance. This time, she wasn't ignored—she was misdiagnosed with terminal lung cancer. That's how bad understanding and awareness of sarcoidosis is. Several doctors mistook it for *terminal lung cancer*. Eventually, of course, the truth was discovered. We've since found that she's far from the only one to suffer through that sort of mistake.

If you want to know more about sarcoidosis, check out this link: https://www.sarcoidosisuk.org

They're committed to informing and supporting sarcoidosis sufferers, as well as funding further research.

What I would love readers to take from this is not necessarily a burning passion for sarcoidosis research (though, on a selfish level, that would be great!). Rather, I want to emphasise how poor attitudes towards chronic illness literally put people's lives in danger. The simple fact is that in our society, no-one takes illness seriously.

It may seem small in some contexts, like disbelieving your chronically ill friend's complaints because "Well, you *look* fine!" But supposedly minor things influence every aspect of our society, including the medical field, because we are all connected and we are only human.

This so-called 'note' is getting very long, so I'm going to rein myself in here. Wishing you all the health and happiness possible,

Talia xx

What's next for Ravenswood? The final story of the series follows the outrageous Zach Davis, the mysterious Rae, and one disturbingly *real* fake relationship...

THAT KIND OF GUY

RAVENSWOOD BOOK 3

She wants a fake relationship. He needs something real.

If there's one thing Rae can't stand, it's pity. She's forty, frazzled, and fed up—so attending an awards ceremony _alone_ while her ex swans about with his new wife? Not an option. To avoid total humiliation, Rae needs a date of her own. And her young, hot-as-hell new best friend is the perfect candidate...

Zach Davis, king of casual hookups, has a secret: the notorious womaniser craves emotional connection, and anonymous encounters leave him feeling hollow. After years of performance, Zach's desperate to be himself. So why does he agree to play Rae's fake boyfriend? And why does it feel so easy?

When the line between pretence and desire blurs, Zach's

forced to face an unexpected truth: there's nothing phoney about his need for Rae. But the jaded divorcée's been hurt by playboy men before. Can a weekend of faking it prove that Zach's for real?

THAT KIND OF GUY: AVAILABLE NOW

ABOUT THE AUTHOR

Talia Hibbert is an award-winning, Black British author who lives in a bedroom full of books. Supposedly, there is a world beyond that room, but she has yet to drum up enough interest to investigate.

She writes sexy, diverse romance because she believes that people of marginalised identities need honest and positive representation. She also rambles intermittently about the romance genre online. Her interests include makeup, junk food, and unnecessary sarcasm.

Talia loves hearing from readers. Follow her social media to connect, or email her directly at hello@taliahibbert.com.

Printed in Great Britain
by Amazon